James Murdo was born and raised in London, where he still lives. He graduated from university with a Master's degree in Physics, which added fuel to his early love of science fiction.

Echoes of Gravity is the first in the Tapache's Promise Trilogy, set in the Sci-Fi Wanderer Universe, alongside many of James' other books.

AVAILABLE BOOKS
By James Murdo

All set in the Wanderer Universe.

Tapache's Promise Trilogy:
Echoes of Gravity (Book 1)

Standalones:
Siouca Remembers
Long Paradise
Fractured Carapace

Wanderers Series:
Gil's World (Book 1)
Searching the Void (Book 2)
Infinite Eyes (Book 3)

www.jamesmurdo.com

Echoes of Gravity
(Tapache's Promise, Book 1)

By
James Murdo

CRANTHORPE
MILLNER

ISBN 978-1-912964-00-0 (Paperback)

www.cranthorpemillner.com

Published by Cranthorpe Millner Publishers (2021)

To Lucca, to whom everything is alien.

Chapter 1
Kera

Kera stood in the centre of a small, dark room, finally alone. Though she could not see it, she could sense Echoes of Gravity, swirling nebulously around her, never revealing itself but always there. She gripped the device tightly in her hand, hoping it was enough; that, somehow, Echoes of Gravity would understand it for what it was. A receptacle for knowledge.

As soon as she returned to Sunsprit, she had felt the inexplicable desire to travel to Echoes of Gravity's hidden dwelling. It had called out to her, drawing her back. She had been called before, but this time was different. She had always had her opinions about Echoes of Gravity; her own theories and musings, just like everyone else who knew of it. But now, for her, some of those thoughts had been validated. Echoes of Gravity was an external presence, with a will of its own. She could feel it.

Thoughts came to her, lifted from the recesses of her mind. Echoes of Gravity was weaving a story for her, from her own memories, as though it were a lonely, orphaned mind, with no memories of its own.

1

Her palms dripped with sweat as she continuously rolled the device about in her hand, reminding herself why she was here.

It probed…and probed…and probed…exploring every part of her mind, weaving its tale. The Source. Tugs. Vaesians. Roranians. Veilers. Great Ships. Tapache. Many other words and concepts she did not understand. Everything was connected, the answers tantalisingly close. Echoes of Gravity was too different; too dissociated to give her the answers itself, but it showed her the way. She needed to go to the Tug Field. Her eyes widened in surprise. Never had Echoes of Gravity been so clear.

Chapter 2
Great Lessons

The cavernous chamber was filled with millions of spherical orbs, each emitting their own distinct auras as they whizzed about the room, floating over the rows on rows of translucent caskets that lined a large portion of the chamber's floor. Small, dark forms could be seen moving lethargically within the caskets.

"Why are you showing me this, Wiln?" Diyan asked impatiently. "I've seen the Great Ship's construction many times before."

"To remind you how far you have come, and to demonstrate your progress."

Alongside the visual simulation of the chamber's construction, historical audio recordings of Wiln talking with a younger Diyan – who was also watching the simulation – were being replayed. Diyan winced as he listened.

"Why are you all referred to as c-automs?" Diyan heard his younger self ask Wiln. "We aren't the same – you're just a spherical ball – but you're still alive, like me."

"C-autom is my type, in the same way that your type is Roranian."

"But you've got so many types!" the exasperated younger Diyan had complained. "You're a c-autom and you're a machine-lect. You're so many things!"

"Many things have many labels." Wiln had spoken softly and in a measured tone, as always. "There are different ways to classify us, that is all. Just like you are a biological sentient and a Roranian. You are both at the same time."

"And I'm Diyan."

"That too."

The present Diyan shook his head in mild exasperation. He squinted, redirecting his attention away from the large swarms of orbs to the individual orbs that flitted about alone. Some ventured close to the caskets at the base of the chamber, their auras reflected on the caskets' casings. Meanwhile, the younger Diyan continued to question the patient Wiln.

"I am Diyan, a member of the Roranian species of biological sentients."

"Correct. And I am Wiln, a member of the Wanderer civilisation of machine-lects. The evolution of the Roranian species, and its ability to be categorised by its genetic precedence, is analogous in many ways to the Wanderer hierarchy of machine-lects."

"But you're a machine-lect and a c-autom!"

"A machine-lect is a sentient machine intelligence, and

a c-autom is a specific category of Wanderer machine-lect."

"And what about Tapache? Tapache's a craft-lect, not a c-autom?"

Diyan winced again. The swarms of orbs in the simulation were throbbing about more energetically than before, with throng-like extensions of adjacent orbs protruding from each swarm, affixing themselves to the chamber's sides. Raw materials were being conducted along the lengths of the extensions, towards the swarm centres; once there, the raw materials were manipulated, the swarms coalescing the materials into large components, many magnitudes larger than the orbs themselves.

"Tapache is a different type of Wanderer machine-lect. Tapache is a craft-lect. Craft-lects create c-automs to aid them in the running of their ships. Tapache created me, for example, and all of the other c-automs you see within this simulation."

"And craft-lects are higher than c-automs in the Wanderer...hierarchy?" the younger Diyan asked.

"Yes. Craft-lects command powerful ships, many times greater than this one. They create subservient c-automs as and when they require the help of a crew on their ships."

"But Tapache doesn't control this ship. Tapache created you, but Tapache isn't here," the younger Diyan protested.

"You are correct. You might consider us an anomaly.

Tapache has given us the Great Ship, so that we may complete a mission on its behalf. That is why we were all created, both you and us. We c-automs have been instructed to teach you—"

"Let's skip some of this, Wiln," the real-life Diyan suggested.

Immediately, the audio moved ahead, and within the simulation, the work of the c-automs jumped in progression. The components fashioned from the raw materials were transformed into great machines and massive structures, and the giant chamber became partitioned into many smaller sections.

Much to Diyan's dismay, the back and forth between the young Diyan and Wiln continued, as the work of the c-automs within the simulation reached completion. The machines used for construction were being disassembled into their constituent materials, and the swarms had split. Individual c-automs now moved about, completing more specific tasks and creating the chamber's finer features.

"How do c-automs interact with the ship?" the persistent young Diyan asked.

"There are a variety of mechanisms through which c-automs can manipulate surrounding matter, and—"

"Does that include how you are speaking with me right now? You haven't got a mouth. What's inside you?"

"Yes, and I will explain that in time. You are not yet ready. First, you need to understand—"

"And your colour, where does that come from?"

"Our auras are the result of complex interactions between cycling quantum fields. Again, you are not yet ready to learn exactly how they are manifested. Suffice to say, for now, the auras are a useful tool, allowing you to distinguish between us."

The activity of the c-automs in the simulation had diminished, and most had stopped completely. Their work was done; the innards of the Great Ship were complete. Everything in the simulation was faintly transparent, allowing Diyan to view the ship in its entirety, though the structure was far too complex to fully comprehend.

"What happens now?" the younger Diyan whispered.

"The final message from Tapache to us. You will be able to hear an audible approximation suitable for Roranians."

A moment later, the deep, rumbling voice of Tapache boomed all around. The recorded message, which all Roranians on the Great Ship had heard so many times before, was being delivered. Tapache's voice was mechanical and perfect.

"The ship is ready, and your most important work begins. You are to be the stewards of the biologicals for as long as that is possible. Tell them what I have promised. Tell them that, conditional upon their return, and having successfully discovered the Source, I shall aid them in understanding what became of the Roranian species."

The communication from Tapache ended and darkness engulfed the Diyan of the present. He was in empty space, a distant observer. A spiral galaxy hung close. One tip of the spiral rotated and expanded; stars and nebulae rushed past him. A single, solitary solar system became the focus of his perception, right at the tip of a spiral arm, the galaxy's extremity. A yellow star orbited by three planets. The planet with the tightest orbit was also the smallest; its dense, red atmosphere, so dark it was almost black, swirled energetically as it rapidly made its way around the star. The central planet was many magnitudes larger, with a far greater orbital period; vivid blue with wide, flat rings, it possessed too many moons for Diyan to count. The third planet was many times further out than the other two, with a swirling, deep green atmosphere.

"What is the Source?" the younger Diyan piped up again.

"What you are to investigate: Tapache's quest. The Source emanates a probability wave that results in the death of machine-lects. We don't know what it is, but we do know that biologicals are unaffected."

"What does it look like?"

"We don't know."

"Maybe it's caused by some sort of technology we can't understand, from the void?"

"Perhaps."

The simulation moved towards the edge of the system and a dark shape resolved in the gloom, against the backdrop of the green planet. It was spheroidal, with tendrils protruding from one end that fizzled with sparks of colour. Tapache's ship.

"What are those wavy things?"

Diyan breathed sharply as his younger self continued to ask questions.

"The protrusions comprise the bloom propulsion unit."

"What does the bloom do?"

"It propels Tapache's ship through space."

"How?"

"I will explain in time—"

"I want to know now!"

"The bloom's individual tendrils branch out fractally, with the finest components small enough to be affected by quantum perturbations. Interactions at that level are harnessed into a powerful force, and that is what is used to propel the ship through space."

The younger Diyan did not immediately respond, and Diyan could not help but smile in victory. The simulation shifted his focus again as it reoriented his vantage point. Tapache's ship expanded as another, smaller object came into view beside it, clearly of the same overall design. There was even a scaled-down version of the bloom extending from one end.

"That's our ship, isn't it?" the younger Diyan asked.

"Yes. It is the Great Ship."

"But why does it look so small? The Great Ship is enormous!"

For once, the Wiln of the past did not reply.

The Great Ship's smaller bloom flicked to the side, moving the ship away from Tapache's larger vessel and the green planet, and outwards from the star at the system's centre. The bloom tightened and straightened, and the Great Ship accelerated, quickly passing through both belts of rock and ice that encircled the system and propelling itself into empty space.

"Wiln," Diyan said, waving to halt the simulation. "I understand I've come a long way. I don't need to hear anymore. I want to stop. What are the others doing?"

"Do you mean to ask what Kera is doing?"

Diyan's simulation disappeared into nothingness. Nearby, Kera was still engulfed in her own. Diyan could see her rough, slim outline within the light purple spherical haze that surrounded her; it was as though he was staring through murky water. She was moving about a little and, every now and then, flashes of light brown escaped the haze as her hands punctured through. The simulation bubble was controlled by her c-autom, Otherness, who hovered above her, its dark purple aura pulsing consistently.

"What is she seeing?" Diyan asked.

Wiln's orb-body moved into Diyan's peripheral vision, settling at shoulder-height, about an arm's width away. Its blue aura did not pulse, instead holding a steady glow.

"Why don't you ask her yourself?"

Diyan huffed, turning to survey the others. Each of

them stood atop their own pale green mound, the mounds spaced just far enough apart that normal conversation could not be heard. The mounds sloped gently up from the base layer of the expanse, reaching a height similar to Diyan's own. Bright, blue-white holo-skies were projected upwards within the enormous expanse, allowing many tens of thousands of Roranians to access their own mounds whenever they wanted.

A warm wind gently ruffled Diyan's thick black hair as he glanced around. Most of the others were still surrounded by their simulation hazes, like Kera, though a few had paused, as he had, and were standing atop their mounds, looking out at the expanse. Every single one was accompanied by their own c-autom.

"Am I far behind the others?" Diyan asked.

"Your question does not make sense. Your schedule is specific to you."

"But why are we starting at the beginning again? Haven't I progressed?"

"Yes, you have, Diyan. It was simply time."

"But…" He unclenched his fists and smiled. "You're trying to make me competitive, aren't you?"

"There are many strategies I employ to teach you and to eventuate certain results. You do not need to concern yourself with my methods."

"Unless that's what I need to hear."

There was a pause.

"You are learning, Diyan."

"Is everything a lesson?"

Wiln's blue aura pulsed in non-audible response. Diyan's perception of reality changed again. The simulation generated by Wiln was truly over. This time, Kera was sitting cross-legged, facing diagonally away from him. Her long, black hair spilled across her shoulders and down her slender back. Like him, her regwear clothes were plain white. He could see the side of her cheek moving in speech, as her c-autom's purple aura pulsed rhythmically. He turned to look at the rest of the expanse. Most of the others were also sitting. Only a few looked to be still engaged in simulations, Diyan had been one of the last to stop. His smile widened.

"You are relieved."

"I am," he replied. "I thought there was something wrong with me."

"There is nothing wrong with you. All Roranians are different, with differing traits. Tapache allowed for a broad genetic variance."

"Why?"

"You are wanted."

"What do you mean?"

The answer became clear without Wiln providing an audible response.

"Finished?" Kera shouted over to him.

"Won't you reply?" Wiln asked.

"Shh!" Diyan hissed from the corner of his mouth. He smiled at Kera in mild surprise. "Oh, you're done already?" he called back, innocently.

"It was excruciating!" she said loudly, with an exaggeratedly pained expression, tilting her head up and rolling her big brown eyes – a feature she shared with all other Roranians – towards the top of her head. "I'm re-listening to myself learning about the Wanderer craft-lects." Her tone became more level and less emotive as she glanced cheekily at her c-autom. "A craft-lect is more than capable of highly complex investigations. The galaxy is a dangerous place, and there are many threats to the Wanderers. Most pernicious of all threats, and that which craft-lects are primarily designed to seek out and destroy, is the Sensespace. However, during its travels around the tip of a spiral arm, Tapache encountered a probability wave that destroys machine sentience, emanating from outside the galaxy. This wave warrants further investigation." She stopped her monotonal mimicry and flashed her c-autom a grin. "I'm sorry, Otherness, but you do drone on!"

Her c-autom flashed bright purple in response.

"Oh, I know all about the probability wave," Diyan replied, equally loudly and with a grin directed at Wiln.

"I do wish we could have met Tapache, though." Kera gestured around and her eyes lit up. "To have created all of this…"

They walked down from their mounds to meet at the valley in-between. Their c-automs rose higher and settled in the air above, close enough that their auras visibly intermingled.

"Tapache is waiting for our return," Diyan said.

"Who knows what we'll find?" Kera grinned. "Maybe we won't want to return at the end. You're finished, right?"

Diyan nodded, and they began to walk along the base of the mounds.

"Look at all this," Diyan mused, pointing at the ground as they walked side by side. "I wonder how it all grows, and what's beneath it." He shuffled across to let some others past. "There's still so much to learn about this chamber, and all the others, and the Great Ship, let alone the Source—"

"And Tapache's promise to us. When we return, Tapache will help us discover what remains of our civilisation, remember?"

"Yes…" He momentarily trailed off. "Did you know that there are almost thirty thousand of us?"

"Ooh," she said, teasingly. "And each of us has a c-autom. That means there are at least thirty thousand c-automs." A pleasant laugh escaped her lips. "Did you know, your eyes widen when you talk about things you find interesting? They almost become circles."

He ignored the jibe. "There are many more c-automs, actually," he replied. Waiting a moment but hearing no response, he turned to her, confused. She had slowed her pace, and her eyes were set a few mounds along, upon someone Diyan did not recognise: a boy, taller and more muscular than the average Roranian, with unkempt, shoulder-length hair. The stranger walked confidently down from his mound, towards three other boys who waited at the bottom, an easy, handsome smile on his face.

"That's Paran," Kera whispered, almost conspiratorially, dipping her head low. "Do you know him?"

"No, why?"

Kera kept her voice low. "He does many of the competitions."

"Why are you telling me this?" Diyan asked. Kera's cheeks reddened, but she did not reply. "Is something wrong?"

A scream from nearby halted their conversation. Both Wiln and Otherness flitted towards the source of the sound as Diyan and Kera rushed up the nearest unoccupied mound.

"One less c-autom," Kera said, sadly. "That's two we've seen today."

Just in front of them, in a valley between mounds, a girl lay sobbing on the ground before a dark orb. Wiln and Otherness circled over her, along with three other c-automs.

"She'll have another," Diyan whispered, weakly.

"I'm going to see if she's okay," Kera said. She rushed down the slope, kneeling to place an arm around the sobbing girl. A hum began to emanate from the five c-automs rotating above and Kera gently pulled the girl back. The circle of c-automs tightened their aerial formation until they were almost touching, allowing their auras to blend together, and descended over the dark orb on the ground. Then, they rose, with the dark orb at their centre, ascending higher and higher, diminishing in size until they disappeared from view.

Diyan watched Kera comfort the sobbing girl. Without the auras of the c-automs, the scene before him appeared somewhat barren. Many others were also watching quietly, from nearby mounds and the surrounding valleys.

The five c-automs reappeared, descending from high above, with their auras so bright Diyan had to shield his eyes. They dimmed as they drew nearer, forming a rotating ring above Kera and the girl. Another light began to shine at their centre, and a new c-autom with a brilliant yellow aura was revealed. The rotating five dispersed. Wiln moved back to Diyan, while Otherness settled a short distance behind Kera, who was still comforting the girl. The new c-autom descended slowly, halting near the girl's face. She raised her head and swatted at it angrily. It moved gently back.

"I don't want you!" she shouted. "I want Selo!"

Kera took the girl's raised arm delicately, putting it by her side, and pulled her up so they were facing. They began talking inaudibly.

"Did her c-autom manage to berth itself in time?" Diyan whispered to Wiln.

"It did not. Unfortunate, but rare."

Chapter 3
Diyan's Rumination

The long, cuboid shape of a light grey skimmer hurtled through the air, travelling up past various levels until it reached the level where Diyan's annexe was located. There, it stopped, the right side of the skimmer folding up as Diyan exited and stepped onto the platform, Wiln zooming out behind him. As Diyan began to walk away, the skimmer's side folded down and it sped off into the distance.

Diyan made his way through the short entrance hall and into his annexe. Immediately, the ship's mechanically created, early evening ambience was gone, and his own preferences took over. A slightly cooler breeze; brighter lights. The walls and ceiling were a vivid, light green, while the floor was obsidian black. In contrast to the brighter corridor, the staircase at the end was dimly lit and narrow.

"Do you think this part's a little too dark?" Diyan asked Wiln, as he wandered down the staircase.

"Depends on what you like."

Reaching the bottom, a white, glowing platform fanned out. The ceiling was many multiples Diyan's own height, extending high above to reach the level of the initial corridor. Aside from the platform, everything in the room was a dark brown, including the walls, ceiling, and pathways that branched off the platform. Directly in front of Diyan was a wide, shallow stairway that wound around to the right, with two passages on either side, leading off to other parts of the annexe.

Diyan strode over to the wide steps opposite him, looking around.

"Hmm…I think it's fine for now. I'll brighten up that staircase another day," he said, gesturing to the back of the room, as he began trudging up the steps.

"You could remove all the lengthy passageways." Wiln flashed brightly.

Diyan shook his head. "Why? They all join up."

"In various ways."

"Exactly."

At the top of the winding stairway, Diyan was greeted by the sounds of splashing water. There were two pools in the room before him: a deep, central pool, running the entire length of the wide room, with jets of water spouting from all sides into the middle, and a smaller pool, which was off to the side. Wiln sped ahead of him, arcing towards the main pool, shooting through the aerial jets, and rapidly completing a circuit of the room before arriving back in front of Diyan, who had paused, sniffing the air.

"You would like to make a change?"

"Yes. Let's remove this scent from the sequence. I'm not sure it suits the water." Diyan sniffed again and smiled. "Much better! What's that? Something Roranian?"

Wiln moved to the side so that it was at head height, an arm's width from him.

"Yes. It's an aroma found at the derelict outpost where Tapache encountered the remnants of your species. It's classified as—"

"Never mind, Tapache's labels are always too long. Let's call it *Water Musk*," Diyan decided, peeling off his regwear.

"You don't want to study anymore today, then?"

Diyan shook his head and leapt into the main pool, splashing noisily in the warm water. Wiln entered as well, circling around Diyan under the surface before breaking into the open air. Diyan kicked about a little, then latched onto the side of the pool and rested his chin on his hands.

"I'm thinking of changing something else," he said.

"Something else? I assume you mean within your annexe? You'll have to be more specific if you want me to change anything." Wiln moved about the room in a lethargic, circling pattern. "Or would you like me to choose?"

"Yes," Diyan replied, after a moment. "You can choose. I like this area, and I like the entrance, but the other parts…they need altering. Not too much, perhaps just change how they connect to each other, in a way that isn't too…" He paused, thinking. "Obvious. Or too short."

Wiln's blue aura pulsed. "Okay."

"Not simple. Not boring."

Wiln's aura pulsed again.

Diyan pursed his lips and stared at the floor. "That won't happen to you, will it?" he asked, quietly.

"You are referring to what happened to that girl's c-autom? It's given name was Selo."

With his chin still resting on his hands, Diyan rocked his head in a vague nod. "And the girl?"

"Her name is Yena."

"Yena," Diyan repeated, as he pulled himself out of the pool. He shook his head and raised his arms as Wiln's aura enveloped and dried him. "Will what happened to Selo happen to you?"

"You know it may. It may happen to any c-autom, at any time. The probability is low, but—"

"But the closer we get to the Source, the more likely it is. The higher the probability is. More c-automs will die."

"Exactly."

"Can you berth yourself now? I'd rather you did that before anything happened. You said that, when Tapache made you stewards of the Great Ship, it gave you permission to self-berth and store yourselves safely."

"Only upon detecting an attack against ourselves."

"Can't you self-berth pre-emptively?"

"No. And if I were to, then who would help you with your annexe? Who—"

"I'm being serious, Wiln." Diyan's regwear clothes rose from their heap on the floor and hung in the air before him; he dismissed them, and they dropped back to the ground. He began to pace about. Some gentle music started to play but he instantly raised his hand and it stopped. "Don't try to distract me!"

Wiln's aura pulsed slowly. "I am grateful for your concern, but even if I were inclined to berth myself, I have my orders from Tapache. I cannot. We may only attempt to self-berth upon detection of an attack against ourselves."

"You already said that."

"Yes, and—"

"And Selo didn't manage it."

"I also said that it was a rare event."

"But the closer we get, the more likely it is that these events will happen! You just admitted that!"

"Selo was unfortunate. Most of us succeed in berthing ourselves when attacked. And besides, the reason for us being on the Great Ship in such numbers, compared with your own species, is to ensure there are sufficient replacements should this kind of thing happen."

"That's a lie. Tapache only sent you because it didn't want to risk going itself!" Diyan argued. "In time, you'll all be gone. You should berth yourselves now."

"I only exist to help you. When you return, if you have not been successful, Tapache will not aid you in finding what remains of your civilisation. That is the promise it has made to you."

"But what about you?" Diyan sighed. "It's not fair…" He looked around aimlessly and clenched his fists. "We will never be able to perform the tasks you do: the Great Ship is far too complex. Roranians and c-automs aren't the same. Tapache may have re-designed us, but there are some things he couldn't change. We are just not capable."

"You have a proclivity for understanding what is around you, and the ability to learn what is required. The ship's systems are simplified far beyond a true Wanderer vessel. In fact, the necessary technologies employed are closer to what Tapache believes your own species was capable of, with some improvements, such as the bloom. We are here to teach you what you need to know."

"What about altering my annexe? I have never understood how you do that."

"That, I am afraid, I cannot teach you. It is not a necessary function of this ship."

Diyan took a slow breath in and out. "I'm sorry, I don't mean to argue. I just don't want to lose you, Wiln."

Wiln moved a little closer. "Don't worry, Diyan. I fully intend to self-berth should I detect an attack against myself."

"How many c-automs…attempted to berth themselves today?"

"Not many."

"Good." Diyan's white regwear rose again in the air and levitated closer to him. He shook his head, once again dismissing them.

"What would you like to wear? You are not planning to go out there naked, are you?"

Diyan laughed. "Your jokes are becoming funnier, Wiln. Don't worry, I am planning to clothe myself. But I'm going to need something a little different. I'm thinking of joining one of the competitions."

"Your apathy towards them has changed? Interesting. Which competition?"

"I…"

A holo appeared in front of Diyan, the same height as him and stretching from one side of the room to the other. Various competitions were displayed. Some were active and physical, others less so. Tapache had uncovered much about Roranian culture from its investigation of the derelict outpost, and had allowed those discoveries to influence Roranian development.

"Might I make a suggestion?"

"Yes," Diyan replied, hesitantly.

"Paran, the boy Kera pointed out to you, takes part in many competitions." The holo changed to display those competitions. One by one, they disappeared, until only one was left. "Combat: typical Roranian style. You have attributes that may help you with certain aspects of this specific competition, when compared to Paran. In time, those attributes could lead you to rank higher."

"Would I beat him?" Diyan asked.

"That depends. Currently, he has more experience and has already reached a high degree of proficiency, so you would need to train extensively. Nevertheless, you have faster upper reflexes and a highly developed sense of balance. Given your physiology, there are techniques you could implement to use his height against him."

"You think I should do this?"

"It would be a good choice, if Kera's attention is what you are after." Wiln began to oscillate about its position.

"Is there something else?" Diyan asked.

"There is. The competition can wait for now."

The white regwear again began to levitate towards Diyan. He dismissed them, but they remained in front of him. He sighed and reached out. "And why is that?"

"Because Kera is requesting your presence."

Diyan looked up. "Now?"

"Shortly. She would like you to accompany her to the casket platform."

"For what reason?"

"Her message does not say. Shall I inform Otherness you would rather—"

Diyan shook his head. "No, tell her it's fine. I'll see her there."

Chapter 4
Peeking in Time

Diyan looked around anxiously. Many others were dotted along the length of the platform, although none too close and none he recognised. He rested his arms on the railing and looked down at the tens of thousands of caskets below. The chamber that housed them was the largest viewable, accessible open space in the Great Ship, dwarfing even those that contained the green mounds.

"Will she be long?" he asked Wiln, who hovered close by.

"Her skimmer is on its way. She'll be here soon."

"Okay."

He half-turned upon hearing footsteps, flashing a quick smile at two others coming through a nearby entrance. Both girls, neither of whom he knew, smiled back pleasantly and resumed their own conversation. They were talking about Tapache's quest. Their two c-automs followed close behind, one glowing with a light grey aura, the other shining a piercing red. They rotated around each other.

"The Source might be something completely unexpected," one girl, the slightly shorter of the two, mused.

"We'll either find what's destroying the machine-lects or not. We don't have a choice anyway," the taller one replied, quickly adding, "Not that I want a choice."

"Tapache didn't have to create us and give us this chance. It saw potential in us."

"You're not getting my point."

They settled between Diyan and the next group along, just close enough that Diyan could still hear their conversation, the topic of which was a far from infrequent point of discussion aboard the ship. He set his eyes on the caskets below. They were all a dark red, just about resolvable from where he was standing. Each was open: a broken sphere, with the top hemisphere hanging off. There was a little space between each of the caskets.

The shorter girl was speaking. "I agree with you. I just think if we don't know what the Source is and how it's attacking machine-lects—"

"It emits a probability wave. Void technology."

"*Void technology*? That's...that's..." She trailed off and laughed. "You do realise Tapache hasn't actually detected anything? The probability wave is just what it calls the whatever-it-is that's destroying the machine-lects. Isn't that right, Corun?"

A more level, considered voice came from her c-autom. "That is correct."

The shorter girl carried on. "Tapache figured out that whatever-it-is is coming from a specific direction, and that its intensity increases exponentially with proximity."

"And how does it know that?" the other girl asked.

"It used c-automs," the shorter girl replied, simply. "Corun told me. Tapache figured out that more c-automs were more likely to be destroyed the closer they were. Hence why Tapache thinks it's a probability wave. A probability wave of death for machine-lects."

"Exactly! That's all we actually know about the Source. That's why it's sending us, biologicals are immune, and the c-automs are training us—"

"I know that!" the shorter girl protested. "But my question is, why us? Why not resurrect another species? Corun won't give me a good answer."

"We're probably extinct. This gives us a second chance."

"From what we've learned about the Wanderers, that isn't something they typically do."

"Who knows why they do what they do? They're machines."

The argument between the two girls quickly became circular. Diyan politely took a step back from the railing and looked around. The group on his other side had moved off, so he shuffled further up the platform, stopping when he could no longer hear them. He sighed and leaned forwards again onto the railing. Wiln circled slowly in a tight ring by his head.

"Is Tapache really waiting for us?" Diyan asked, quietly.

"That is its promise. It waits at the edge of the galaxy for you to return, and then it will aid you in searching for the remnants of your civilisation. That is what these caskets remain here for, to remind you where you came from."

"So that we don't forget."

"Exactly."

"Will there be any others?"

"No. You were all created to last."

"If we're extinct, what's the point?"

"It's possible the outpost where Tapache found the remnants of your species was just a remote part of your civilisation. Your species may still exist."

"And if it doesn't?"

"Then you're still not extinct. There are tens of thousands of you now."

"And all we have to do is find this Source, and then what? Destroy it? Tell Tapache what we've found?"

"That has purposely been left vague by Tapache, considering it does not know what you will find."

"So, it's up to our discretion?"

"You could say that."

"Do we have weapons?"

"The ship does."

"And we'll learn how to use them?"

"In time, Diyan. Kera is nearly here. Her skimmer has docked at the entrance and she is about to walk through."

"Shh." Diyan automatically turned his head towards the sound of nearby footsteps.

"Those are not Kera's. She can't hear us yet, and we're far enough away from anyone—"

"Wiln!"

The c-autom stopped communicating, instead bobbing innocently up and down in the air.

Diyan turned forwards again and squinted, fixing his eyes on one of the caskets down below. Footsteps and a faint whirring sound came from behind. His hands tightened their grip on the railing.

"Diyan."

The familiar voice of Kera. Diyan turned around with a half-smile. Otherness whizzed about in the air above Kera, its aura briefly mixing with Wiln's, who began to fly about in a similar pattern.

"Hello, Kera." Diyan looked up. "And hello, Otherness."

"We're sorry to have kept you waiting," Kera said. In contrast to Diyan's simple white regwear, Kera was cocooned in a dark ensemble that wafted about her as she moved. Every now and then, her outfit all wafted in the same direction, outlining her slender frame.

"I wasn't waiting," Diyan replied, a little too quickly. "I wanted to come before…to look at them. That's why you wanted to come too, isn't it?" He gestured at the caskets below.

Kera looked down and moved beside Diyan, pressing her body against the railing, her delicate lips pursed a little tighter than usual. "Oh, yes, of course." She was nearly a head shorter than Diyan. "Do you like it?"

Diyan looked at the scene below them. "They're interesting, yes. I was just talking with Wiln about them. Did you know, Tapache made our adolescences far more prolonged than was typical for our species? We've been learning for a very long time. The purpose of the caskets remaining here is to remind us where we came from, despite all the time that has passed, and that we are as much a part of the Great Ship as Wiln, Otherness, and all the other c-automs. Tapache resurrected our species from the remains and records it found at the derelict outpost-"

"Not the caskets, silly!" Kera interrupted him with a giggle. "Your eyes are so wide, Diyan. It's so funny!" She shook her head, smiling in amusement, before thrusting her hands forward, shaking them so that her sleeves floated gently down her arms. "I meant this! What do you think? It's something Otherness found for me in the ship's databanks. Gronwenthian cloth, I think."

Otherness' aura flashed brighter. "That is correct."

Kera nodded. "The Gronwenthians were not so different to us, apparently, and they designed their clothing this way. It's very different to our regwear; the cloth is meant to be light, to ruffle about. There's less thermal regulation, but I don't really mind." Her arms moved back to her sides. The Gronwenthian cloth drifted lethargically behind, as though unsure whether it was supposed to move.

"I like it," Diyan said, with an awkward smile. "Suits you."

She smiled, looking down. "Thank you."

There was an odd quietness between them. The c-automs flitted about, seemingly unconcerned. Finally, Kera broke the silence.

"It's been some time since we came out from the caskets, hasn't it?"

Diyan nodded. "Wiln tells me our bodies are almost mature."

Wiln responded. "But not your minds."

Otherness followed. "There's still some way to go with them."

Kera swatted at Otherness, with an amused scowl. "On the mounds we have our answers," she said, lightly.

"You like that phrase, don't you," Diyan observed. "On the mounds we have our answers."

"Because it's true, isn't it?" Kera replied. "We learn everywhere. Our c-automs teach us wherever we go, through everything we do. But it's on those green mounds that we really learn. When we are all together; when we can feel everyone else learning alongside us."

Diyan laughed. "I suppose."

"I'm going to watch some of the competitions later,

with Yena." Her tone was suddenly vague, as though she was hoping for his approval.

"Yena?"

"The girl who lost her c-autom earlier. Selo."

"Ah, yes. She has a new c-autom now."

"Which she's not yet named," Kera said, looking sad.

"You're friends now, then?"

"Yes."

Diyan looked about, feeling foolish. "Is that what you wanted to tell me? If you'd rather I didn't watch any of the competitions with you, that's fine. I was thinking of entering some myself. It's time I learned, and..." He stopped as she turned to face him, looking bemused.

"Of course not, I assumed you'd want to come with me." She frowned. "Is everything okay?"

His cheeks flushed a shade darker. "Yes, everything's fine. I just misunderstood."

She punched his arm playfully. "Good, I'm glad. There's something else I wanted your help with. But if you'd rather practice for your competition, then don't worry."

"No, of course not. What is it?" he asked.

"It's Paran."

Diyan's jaw clenched. "Paran," he repeated.

She nodded. Her voice became quieter. "Can you help me compose a message to him? I've tried myself, but...well...I don't know how these things work, and...you're a..."

Diyan frowned, then looked at her when he realised nothing else was forthcoming. "A message? For what?"

She shuffled self-consciously. "To introduce myself."

Diyan's frown remained. "What do you want it to say?"

"That's what I'd like you to help me with." She looked nervous.

"And that's why we're here?" he asked, softly.

"I just thought you'd be able to help." She turned her head to the side and squinted at Otherness. "Nothing we've come up with seems to be…right."

"Of course, I'll help." Diyan forced a smile.

"See!" Kera exclaimed to Otherness. "I told you he'd want to help!"

*

Having stormed back to his annexe, Diyan tore off his regwear clothes and threw them into the central pool, where they proceeded to move inconspicuously to the side, before rising into the air and drifting out of sight. Wiln followed Diyan, its blue aura dimmer than usual.

"Wiln, can you stop those? I need to think!" Diyan shouted, pointing at the water jets spouting around the pool. The noise emanating from them dissipated to nothing, although the jets themselves carried on.

"Paran!" Diyan fumed, sinking into the pool and holding the side. "Why him? He's stupid, and that ridiculous—"

Wiln's reply was measured. "You have never spoken with Paran. His c-autom informs me that he is calm and thoughtful."

"You contacted his c-autom?" Diyan shouted, turning to Wiln, hitting the surface of the water with his hand.

"You know many c-automs communicate with each other, Diyan. Like you, we have our friendships, and—"

"But now he'll know you've enquired about him!" He pulled his body half out of the water to glower at Wiln, who did not move, instead oscillating gently around a fixed position, out of arm's reach.

"Paran's c-autom, Loten, will not mention that we have communicated. I explicitly asked for that. We can be very discrete."

Diyan sunk back into the water and turned to face the centre of the pool. "Paran," he muttered.

"Might I suggest you focus on something else, for now?"

"Like what?"

Dark, thickly padded regwear appeared in Diyan's peripheral vision and hovered in front of him, somehow avoiding becoming damp despite the jets of water splashing against it.

"Like the competition we spoke of earlier. Paran is a level seven already, out of twenty. But I do not calculate it will take you as long as it took him to pass each level. If you want to display your attributes to Kera, then competing against Paran is what I suggest we do."

Diyan's eyebrows raised in the middle. "And you think this will work?"

"If by work you mean increase your favour with Kera, it is possible. You biologicals are complex beings, and the information contained within the databanks given to us by Tapache is not extensive enough to know for certain. But it does appear to be reasonably likely."

"Wiln, there is another thing?"

"Yes, Diyan?"

"What is it that Kera notices about my eyes? They're normal, aren't they?"

"They are within normal parameters, Diyan. Perhaps, you should ask her what she means."

Chapter 5
Changing Destiny

Diyan clenched his fists. Paran, opposite, did the same, both their faces impassive. They began to circle the perimeter of the combat zone, represented by the thin blue line traced on the ground around them. They were surrounded by other combat rings, all filled with competitors engrossed in their own battles. Their fight was just beginning.

Paran's hair was tied behind his head and his eyes were focused on Diyan, scanning his opponent from head to toe. Likewise, Diyan watched Paran for any signs of weakness. Kera, Yena, and all their c-automs watched from outside the combat zone, along with a couple of other wandering spectators. There was a loud clamour coming from all the other fights, a mixture of grunting, shouting, and cries of victory and defeat. But Diyan and Paran moved in silence.

Paran flinched, his arm moving briefly to the side and back. A ruse? Nerves? Diyan took a step closer. Paran mirrored him. They circled around a tighter ring. Both began to make deliberate, obvious feints. They were testing each other. The fight had begun.

*

Grinning, Diyan extended a well-muscled, sweaty arm to Paran, who took it after a moment's hesitation and hauled himself up. They embraced one another, each giving a brief murmur of approval. While still shorter than Paran, Diyan's frame was bulkier.

"That makes us even, doesn't it?" Paran said, his easy smile appearing as usual, as he took the fastener from his hair and shook it loose. "One each."

"It does," Diyan replied. "We've both won. And you still have enough points to go through too."

"Perhaps we'll face each other again in the final rounds before we reach level twelve."

"Perhaps."

"You caught up quickly, you're a fast learner."

Diyan smiled. "Thank you. You're not so bad either, you know."

"At least you'll talk to me now. That's why I let you win."

"Careful, or I may decide to put you down again."

Paran laughed loudly. "Whatever we find in the space

between galaxies, we'll fight it side-by-side."

Loten hovered beside Paran. Its aura was akin to Wiln's, if not a slightly deeper, darker blue. "The scores have been transmitted."

Paran raised his arms defensively at Diyan. "No cheating here!"

The bright blue line designating the combat area around them disappeared and Kera rushed over, grabbing Paran's arm. Otherness and Wiln followed, settling a short distance above them.

"I hope you didn't hurt him!" Kera glared jokingly at Diyan.

"I tried not to," Diyan replied. "And no more than you do, anyway. I've seen the way you train with him!" He turned away politely as Kera kissed Paran on the lips.

"But I don't hurt him," she cooed.

"Kera will be up at your levels soon enough," Yena added cheerily, also stepping into the combat zone. Like Kera, she wore her hair long, though it was a dark brown with streaks of blonde, compared to Kera's pure black. Her features were also more rounded, and her quizzical eyes and slightly upturned nose suited her smaller stature. Her c-autom, with its bright yellow shimmering aura, floated alongside her.

Diyan smirked at her. "And what about you? When will you join the competition?"

"You wouldn't like that," Yena replied, stepping back to show off the standard combat regwear she had chosen to wear. "But I thought you would appreciate the solidarity."

"Then she'll be the one doing the hurting!" Kera grinned.

They continued joking for some time, until Yena cleared her throat, but said nothing. They fell silent, looking at her. Yena took a deep breath, as though recovering from a long run. She seemed suddenly nervous; less assertive than usual.

"I've something to tell you. We both do." She gestured to her c-autom. "We've decided on a name."

"What is it?" Kera asked.

"Rememox," she said. "It's a mixture of words, to remind me of Selo, but also, it's a new word. Because Rememox isn't just a copy." She smiled at her c-autom. "It just took some time to get over Selo."

Rememox hovered closer to her. "Understandable."

"I'm glad," Kera said. "Rememox is a lovely name." She looked pointedly at Paran and then Diyan. "Isn't it?"

They both nodded, quickly, in agreement.

"Well, seeing as we're all friends now." She glowered at Paran and Diyan again, "And Rememox has its name, why don't we celebrate?"

"How?" Diyan asked. "What do you want to do?"

Kera smiled. "Something we've never done before. Come on, let's grab some skimmers."

*

Kera, Yena, Diyan, and Paran – along with their respective c-automs, Otherness, Rememox, Wiln, and Loten – had congregated on the long viewing platform overlooking the chamber of caskets. For once, the entire platform was empty. It was just them.

"Why are we here?" Diyan asked.

Kera smirked.

Paran shrugged casually. "She hasn't told me." He looked at Otherness, whose aura flashed brighter as it circled about over Kera.

"I thought you didn't like cheating," Kera teased him.

"Isn't it obvious?" Yena asked, blushing. They all looked to her, except Kera, who was leaning on the platform's railings, facing away from them. "It's almost the only thing we've never considered. No one's considered it, we'd be the first, in a way." She gestured down to the caskets. "She wants to go there."

"That's not going to happen," Paran replied with a short, uncertain laugh. For once, he looked unsure.

"Who says so?" Kera responded, still facing away.

"Wiln," Diyan said. "Has anyone ever gone down there?"

"No. You would be the first."

"And it's allowed?"

"It isn't disallowed. However, there are no rules explicitly allowing it either. We constantly re-evaluate and change rules and procedures based upon your

40

behaviours."

"And who decides?" Yena asked.

Rememox replied. "We all do. We are here to care for you and the Great Ship, for as long as we can."

"Will you let us?" Diyan asked.

"And how do we get there?" Paran added, before any of the c-automs had the chance to reply. "There's no way down. The c-automs rerouted access when it was no longer needed."

"Like this," Kera said softly.

They looked to her as she jumped over the railing. With cries of fear and astonishment, they rushed to the railing to look over. She was fine, hovering a short distance below them. Her lower half was enveloped in a strong dark purple aura, emitted by Otherness, who hovered at the side of her feet. She was smiling with delight.

"I knew it!" she cried. Her body rose upwards, bringing her head level with the platform railing. Her legs squirmed. "Oh, come on, Otherness, give me some room!"

"Do not do that again without consulting me first." Otherness' tone was serious.

The victorious smile disappeared briefly from Kera's face, before cracking into an apologetic grin. "But I knew you'd catch me."

"And what if I had been attacked, unable to reach you? The probability of your death was not zero."

"The Great Ship has other mechanisms to protect me."

"Kera—"

"Okay, okay." She raised her arms and wriggled her body jovially in the air; evidently Otherness had released its tight hold over her legs. "I won't do it again. I was foolish, I apologise." She looked at the others. "Well, what are you waiting for?"

One by one, they jumped from the ledge, briefly gasping before they were caught and embraced by the warm auras of their respective c-automs. They descended simultaneously to the floor below until, upon reaching ground level, the c-automs' auras returned to normal, and they were released.

The caskets were arranged in rows, forming a giant lattice that spanned across the enormous floor. All half-opened, they looked like comically large, dark red c-automs. The open hemispheres revealed equally dark red internal features, with the only difference, just about visible upon closer inspection, being the small black circles patterned across the inner surfaces. The caskets were each set upon raised, knee-height, square blocks.

The four of them stood together at the corner of one of the caskets, staring. Kera stepped onto the square block and peered directly into the casket. She turned around, grinning.

"Back where we all started, eh!"

They began investigating other nearby caskets with interest. Yena yelped, causing them all to turn around in alarm.

"It's soft!" she exclaimed, padding her hand against a casket's interior. "We must have been comfortable here!"

"Makes sense," Paran replied. "We were grown inside these until we were ready to leave and the c-automs were assigned to us."

"Our annexes are just larger caskets," Diyan added.

"They still look big enough to fit inside, even now!" Kera said, with glee, jumping up to hoist herself inside the one she had been inspecting. She fit easily, with her legs bent slightly at the knee. "Oh, look! They're actually quite transparent from the inside, how interesting!"

"Ready to give up your annexe?" Paran asked, as he and the others climbed into caskets too.

"They really are transparent," Diyan commented, looking around the inside of the casket enthusiastically.

"Look!" Yena shouted, pointing up towards the platform they had descended from.

High above, a throng had gathered, watching them. The haze of auras from the c-automs floating above the top of the throng made it look as though they stood beneath a multihued ocean.

"Think they'll come and join us?" Kera asked, rolling out of her casket. She stood straight up beside it and waved. "Perhaps this is how it will feel when we meet Tapache, after everything."

Paran rolled his eyes animatedly at the others. "That's a long time from now."

Kera continued, unperturbed. "We'll reach the Source

and stop it, then Tapache will take us home."

"If there is a home to go to," Diyan muttered.

"Tapache only said we had to discover the Source," Yena added. "Who knows what we'll have to do when we find it."

"We'll destroy it, and then we'll be with the rest of the Roranian civilisation!" Kera replied, defiantly.

"There's just the simple matter of destroying the Source first then," Paran said, cheekily. "Aren't we lucky Tapache's designed us to live for so long?"

A deafening roar coursed through the chamber, causing everything to vibrate erratically. The caskets suddenly closed. Outside the caskets, Otherness cast a thick, purple aura over Kera. Similarly, the ocean of auras up on the viewing platform became thicker and more vivid. Bright, blue, searing lights began stabbing through various parts of the chamber, all diagonally downwards from the far side of the ship, away from the viewing platform. There was an even brighter flash, and the casket walls became opaque.

"Kera!" Diyan shouted from within his casket, immersed in dark red light. He pushed against it, trying unsuccessfully to force it open.

"I'm taking protective action." Wiln's voice sounded from around him. "I believe we are being attacked."

"What's going on out there? Where's Kera?"

"I'm sorry, Diyan, I don't know. I'm going to need to use all my capacity for now."

"What's happening? Kera! Please, tell me she's okay?"

"I can't."

With that, Wiln stopped communicating. No matter what Diyan said, he received no response. He was alone, in the darkness.

Chapter 6
Reimagined Dawn

Diyan awoke to a gentle, faintly red light. He was still in the casket, lying with his back against its curved surface, his legs bent. The walls of the casket were opaque. His breathing became erratic as he squirmed about.

"Don't panic, Diyan." It was Wiln. "You should be comfortable."

"What happened? Is Kera okay?"

"I don't have all the details. As I told you before, it seems we were attacked. Kera is still missing, as is everyone aside from yourself, Yena, and Paran."

"Everyone?" he cried in disbelief. "Everyone on the Great Ship?"

"Yes. Yena and Paran are under the care of Rememox and Loten, but we have no contact with the other Roranians or c-automs. It is just us."

"That can't be right." Diyan blinked, tears forming in

the corners of his eyes. "There was a bright light, then Kera vanished...they all vanished!" He began to flail his fists against the casket walls. "Kera..."

"I'm going to stabilise your response."

"Stabilise..." Diyan slowed his flailing and repeated the word, dumbly.

"The casket allows me a high degree of control over your physiology, and—"

"No, no. Don't do that," Diyan begged, shaking his head, suddenly becoming calmer. "Just, tell me what you know."

"You are currently within a casket, outside of the Great Ship. I am externally affixed to the casket, which I can control and manoeuvre. The same is true for Yena and Paran. We are clustered together, trailing the Great Ship, gathering what data we can."

Diyan took a deep breath. "You're trailing the Great Ship...and...we are outside, in open space?"

"Yes. The casket is more than capable of sustaining you for as long as necessary. We took the decision to evacuate you from one of the apertures in the hull, created during the attack."

"Is the attack still ongoing? Why can't we go back to the Great Ship? Who attacked us?"

"It will be simpler to show you."

The walls of the casket near Diyan's feet shimmered and faded to transparency. Small stars twinkled in the distance, in the same way they always had. He knew he was still in the gulf between galaxies. Empty space. He planted his hands against the walls to steady himself. Some malformed skimmers were easily visible, not too far away in the nothingness, half-melted, and broken. His eyes glided over other nearby debris, then passed it all. He gasped. There were two adjacent leviathan ships. Both looked like the Great Ship.

One was immediately recognisable from countless simulations as the enormous vessel he had lived his entire life within, the bulk of its great, spheroidal body bespeckled with light silvery patches, incongruous with the rest of the smooth hull. The Great Ship. Some of the silvery patches were crossed with fine lattices that looked to have extended out from the surrounding hull plating: presumably attempts at self-repair, albeit short-lived. Debris trailed around the ship's stern, and alongside the great tendrils of the bloom unit dangling behind it, propelling it through space. The tendrils sparkled with colourful cascades of light, as they were supposed to, seemingly unconcerned by the carnage affecting the rest of the ship. Every now and then, small pieces of rubble impacted against the bloom, being violently flung away, or disappearing in the blink of an eye.

The other vessel was surprisingly similar, although appeared to be in far worse condition. It had the same proportions, but its hull was battered and bashed, as though the ship had been rammed repeatedly and viciously. It was bespeckled with dark patches that looked entirely out of place, like breaches that had been incorrectly repaired. The ship also had a bloom, with fewer, shorter tendrils that emitted less energic displays of light than that of the Great Ship. There was no debris around or trailing the second ship. Both ships were adjacent to each other, almost touching.

"That attacked us? A Wanderer ship? Another Great Ship?" Diyan exclaimed, aghast. "Other Roranians?"

"My sensors are not capable of detailed analysis at this range. However, its general appearance indicates that you may be correct. The ship is highly likely to be a Wanderer vessel."

"We were attacked by Wanderers!"

"Whoever attacked us appears to have a Wanderer ship in their possession, but that does not mean they are Wanderers themselves."

"Why do you say that?"

"The Wanderer civilisation is predominantly led by machine-lects, not biologicals such as yourself, as you know. Single machine-lects can control entire ships that would make ours appear insignificant by all comparisons. Tapache created our ship to investigate the Source and could create many more without issue, should it decide to. Wanderers do not need to scavenge resources from other Wanderers."

"But you're a Wanderer," Diyan protested. "Not all Wanderers can do what Tapache can."

"I am, but like all c-automs, I was created for a specific

set of tasks. Besides, this is a dangerous area of space for machine-lects, considering the presence of the probability wave of death. It does not make rational sense for a machine-lect, Wanderer or otherwise, whether a singular entity or a group, to attack and overcome us, only to lead us directly along the same path, possibly to self-destruction."

"Then who attacked us?"

"There are many possibilities. Clearly, the other ship has a level of technological sophistication at least comparable with ours, considering the attack. It appears to be close enough that you might mistake it for our own Great Ship, were it not damaged. However, the attack was not as efficiently carried out as it could have been, and the subsequent repairs are not perfect, on either ship, though theirs appears to be in far worse condition. Most likely, we were attacked by biologicals."

"They couldn't repair their own Great Ship and wanted ours?"

"Perhaps, or perhaps not. There could be other reasons for acquiring ours."

Diyan's rate of breathing intensified again. "Is it possible anyone else survived?" he asked, quietly.

"Before leaving our ship, I was able to ascertain that most c-automs were immediately destroyed, along with their biological charges. I'm sorry, Diyan."

"But Kera…" Diyan turned his head to the side and vomited, partly on himself and partly against the casket wall. The vomit slid off his clothing and disappeared. Wiln said nothing more. Diyan stared despondently out at the two ships. The trailing debris behind the Great Ship made it look like a strange comet.

"Paran and Yena?" Diyan muttered, weakly.

Despite the entire casket around him becoming transparent, he said nothing, simply watching. There were two other caskets, one on either side of his own, forming part of the extremity of their home ship's debris tail. Everything was set within a blanket of darkness.

"Would you like to speak with them?"

Diyan did not reply. He clenched his jaw and closed his eyes, allowing tears to run down his cheeks. When he awoke, the two ships ahead looked just as before. Wiln informed him again that communication channels could be opened with Paran and Yena in the other two caskets, which the c-autom was highly certain would be shielded from whomever resided within the attacking ship. They began to talk. Each of them was curled up in their casket, facing the two ships ahead.

"We've established we're still on the trajectory set by Tapache." Wiln's voice filtered through to all three.

"I'm glad that hasn't changed," Paran murmured, bitterly, his easy smile gone.

Diyan grumbled a similar response.

"Are we shielded?" Yena whispered, accompanied by some ruffling noises. She was shifting up from her curled position, becoming more upright, with her arms around her knees and her chin resting between them. Diyan and Paran were both too large to attempt the same position. "I assume we must be?"

Rememox replied. "Yes. The caskets were originally designed to protect you from a wide variety of incursions, and to keep you alive for as long as required. They continue to function well."

"I mean, are we shielded from the ship? Ships. Both of them."

"We are quite certain these caskets are safely concealed. To all observers, they will appear as devoid of life as everything else in this debris stream."

"What now?" Paran asked, despondently.

Loten replied. "A change in our trajectories might lead to our discovery."

"We just follow and watch?" Diyan asked.

Loten continued. "We propose stasis."

"You want us to sleep?"

"Tapache adapted your bodies to survive for vast periods of time, far longer than your species' natural lifespan, but not confined to these caskets. You have needs beyond the physical, and these environments are poorly suited to them in your current state. We have resources that we can utilise, but stasis would be most prudent. It is your choice, of course, and you have time to consider it."

"Needs beyond the physical?" Paran repeated.

"Our minds," Yena answered. "Being locked in these

caskets."

Wiln's voice sounded. "We will awaken you when we understand more about what has happened."

"What about you three?" Diyan asked. "The intensity of the probability wave will be increasing."

"It's highly unlikely all three of us will be impacted at the same time. Our calculations indicate we are still relatively assured of being unaffected."

Diyan, Yena, and Paran looked across at each other, and then nodded, one by one.

Chapter 7
Long Awakening

Diyan's eyelids flickered. His outstretched legs twitched, and he began to repeatedly curl his hands into fists and straighten them again. His breathing intensified as noise began to fill his mind.

"Diyan, it's time to wake up."

Other names were being spoken too, by familiar voices. Paran. Yena.

Diyan opened his eyes and lifted his head up. He was no longer curled up in the casket. Paran and Yena were with him, looking around as he was, their faces marked with frowns of confusion and concern. The three of them were in a large, spherical room, spaced equidistantly apart; if they reached out, they were still a few arm's lengths away from each other. From Diyan's vantage point, both Paran and Yena should have rolled down the sides of the room towards him, but they were all somehow rooted to their

Echoes of Gravity

own positions. The light was the same as it had been inside the caskets – red-tinged – and the walls were dotted with small, black circles.

Shakily, Diyan rose to his feet. There was easily enough room for him to stand tall, the total diameter of the sphere was about three times his own height.

"We've combined the caskets to create a larger ship." It was Loten speaking to them.

Wiln's voice followed. "It took some time. We operated gradually to ensure our work was not discovered."

"How long were we asleep?" Diyan muttered.

"Three hundred standard years."

"There must be some mistake…"

Paran also rose to his feet, followed by Yena, who immediately began pacing around.

"Gravity's been tweaked," Paran muttered.

"Configured to operate spherically."

Yena's eyes widened. "Rememox?" she asked.

"I am here, Yena."

She sighed, looking relieved, flicking her light brown hair back from her eyes.

"Kera?" Paran asked.

Loten replied. "I am sorry, Paran. We have not encountered any other survivors."

Diyan shook his head. He walked towards Yena and Paran and they all drew together.

Yena squeezed both of their hands. "If anyone

55

survived, it would be Kera," she whispered.

"Three hundred years…" Paran sighed heavily. "That can't be right…"

"Are we still trailing the ships?" Diyan asked.

They turned to face the small holo that appeared in the middle of the chamber, sitting down beside each other as it gently expanded to fill much of the casket-ship's central space. The holo displayed the two large ships they had been trailing behind, outlined in blue. As they watched, the hologram zoomed in on the ship that had attacked the Great Ship. It no longer appeared as ravaged as before; its hull had smoothed out, becoming less uneven and more uniform. Its bloom propulsion unit was still more sparsely tendrilled by comparison, but the rest of the ship appeared in better condition. More like a copy of their Great Ship. The new ship's holo representation reduced and disappeared, replaced by their original Great Ship. It was changed. There were various dark, blocky structures attached to the outside of the hull.

"What are they?" Paran asked, pointing to one of the larger blocks.

"We don't know. They cover over ten percent of the ship's surface, excluding the bloom."

"They are directly over where repair mechanisms tried to patch holes," Yena stated. "The silvery patches are gone; these have been built over them."

"You are correct, Yena. We observed the patches expand and darken to form these structures."

"That means they're some kind of containment measure," she said.

"Or for communications?" Diyan suggested.

"Maybe weapons," Paran added.

"Why doesn't the other ship have them then?" Yena questioned.

Rememox answered Yena. "It is possible that our attackers acquired the Great Ship to do something theirs could not. Either way, we should find out soon enough."

"What do you mean?"

The holo of the Great Ship reduced to about a third of its previous size, and the other ship came into view again. Then, both ships were minimised further, until they were represented only as small blue points. Other points appeared in the holo: three of them, this time red in colour. They appeared to be some way away, in a rough line, directly in the path of the two blue points.

Rememox continued. "From what we can ascertain, there are three structures in our path."

"The Source?" Yena glanced at Diyan and Paran, and they shuffled nervously, waiting for the c-automs to respond.

"Ships, we believe. We don't know if they are the Source or not."

"More ships? Other Great Ships?" Diyan asked.

"They must be the Source," Paran said. "There's not supposed to be anything else out here."

Yena gestured to the red points. "What do we know

about them?"

"Little. We are only passively receiving information about them. However, a scenario to consider is that the ship that attacked us is going to attack them."

"Attack?" Diyan asked, horrified.

"The ship that attacked us managed to hide itself beforehand..." Yena began. "If those are three ships, and they are allied to it, presumably they would also be capable of hiding themselves. But if we can detect them, then it's possible they can't hide themselves in the same way, so they probably aren't allied. That's why you think our attackers are going to attack them, isn't it?"

Wiln responded. "More or less."

"And if they aren't the Source, they might be protecting the Source," Diyan suggested.

"That is also a possibility."

Paran cleared his throat and spoke slowly. "But either way, we're almost there, aren't we? We're close. It's getting more and more dangerous for you three, isn't it?"

"Can we turn back?" Yena asked, alarmed.

"We cannot." Loten's voice answered her. "However, we have made upgrades to this casket-ship. We have created a repository for our intellects to be berthed, should we detect an attack against ourselves."

Yena's heavy breathing quietened. Diyan placed a hand on her shoulder and squeezed gently.

"What now then?" Paran asked, grimacing. "We sit back and wait for this attack?"

"Would you like to be put back into stasis?"

They each shook their heads.

"Then, we wait."

*

Via the holo, they could see the two ships drawing ever closer to the three potentially unsuspecting structures in their path. According to the c-automs – using typical Roranian timekeeping – many standard days had passed, and conversation had run dry. Suddenly, Yena leapt up, looking part-excited, part-terrified, in equal measure. She was staring at the holo. Before she could say anything, Rememox' voice sounded.

"Another structure has been detected."

Diyan and Paran looked at the holo. There were now four red points. The new addition was above the previous central point. The holo rotated, and the curvature was evident.

"They're not in a line," Yena exclaimed. "They're surrounding something, aren't they?"

"We suspect more structures will reveal themselves. They may be part of a spherical lattice of structures. From slight deviations in the positions of the three original structures, we believe it is accurate to conclude that they are ships."

"Ships in a lattice surrounding something," Paran suggested, standing up.

"Must be the Source," Yena concluded.

A few moments later, further additions were made to the lattice: more red points, representing even more ships. A great, curved surface began to be revealed. The points were not always equidistant; some were packed close together, and the holo began to magnify these clusters of points, displaying the vague outlines of the ships they represented.

Wiln narrated what was being shown. "They are in various states of disrepair; it seems they have all been in battles. Most of the ships we can examine from this distance are highly alike."

"Very like our Great Ship," Paran remarked.

"They're Roranian…Wanderer," Yena said, correcting herself. "Wanderer vessels, just like ours."

Rememox answered. "Yes. They have the same basic structure, and most have their own blooms. However, there are others we cannot identify. We may be able to obtain better information about them as we move closer—"

Yena jolted as though stunned. "Rememox?" she whispered.

There was no response from any of the c-automs.

"Wiln?" Diyan said shakily.

"Loten?" Paran asked.

"We are here, Loten and I."

It was Wiln. Diyan sighed with relief.

"Unfortunately, Rememox is not."

Fear spread across Yena's face.

"Berthed?" Diyan asked softly.

"Yes. Rememox is berthed, stored securely, and as intact as any of us are. Do not fear, Yena. Rememox is safe."

Yena nodded, glancing at the other two, their eyes reflecting the sadness in her own.

*

Yet more ships had been revealed. Although they had initially appeared to be of Wanderer design, it had become apparent that the vast majority were nothing like their own Great Ship, and the c-automs could only guess at their origins.

Diyan stared at the two blue points representing their Great Ship and its strange, twinned vessel. He blinked and rubbed his eyes.

"What the...?" Paran muttered.

"Wiln?" Diyan asked.

More blue points had appeared nearby, swooping into view, seemingly from nowhere.

"Eleven additional ships alongside our own." It was Loten, not Wiln, speaking.

"Wiln?" Diyan repeated, louder than before.

"Wiln has just detected an attack against itself and has successfully berthed. We appear to be part of a hidden fleet that has revealed itself."

A bright green point appeared, behind the two front ships and near the centre of the total mass of ships.

"That is us. Our casket-ship is trailing the two front ships and is currently surrounded by the newcomer vessels."

Diyan looked about hopelessly. Yena grabbed his arm, squeezing it, while Paran looked at him almost apologetically.

Loten carried on. "The fleet is accelerating, and gravitational eddies from the blooms are sweeping us in their wake. I anticipate we are going to intercept the lattice ships far sooner than previously anticipated. I'm reducing non-essential capabilities and diverting all my resources to emergency navigational manoeuvres."

Following Loten's words, the blue points representing the supposed attacking fleet reduced the distance to the red lattice ships by almost a third. The three friends remained frozen, staring at the holo. All too soon, the distance between the forces was reduced by a half. Thin blue lines traced between the blue points.

"Are they attacking each other?" Yena asked.

"It does not appear so. I cannot ascertain what those energy signatures refer to."

As though the remaining distance was nothing, the front two ships accelerated even harder, reaching the lattice a moment later. The rest of the blue fleet was close behind. Upon reaching the lattice, the two ships – their Great Ship and the one that had commandeered it – came to an abrupt halt.

"Is that a glitch?" Paran asked hopefully.

"No. A hard deceleration – very dangerous tactic."

"Are you in danger, Loten? Will you berth yourself?"

"The probability is extremely high that I will need to attempt to do so soon. But we are all in extreme danger."

The red point before them disappeared. Immediately, other red ships nearby moved to join the battle. Yena, Paran, and Diyan watched as the lattice of ships in the path of the blue fleet rapidly densified. The rest of the blue fleet caught up, spreading out slightly around the front two ships, albeit maintaining a tight formation. The green point showing their own location was fortunately positioned off to the side, away from the brunt of the battle, though the lattice of red ships still looked densely packed ahead of them. Each of the ships in the blue fleet appeared to undergo aggressively hard decelerations upon reaching the red lattice, halting almost immediately as they reached the blockade. In places, some of the blue ships managed to push forwards slightly, but for the most part, the red ships kept them at bay.

"We're not feeling anything," Yena remarked.

"Inertial dampeners. I'm going to try to manoeuvre us through."

"Through the lattice?" Paran asked. "Loten?"

The c-autom did not respond.

"Loten?" Paran began shouting.

"Look!" Yena was pointing at the holo. The blue point

depicting their original ship had disappeared. The colour drained from Yena's face. "It's...gone."

A number of blue ships, which had previously been positioned alongside the Great Ship, had managed to break part-way through the red lattice, before being forced back, disappearing as the Great Ship had done only moments before.

"The Great Ship is gone."

"And the attack is failing," Diyan said, breathing heavily, watching as the blue points continued to disappear, one by one. Soon, they were all gone. Only the red lattice remained.

"Anyone who was left on the Great Ship is gone," Paran murmured miserably, slumping down to the floor. "And Loten's gone."

The holo pointing out their location showed the casket-ship had somehow punctured through the lattice and was at the exact level where the other blue ships had been destroyed.

"Even if Loten berthed, we're about to be destroyed anyway. And Kera...Kera..."

"Wait." Yena grabbed Paran's shoulder and pointed upwards. Diyan stood beside her, staring.

Behind the lattice of red ships, their green-marked casket-ship was heading towards a new feature on the holo. A solid, red sphere.

"What is it?" Diyan asked. "Do you think it could be..."

"A star?" Paran asked feebly.

"Or the Source, whatever it is," Yena replied.

They watched as the casket-ship moved closer to the red sphere, unhindered by the lattice ships. Then, suddenly, it moved through the surface of the red sphere. The lattice ships immediately disappeared, as did every other feature on the holo. They waited, silent. A ripple flowed across the blank holo, as though there was a ripple in reality itself, and a faint, red structure emerged, almost too indistinct to make out. It appeared to be comprised of two oddly shaped rings, immersed in a faint, reddish haze. There was a vertical inner ring, its sides squashed together in the middle, and a perfectly circular, horizontal outer ring, orbiting around the inner ring's squashed sides. The inner ring looked like a cylindrical tube that had been connected at the ends, while the outer ring was flat.

The holo rippled again, then disappeared. A moment later, they began to rise off the sides of the casket-ship.

"Gravity's gone," Diyan muttered.

Chapter 8
Kera

There were few others in the Tug Field. News of what she had done in Fadin had not yet reached Sunsprit, but time was running out. She had explained the minimum, but more questions would soon be asked. Kera had to be quick. She needed to do whatever it was that Echoes of Gravity intended for her to do here. Once the Vaesians truly understood, they might try to stop her, and she could not take that chance. This was too important.

She raised a hand in greeting to some of the nearby Vaesians, before wading into the gloom at a measured pace, alone. Although perfectly attuned to the contours of her head, the mask felt too tight. Her breathing was rapid. The device still rotated in her hand, pushed around by her sweaty fingers. Only she understood its significance.

Her elation at having seen the others – Diyan, Paran, and Yena – had been short-lived. Torturously fleeting. Immediately, she had realised what that meant. Her time had come. The waiting was over. She was able to access those initial levels of the Administration denied to her, and the rest had been easy. She still remembered her reasons for entering the Source. She had not forgotten. Events had not yet been set in motion; only she could foresee their conclusion. It was a gift she had always had, presumably given by Tapache, honed by the Nesch. Her work was for everyone, a necessary act of betrayal.

Chapter 9
Settling Down

Diyan's feet touched against the surface of the casket-ship, and his knees bent gently. Yena and Paran floated down lightly next to him. The holo had not returned, and their calls to Loten had gone unanswered. The lighting within the casket-ship had dimmed.

"Gravity's coming back," Yena said, sweeping her long, unruly brown hair back from her face.

"And it's getting stronger," Diyan added, with a nod. "It's not spherical and we can't walk around the ship, so it must be coming from outside."

Paran slumped down. "Do you think Loten berthed in time?"

"I do," Yena reassured him, as she and Diyan huddled down beside him. Soon, they began to shiver, holding each other tightly for warmth.

"I hope the ship's not malfunctioning," Yena

murmured.

"At least we're all wearing combat regwear. And lucky you decided to wear it to watch our fight," Diyan replied.

"Up to level thirteen, anyone could access it," Yena replied. "And besides, it's surprisingly comfortable."

Despite the situation, they laughed.

"Seems like a lifetime ago," Paran whispered. "I can't believe all that's happened. Three hundred years, that's what Loten told us."

"We still have each other," Diyan said.

Paran raised an arm, as though testing an imperceptible wind. "Gravity's getting even stronger, maybe soon it'll be normal."

"Normal?" Yena chuckled, though her tone became more serious. "Let's hope it doesn't go even further than that. There would be nothing we could do. And for gravity to be increasing, you know what that means?"

"It means we're probably approaching whatever it is that we saw in the holo," Diyan replied. "We just have to hope that the casket-ship is capable of landing us safely, or at least has working inertial dampening systems."

"It must have," Paran said. "We've barely felt anything so far. From what I've learned from all the simulations, if inertial dampening isn't working during entry into a new atmosphere—"

"There might not be an atmosphere."

"We would feel *something*, though."

"We'll see," Yena said, her eyes betraying the calmness

of her voice. "Any thoughts about the Source?"

"It was a ring," Diyan answered. "Drawn in on two sides, like it was squashed inwards. And there was another, flatter ring surrounding it. That's what the lattice fleet was guarding."

"There was a mist of some sort surrounding it all too," Paran added. "Unless that was just the holo malfunctioning."

The ship began to vibrate softly. They hugged each other more tightly, in silence. A short time later, the vibration abruptly stopped. They stayed as they were, watching and waiting.

"Have we landed?" Paran asked. "I didn't feel anything."

They slowly stood up.

"I don't think we're moving anymore," Yena offered, cautiously.

"It's impossible to tell," Diyan said, placing his ear to the casket wall. "But I don't think gravity is changing. I think we've landed, or docked, or whatever the correct term is."

They each moved around the casket-ship, inspecting the walls, looking for anything that might give them an insight into what was happening.

"It's still getting colder," Yena said, rubbing her hands together. "How are we supposed to leave?"

"If it's safe to leave…" Diyan murmured.

They continued to inspect the walls for any sign of an

exit, before giving up and settling back down together on the floor.

Diyan became increasingly aware of a tremendous noise coming from outside the casket-ship, reverberating all around like a sequence of explosions. He frowned, turning his head to try to escape the noise, but the sound was all-encompassing. He tried to bring his hands up to cover his ears, but his arms seemed sluggish. The loud noise died down, replaced by a brief crackling. Gentle white light shone through his eyelids. He shook his head and opened his eyes, blinking slowly. Pushing himself upright, he saw Yena doing the same. They both shielded their eyes from the bright light. Paran was on Diyan's other side, muttering something groggily, as though he had just been woken up. They looked around, confused. The ship was different. Parts of the walls were indented, as though something had tried to force its way in.

"Were we...we must have...fallen asleep," Yena murmured, confused.

"What was that?" Diyan asked, removing his hand from his eyes. He froze. There was an opening on the far side of the ship, and a face was peering through.

"Brr, it's cold in here," came a familiar voice.

Chapter 10
Strange Reunion

Paran rushed towards Kera, stopping a half-stride in front of her and falling to the ground. She knelt down beside him, cradling the back of his neck. His sobbing was muffled as Kera rested her chin on his shoulder and looked over at Diyan and Yena, who stood with their backs to the circular hole in the casket-ship from which they had exited only moments before.

Aside from the twinkling lights glittering not too far away, there was nothing within the dark, barren, flat landscape. It was akin to the simulated night they had experienced when they had all been living on the Great Ship. Fine, yellow debris blew gently all around, rising to knee-height in the air.

One of the convex slabs which made up the casket-ship's continuous wall was currently attached to the front of a large, bulky, bright yellow machine, that was about as large and had the same dimensions as a skimmer, cut in half. It looked heavy, depressed about a finger's length into the ground, with debris pooled around its cratered base. Next to the casket-ship, the machine looked comically obsolete, a primitive tool for making holes.

From the outside, the casket-ship appeared like an enormous individual casket. Its surface was a dark red, and deeply pitted at various points, as though it had experienced multiple powerful impacts.

"It's rather fitting that we should meet beside a great big casket, isn't it?" Kera said, softly.

She wore an all-black, tight-fitting ensemble that extended from her feet upwards, with a loose piece of fabric wafting about her neck. Her hair, once so long, had been cut short, and was neatly tied in a bun. Her face was still mesmerizingly beautiful.

"And I can see that I wasn't the first to find you." She gestured to the impact craters across the casket-ship's surface. "Lucky these caskets are triamond-derivatives. Near impossible to cut through, without one of those." She flicked her head towards the large cutting machine, with its circular slab of casket-ship wall still attached.

There were two others with Kera, both wearing similar, though slightly thicker-looking, all-black ensembles. Unlike Kera, they had pulled the loose neck fabric up around the lower parts of their faces, hiding their mouths. Both were female. The taller one stood by the side of the cutting machine. She was using the chest-height controls, causing the front part of the machine to tip forwards. The slab of casket-ship fell heavily to the ground with an audible thud, sending up a thick cloud of debris. The circular part of the machine, which had previously held the slab, had a series of whirring needles the same colour as the casket-ship, which slowly came to a stop. The female in charge of the machine pressed some more controls, and a loud, irregular rattling sounded, followed by a consistent, quieter buzzing. The base of the machine proceeded to rise to ankle height, and she was able to manoeuvre it to the side.

Kera's shorter, stockier companion was pushing a tall rod into the ground, the last of three rods that were now sticking out of the ground, completing a triangle. The three rods all had five blue lights along their length that slowly flashed in sequence. When the shorter companion was done, she joined the taller one by the machine, helping manoeuvre it around the casket-ship. Once it was in its next position, the buzzing stopped, and another cloud of debris was brought up as the machine slumped to the ground. The front dipped forwards so that it was pressed against the front of the casket-ship, and a loud whirring began.

"What's going on?" Yena asked, alarmed.

Kera shook her head comfortingly as she rose to her feet, pulling Paran up with her. "It's good to see you again," she said with a smile.

Diyan flinched, casting a furtive glance at Kera's two

companions.

"It's okay," Kera continued. "Soji and Irido are with me." Letting go of Paran's hand, she walked to Diyan and Yena, briefly resting her hands on their shoulders. "It's so good to see you all."

"What happened to you?" Diyan asked.

"That's a long story. I'd like to know what happened to you three as well, and how you managed to survive." She gestured to their ship again. "Judging by the impact marks, you're lucky the ship held. Most aren't so lucky when the Breaker knocks." She glanced nervously at the triangle of poles.

"Where are we, Kera? Is this the Source?" Yena asked. Her voice was faint, as though she were far away. "And who is the Breaker?"

Kera waved a hand. "We have much to tell each other. But we don't have time now. The Haze Rings will be moving shortly, and we'll be stuck here in the daytime, which is not advisable. Come." She pointed at the nearby twinkling lights. "We'll wait in my ship while Soji and Irido finish doing what they can with yours."

"Haze Rings?" Paran repeated.

"Finish doing what they can with our ship?" Yena also repeated, confused by Kera's words. A thud caught their attention as another circular slab of the casket-ship was dropped to the ground, and the buzzing began again. Quicker this time, the machine operated by Kera's companions was moved to its third position. The blue lights on the three triangular poles momentarily flashed more rapidly, but quickly slowed down again, continuing their lethargic routine.

"We're collecting resources. Not very exciting, but it can pay quite well, if you're lucky," Kera said, as though it were obvious. She smacked her forehead. "Yena, did you think we came for you? Did you all?" She looked at them with an awkward, lopsided smile. "Believe me, I'm happy to have found you, more than anything, but we came to scavenge the resources we'd located. This is as much a surprise for me as it is for you, though judging by the condition I found you in, I'm guessing you know less about our situation than we do. Are you aware that you're in Barrenscape?"

The three of them shook their heads.

"We've only just arrived," Diyan said.

Kera frowned and looked at their ship, staring pointedly at the impact marks. "No, by the looks of it, you've been here for some time. I think you must have been in stasis. We're taking that ship—" She stopped and corrected herself. "*Your* ship apart, to bring with us. You may not have noticed, but there isn't too much around here." She glanced at Soji and Irido, who were disappearing around the side of the casket-ship, which now had a sequence of large holes cut into it. "We need to be quick. Come on, let's go to my ship. They can work just as fast without me. Our second cutter broke a few trips back." She gestured for them to walk towards her ship.

"But Rememox…" Yena protested.

"We recognised the c-autom orb-bodies affixed to the outside. They created some type of repository to berth themselves in, didn't they?" Kera asked.

Yena nodded in response.

"We've seen this before. A few others escaped the initial attack on our ship in similar structures, and some of the other Great Ships had c-automs too."

"Great Ships?" Diyan asked. "So, there are others."

Kera nodded. "I know there's a lot you don't understand yet. Don't worry, we've already taken the c-autom repository." She pointed towards her ship. "If we ever find a way to awaken them, they'll be included."

"Can you tell how many c-automs are berthed in the repository?" Paran asked, anxiously, looking at the ground. "I want to know about Loten…I'm not certain there was time for it to save itself."

Kera placed a hand on Paran's shoulder and looked him in the eyes. "When we're back in Fadin, you'll be able to find out. Now, come. It's safer inside."

As they drew nearer, the bright lights of Kera's ship obscured its features less. It was immediately clear that the ship was an amalgamation of components never intended for combination. There was a battered front cube that was far taller than seemed practical, the outermost side of which, facing away from the rest of the Kera's ship, was fully transparent. The cube also had various irregularly shaped transparent windows dotted about the other two sides, through which a raft of worn-looking controls could be seen. The cube was connected at the back to the rest of the ship, which predominantly consisted of a large, equally-battered-looking container that was many times larger than the front section, presumably for storing cargo. The back container had no windows, but the two sections of the side facing them were open, and ramps descended to ground level.

The inside was dark and unlit, appearing mostly empty. The main parts of the ship were raised off the ground just enough that Paran, the tallest of them, would have nearly been able to scrape the bottom with his fingers. Underneath, the bulk was sparsely supported by eight rods, each about the thickness of an arm, and each concerningly bent at points. Halfway down the rods, a chunky piece of equipment was welded in place. Various pipes and funnels extended away from it at all angles.

"That's your ship?" Diyan asked, horrified. "And that's the propulsion unit?"

Kera chuckled as they drew closer. "No bloom on this one, I'm afraid."

The others chuckled too.

"You'll find things are very different here compared to what you're used to."

"Who would design a ship this way?" Paran asked.

"It's just a salvage vessel," Kera protested. "And we're constrained by the resources we can get." The closest side of the front cube began to swing down. "At least it's got soft-gravity emulators. You should see some of the others!"

"It looks like it's falling apart!" Yena blurted out.

As soon as the ramp was in place, a loud, high-pitched sound pierced the air. Kera turned and stared at the triangular poles. Both Soji and Irido ran around the side of the casket-ship. One pole was flashing red; two excitedly flickering blue. A moment later, the sound was extinguished and all three flashed a slow, blue sequence again. Kera's companions walked back around the casket-ship, their heavy breathing evident through their tight suits.

"What was that?" Yena asked, alarmed.

"Gravitational anomaly, probably. Happens sometimes in Barrenscape." Kera led them up the ramp, which vibrated noisily under their weight. "The alarm is for the Breaker. The rods are proximity sensors; they detect gravitational disturbances. We're in no danger, don't worry. If the alarm really goes off, we should have more than enough time to leave safely."

The inside of the cube was as haphazard as the outside. There were two simple seats at the front, consisting of metallic sheets bent perpendicularly in two places, welded unevenly to the floor. Only one still had fabric stretched across it, and that was sparse and heavily frayed. A bank of controls lay in front of the seats, seemingly an odd mixture of touch-sensitive and mechanical buttons, with various markings and grooves, many of which had been smoothed down or worn away. Clusters of cubed crates were piled behind the front seats, filling up most of the rest of the compartment. They were all the same height, rising a little higher than the front seats, with flashing red buttons attached messily near their bases.

"Electro-clamps," Kera explained. "They automatically engage once we're in flight. The inertial dampeners aren't great." She looked apologetically at them. "Please, make yourselves comfortable."

Diyan pointed towards Soji and Irido, who were just about visible coming around the other side of the casket-ship with the cutter. "Are they alright?" he asked, concerned.

Despite the large cuts in the casket-ship, the top part had still not fallen, and it appeared as stable as before.

"They'll be fine. We'll come back again tomorrow and finish off if there's anything left. It depends on whether the Breaker finds it first. It doesn't tend to leave too much behind. But then again, it has clearly already failed to break in, so maybe it wasn't interested."

"Who or what is the Breaker?" Yena asked, moving to the far side of the compartment. She pushed one of the crates right up against the wall and sat down. Diyan pushed another crate beside hers, leaving enough room for her legs to dangle down. Paran remained standing beside Kera.

"No one knows, exactly, and no one survives their

encounter with it. They just disappear. You might find the odd part leftover, but that's about it." She smiled uneasily at their horrified faces. "Our sensors can't accurately image or scan it, and it moves fast, but we can detect its rough location."

"Maybe it's looking for something?" Diyan suggested.

She shrugged. "All we know is that it can manipulate gravity. We don't know how it got here, or why. But one thing's for certain." She gestured for Paran to sit down on the crate beside Diyan as she also sat down. "You'd better be gone when it comes for you. That old combat regwear you're wearing won't save you."

An awkward pause descended as Kera looked at all three of them, as though suddenly unsure of how to continue, and they looked back.

Paran ended the silence. "So, what now?"

"Soon, it'll be daytime, meaning it'll be too dangerous to fly. We'll let those two finish collecting as much as they can, load up the ship, and then, we leave Barrenscape." She heaved a sigh. "So...tell me what happened to you."

Chapter 11
Starting Wonders

Kera's two companions, Irido and Soji, sat at the front of the compartment, working the ship's controls. They had changed into the same, less bulky, all-black regwear as Kera's upon finishing with the casket-ship, though they both still covered the lower parts of their faces. They had yet to speak, entering quietly before fastidiously preparing the ship to leave. One of the blue rods had momentarily flashed red again, and although it was another false alarm, they clearly wanted to leave quickly. Soji kept glancing up nervously at the sky outside: it was lighter than before.

Kera was staring at the floor. One of her hands was tapping her knee, and she nodded slowly. "That's quite a story." She looked up at Diyan, Paran, and Yena. "I always wondered what had happened, and if you'd survived. Over time, I lost hope." The ship began to vibrate. Kera smiled. "But I'm glad, really glad."

"Kera," Diyan began. "How long do you think we were in stasis for down here?"

Kera rolled her head from side to side. "Overall? Based on what you've told me, it must have been at least hundreds of standard years. Maybe even as far back as the very beginning, three hundred years ago, when we first came here, before Fadin was established. The casket-ship probably hid you from search expeditions. The Breaker must have only recently found you, damaging you enough for us to spot you."

"So, we slept for three hundred years while we trailed the Great Ship, then another three hundred years down here..." Yena trailed off.

Kera nodded. "Seems like it. You've been asleep considerably longer than you've been awake, by some way."

Yena's face drained of colour. She looked uncharacteristically hesitant. "And you've been awake this whole time..."

Kera nodded.

The four of them stood in silence for some time, before eventually continuing their conversation.

"What about you?" Paran asked, placing a hand on Kera's shoulder. The same, easy smile that had long since left Paran's face had returned, though it did not quite reach his eyes.

Kera spoke quietly, almost whispering, looking down again. "I didn't make it down here for a long time." She paused, a single tear falling from her cheek. "A few made it through when our ship was destroyed; their c-automs managed to keep them safe, like yours did, creating protective barriers within various parts of the ship. When the Great Ship was destroyed, some of the debris made it through in one piece, carrying survivors inside. By the time I arrived, we had already built up quite a presence here."

When she did not continue, Paran rubbed his large hand across her back. "How come you didn't make it through with the others?"

Kera's head moved from side to side, meandering through the air, as though she could not decide how to respond. "I was captured; made to fight."

"But the whole ship was destroyed!" Yena exclaimed. "We saw the blue beams piercing the hull, they went right through..." She stopped abruptly.

Kera's head continued to drift from side to side, and her eyes had glazed over. "Graviton tugs. They evaporated parts of the hull and sucked us right out, into their ship, removing as many as they could. They wanted us for their army. Our ship was only ever going to be a decoy; a shining emblem to draw their enemies in."

"Camouflage," Yena sighed. "That's what the additions were – the structures they built on the hull of the Great Ship. Obvious weaponry of some kind?"

Kera nodded. "They wanted to draw their enemies' attention, so they could attack and destroy the Source, if that's even possible." She took a deep breath. "It was a species called the Nesch – the ones who took us; the ones who destroyed the Great Ship. They were part of a coalition fleet, seeking to destroy the ships defending the Source, and then the Source itself. That particular Nesch ship had been tasked with scouting for resources to aid the fleet, and it was our misfortune that they found us…" She clasped her hands together wearily. "Anyway, when the coalition fleet attacked the enemy ships in the lattice, those enemy ships concentrated on the heavily fortified ship the Nesch had taken from us – our Great Ship. And while the enemy's focus was on the Great Ship, the coalition fleet focused on infiltrating the enemy vessels. They pushed their armies aboard using reverse graviton tugs, leaving the coalition ships empty. And as the coalition's ships were destroyed, the enemy ships were quietly subverted."

"They transferred themselves to the enemy ships and took control from the inside?" Paran asked.

Kera nodded.

"You keep talking about enemy ships…" Yena began.

"The Nesch trained me, and all the others they captured. Biological life is important here because the Source doesn't destroy us; only intelligent machines cannot survive. That's why Tapache sent us. We became the soldiers of the Nesch; joined them; fought for them, as we spread through the ships in the lattice. It was that or die."

"Why do the Nesch want to destroy the Source?"

"Why not? Isn't that what we were also sent here to do? Many Roranians thought so; Tapache wasn't clear. The Source is dangerous, and we can't understand it, so it makes sense that some would want to destroy it, while others would seek to protect it and learn more."

"Did you win?" Paran asked.

Kera laughed, bitterly, drawing herself upright and leaning her back against the compartment wall. "The battle is still ongoing out there, I'm sure. It's no longer my concern."

They were distracted as Soji and Irido simultaneously pulled the black fabric down from their faces and twisted their heads around from the front seats. The taller and slimmer of the two was very pretty, with dark skin and thin, wide lips that stretched across her face.

"Ship's ready to go," she said sternly, her voice a complete contrast to her appearance. She cast an impassive glance over the newcomers.

Kera nodded. "Take us up then, Soji."

Soji turned back, grabbed the central throttle in front of her and began twisting it. "Doing it now."

The shorter one – evidently Irido – took a longer look at them. She bore a small, irregular patch of pure white skin on her cheek, and though not as pretty as Soji, her smile was bright and pleasant. She looked as though she wanted to speak, but Soji shot her a sharp look as the ship began vibrating, so Irido simply nodded at them, before turning back around.

The ship's vibrating increased, somewhat erratically.

"You'll get used to it," Kera shouted over the noise, her voice tinged with humour.

Paran, Yena, and Diyan grabbed the sides of the crates they were sitting on as the ship accelerated jerkily upwards. Outside, it was becoming brighter.

As the ship rose higher, the topography of the bleak landscape below them became apparent. The ground curved around in an oddly linear fashion, as though they were flying over a large, cylindrical tube. The three newcomers stared out of the windows, craning their necks to capture as much as possible. In the distance, the landscape disappeared into the hazy air.

"It's not a planet, is it?" Yena shouted.

"We call it Barrenscape, because there's mostly nothing there," Kera replied. "Remember you told me you saw two rings on the casket-ship's holo? One central one, with two sides bent towards each other, and an outer flat one? This is the central ring."

"How big is it?" Diyan asked, turning to Kera.

"Vast."

"Does it orbit anything?"

"No."

"And the outer ring?"

"Ringscape. That's where we're going, to a city called Fadin." Kera stood up and shuffled in between Soji and Irido to look at the controls, then returned to her crate.

"It's not quite the Great Ship," she grinned, "But it works."

"And this is the Source – Barrenscape and Ringscape?" Paran shouted. Midway through his question, the noise died down as the acceleration of the ship eased, and they began to move at a constant speed. "This is what Tapache sent us here for?"

"Almost," Kera replied. "Almost."

"What do you mean?"

Yena stood up, wobbling slightly as she struggled to balance. Her eyes were fixed on Barrenscape. Paran and Diyan looked out of the window, trying to determine what had taken her attention. There was nothing there, just the brightening sky.

"Where's it gone?" Yena asked incredulously. "Where's Barrenscape gone?"

"Gone to the haze," Irido answered excitedly, whilst remaining diligently focused on the controls.

Kera gestured all around. "The third part of the Source: the Haze Rings. They are the rotating structures around Ringscape and Barrenscape; they keep us here and keep everything else out. They create the light and the winds, functioning in a similar way to a star, just without the dangerous radiation. They also have some strange effects. Signals within the confines of the Haze Rings are scattered as they travel through the air. Even visible light becomes dispersed; that's why we can't see Barrenscape anymore. Some call the effect a *thick atmosphere*, but it's more than that. It's almost impossible to efficiently transfer any information long-distance, by any medium other than *us*. It's all limited."

"What are the Haze Rings?" Diyan asked.

"If we fly close enough, you can see for yourself," Kera replied, with a mischievous grin. The ship began to rattle again, and they all fell back, grabbing the crates more firmly.

"Turbulence?" Yena asked.

"Haze winds picking up," explained Kera. "It's going to get a lot noisier again. Full daytime brings the strongest haze winds, and we don't want to be out in them." She chuckled at their worried expressions. "Don't worry, we'll be in Fadin before that."

The ship rattled even more fiercely. "Why didn't we wait for longer in Barrenscape instead?"

"And sit there hoping the Breaker doesn't find us? Many have died by that gamble."

The ship's shudders increased in frequency and intensity, the noise making further conversation impossible.

After a while, Yena jerked her arm towards something resolving in the distance, in the opposite direction to Barrenscape. A group of dark objects were becoming visible: three of them, in a rough line, with great wedges of space between them. Each was enormous – many magnitudes larger than Kera's ship – and comprised of a great cylindrical axis, with two large, corrugated platforms fanning out on either side, almost as thick as the axis itself. The cylindrical axes and their platforms were all parallel, and immense grills were plastered across the platforms, covering every possible unit of surface area. Some of the grill slits appeared wide enough that their entire ship could have passed through; others were tiny. One of the central structure's platforms seemed to shimmer as the grills began moving fluidly across its corrugated surface.

"They're reorganising," Kera shouted over the noise. "They suck up the debris around them."

"What are they?" Paran yelled.

"Sky-factories, for manufacturing. That's where the parts we managed to cut from your ship will end up."

"Sky-factories from Fadin?" Yena asked.

"They're what's allowed the city to thrive. They're very noisy and they generate a lot of heat, so it makes sense to keep them out here."

Paran pointed to some small objects orbiting the sky-factories in tight formations, with flickers of light trailing them. "What're those?"

"Drones, for defence. The sky-factories are important to Fadin."

The noise from the winds died down, and as their ship moved closer they could see multiple taut, giant, metallic tethers extending away from the sky-factories. Like the grills that moved across the sky-factory surface, the tethers also shimmered. Dark silver capsules were affixed around them, moving rapidly up and down. All the tethers pointed in the same direction, where something else was also coming into view.

This time, there was no yellowy, desolate expanse; instead, a dark brown landscape lay before them. The tethers continued into the distance, stretching over the terrain and looking to meet the ground somewhere further along. The landscape they approached was bordered by a straight edge, where the surface dropped off spectacularly, as clearly defined as the angled bends of the metallic chairs that Soji and Irido sat upon. The drop was perpendicular, and the surface that continued down was similarly dark brown and planar. There was a sharp intake of breath from the three newcomers.

"The edge of Ringscape." Kera pointed along the surface, where the tethers disappeared from view. "Up there is one part of Fadin. It's newer, we call it Under-Fadin, as this is the underside of Ringscape."

Lights glinted in the distance.

"What're those?" Diyan asked, pointing to the thin, arrayed structures that ran down the edge of Ringscape. As the ship drew closer, it became apparent that the entire edge was lined with the structures, as far as they could see. On the surface of Ringscape, the arrays periodically joined up into three, large, thick rails that ran directly away from the edge, pointing towards Fadin. There looked to be other structures alongside the rails, but they were too far away to make out clearly.

"Power generation, for Fadin," Kera explained. "Some

communications too. Very power heavy, and the data bandwidths are low, but good enough."

"How do they work?"

Before Kera could reply, Paran interrupted. "You said that this is just Under-Fadin, on Ringscape's underside. Where's the rest?"

Irido giggled from the front. "You mean Upper-Fadin?" she smirked.

Suddenly, Ringscape twisted around, and the ship banked up what appeared to be a never-ending, sheer wall of dark brown. The force of the acceleration pushed them against the ship's sides until, finally, the ship crossed up and over the edge and began flying over another dark brown landscape, as the edge of Ringscape rapidly disappeared behind them. Diyan clenched his jaw shut, taking a moment to recover his composure.

Kera and Irido chuckled. "Here, on this side of Ringscape, the upperside."

Soji flashed an apologetic smile at the three newcomers, as Yena wiped stray strands of hair back from her face, staring eagerly out of the window. Diyan and Paran did the same.

"There's Upper-Fadin," Soji informed them.

Ships in the distance were headed in their direction; though they were too small to properly distinguish, they looked similar in size to Kera's vessel.

"Who are they?" Yena asked.

"Business traffic, I assume," Kera replied. "They'll be

going down the edge to Under-Fadin."

"From Upper-Fadin?"

"Yes." Kera nodded.

The silhouette of Upper-Fadin came into view as the gentle light of day grew brighter and brighter. None of the structures in the city were very high, aside from the three tethers, which could be seen descending from somewhere in the sky and plunging into the city.

"Is that really it?" Paran asked. "It's all so...low."

Kera nodded and pointed to the three tethers. "Each side has three sky-factories."

Capsules moved up and down the three tethers, each of which had smaller, thinner support tethers that branched off to other parts of the city.

Drawing closer, they noticed that the city had an organic, haphazard look to it. Various structures were built alongside each other, separated by brightly lit routes. There were many large, white, circular domes, joined together by similarly coloured conduits. They looked to be recent features, brighter and less weathered than everything else. Other buildings, all emitting a strong green light, were dotted about, although predominantly concentrated around what appeared to be the centre of Upper-Fadin. Soji and Irido seemed to be taking the ship to a large open space that was bordered by a high wall, halfway between the city centre and the closest discernible periphery. A few other ships, mostly similar in appearance to Kera's, came into view, apparently sharing the same general trajectories. A shipyard.

"Where are the local transports?" Paran asked, tilting his head to the side, and squinting as he stared down. "How will we get around?"

"You can always walk," Kera replied, cheekily. "Or use the ground-based transports that we typically use here. They're skimmers, although not as functional as you're used to, but we've done what we can with them. None of the cities here are quite like what you're used to."

"The layout looks similar to the holos of the Roranian ruins Tapache found," Diyan said.

Kera shrugged. "Makes sense. We built this, after all."

"It's just so strange how it's all so flat," Yena murmured.

"You'll get used to living on the ground, it doesn't take long."

Diyan looked around. Now they were flying over the city, Upper-Fadin seemed like an endless sprawl. No edges of Ringscape were visible and most of the brown landscape had been built over.

"This stretches all around Ringscape, does it?" Diyan asked.

"Not this." Kera laughed. "It's just one city, and this is only part of it. But yes, Ringscape is a ring that circles around. If you were to walk along it for long enough, you would arrive back where you started." The ship began to descend lower. "I would like to welcome you all to Fadin, the greatest city on Ringscape, named after the c-autom of one of the founders." There was a hint of something approaching sarcasm in her voice. "But before you start exploring, we need to take you to an influx node."

Chapter 12
Fadin Awaits

The final manoeuvres for the ship's docking sequence had been completed, without Soji or Irido lifting a finger. The ship had connected to what Kera had called the influx network, which took over control of the ship, ensuring landing was executed smoothly. Once docked, they exited the ship, walking down the ramp attached to the front cabin to find themselves in a large shipyard, packed to the brim with ships, albeit neatly ordered and with thin lanes between them. Whilst some of the ships looked fairly new, most had seen better days and had clearly been battered and bashed about, with many exhibiting multiple scrapes and copious repair works. As they watched, a few other ships descended in other parts of the shipyard, though the hustle and bustle seemed to be winding down.

Soji and Irido walked to the side of the ship and waited for the ramps to descend, before rushing up and disappearing into the ship's cargo area. Diyan, Yena, and Paran stared at the other individuals walking about the shipyard, who were weaving around the ships in the same overall direction. Most wore the same black regwear as Kera, Soji, and Irido, and whilst some walked stony-faced, others smiled and laughed together in groups.

"It's almost like being back on our ship," Paran mumbled.

Diyan nodded. "I know what you mean." Aside from the odd glance, no one was paying them much attention. "What's that?" Diyan asked, pointing to one of the newer-looking ships.

While its overall design was the same as Kera's, it did not have a bare undercarriage holding a propulsion unit. Instead, it was lower to the ground, with its aft covered by a dark, solid casing that extended some way back. It was also docked with more space around it than most other ships they could see.

"Bloom units," Kera explained, gesturing almost absentmindedly to the hazy air that could just about be seen escaping from the rim of the solid casing, as she inspected a device in her hand that projected a small holo screen into the air. "Only the most recent vessels have them; mostly they're used for military ships or the drones defending the sky-factories." She looked up and pointed to the sky. "When parts of the Great Ships make it through, their blooms occasionally also come through in parts, all broken up. Since we can't do that ourselves, it's assumed the breakages are caused by interactions with the Haze Rings. It's only recently become possible for us to collect and use those parts, and that's partly because so many pieces of our own Great Ship's bloom happened to make it through. Before that, the Vaesians used to push the bloom fragments against the Haze Rings, as they were too difficult to contain." Kera cast another glance at the holo screen projected from the device she held. "Irido," she shouted. A muffled 'yes' came from inside the ship's cargo area. "You forgot to peg the ship site as ours, again. I'm doing it now." An even quieter response came back, too inaudible for the others to make out, though Kera seemed satisfied.

"What do you mean?" Yena asked.

Kera frowned. "About what?" Her eyes opened. "Oh, the bloom fragments. They used to cause havoc when they rained down on Ringscape. Great efforts were undertaken to take them back up and push them against the Haze Rings, to destroy them. Nothing else down here can destroy a bloom. Fortunately, now, we can use them for our ships."

"I wasn't talking about the bloom fragments," Yena said, somewhat impatiently. "I don't understand anything you just said. These other Great Ships, what's that about? Who are all these people? Why did it take us so long to get here? Everything is so confusing!" Yena's eyes bulged as she looked about exaggeratedly.

"It's a lot to take in, I know." Kera smiled

apologetically, cancelling the device's holo screen and putting it back into her pocket. "You'll understand more when we get to the shipyard entrance." She pointed to the place everyone else in the shipyard was heading towards. "We can register you at an influx node. The influx network contains all the information you need and will explain everything much better than I can." Kera disappeared briefly up the cargo ramp to speak with Irido and Soji, before returning. "They'll make sure your c-automs are stored safely."

"Did Loten berth itself in time?" Paran asked.

"We'll know soon enough. Come on, let's go."

As the three of them weaved around the ships, following Kera closely, they could not help but notice the blue indicator markings on the floor, akin to those that had outlined the combat zones on the Great Ship. They passed a group of Roranians, standing beside a ship, chatting. Three males, in the same black regwear as Kera, Soji, and Irido. Two were leaning with their backs against the ship's propulsion framework, one was gesticulating wildly, and they all began laughing loudly. The gesticulating man suddenly stopped and turned around, shouting something at the four of them and pointing at their combat regwear, before pulling up the fabric around his neck to cover his mouth and nose, then turning back to his friends.

"What's he doing?" Paran asked, puffing his chest and glaring.

"Nothing," Kera replied.

Paran glared back at the man. "He said something about us joining silver things…"

Kera chuckled. "Calm down, all he did was pull his facepiece up. Maybe he prefers filtered air."

Paran grunted and turned back.

"Haven't they seen combat regwear before?" Yena asked, looking back at the many curious expressions behind them as she drew level with Kera.

Kera shook her head. "Probably not. Time has passed while you slept, I'm afraid. Most of the old technologies and materials have been recycled and repurposed. You can change out of them soon."

"Surely they remember," Paran said.

"Remember?"

"From the Great Ship? They were there too."

Kera shook her head. "Most of those who live in Fadin were never on that ship."

"What?" Yena asked, surprised.

"There have been more Roranians born here than made it through in the first place. The population growth was rapid, at first. Some are thirteenth or fourteenth generation now."

"We've procreated?" Yena still sounded shocked. "On the ship it wasn't possible."

"Tapache blocked it, but not now. Soji and Irido were born here, eleventh generation, both of them."

"Really?"

"Yes, and if you want some advice, while we're on this topic, don't tell anyone that you've just arrived here, unless you have to. It leads to too many questions."

"Does that mean we can die, too?"

"We still have the long life Tapache gave us. No Roranians have succumbed to old age, yet."

"And you watched Fadin grow all this time? From nothing to this?"

"I wasn't here at the start. I was made to fight, outside the Source, as I told you." Her face was momentarily serious. "But I've still been here a lot longer than you."

The end of the shipyard loomed nearby. There were two tall, cylindrical buildings, fanning outwards higher up. Each had wide circular plateaus at the top that dipped, curling down at the sides, casting wide, rounded shadows on the shipyard floor. High walls, attached halfway up their outer sides, looped right around the shipyard. A thick, shoulder-height barrier crossed the ground between the two buildings. Sections rippled up vertically in discrete, pole-like segments, allowing those leaving and entering the shipyard to pass unimpeded.

Kera pointed at the barrier. "That's the usual way in and out," she told them, before pointing to the left building. "But we need to go and complete your registration first. The influx network is expecting you; we've already submitted the salvage overview."

The four of them headed towards the tall building on the left, stepping into its shadow. The surface of the building was white and appeared smooth, like the large domes they had seen as they flew over the city. The base of the building was dark grey and bulged outwards. When Kera was close, a section comfortably wide enough for her to walk through rippled up, in the same manner as the barrier. She stood below the ripples and gestured them inside.

"This way."

They followed, with additional segments rippling up to accommodate their entry.

The inside hall was pristine and appeared to span most of the building's lowest level. Almost everything was bright white, though there were some smaller entrances to the left that were individually covered with the same grey mechanisms they had just walked through, and a larger entrance on the opposite side of the room.

Aside from the four of them, there were three others standing in the vast room, each clad in dark navy uniforms strikingly similar to the combat regwear they themselves wore, albeit far bulkier. They wore masks wrapped around their heads, with two bright yellow circles where their eyes looked through. Each held a selection of large items that looked menacingly like weapons, and stood completely still, neither looking at, nor acknowledging, anything.

"They're guards," Kera said.

One of the guards moved to the side, away from one of the smaller entrances. A moment later, it rippled open and a woman walked through, wearing casual, loose clothing. She glanced at the four of them with a slight look of surprise, before walking briskly through to the larger exit on the other side. It rippled up and she stepped out, but just before resealing, some small, light grey transport vehicles were briefly visible, hovering a short distance above the ground on the other side.

"Those were skimmers," Paran said, brightly.

"But not as you remember them," Kera said.

"You said they're only ground-based now?" Diyan asked. "They can no longer fly?"

"Unfortunately, not."

"Where's this influx node we're supposed to register at?" Yena asked.

Kera strode over to the near wall on the right. A circular segment rose from the floor, stopping just below her chest height. Four small stools also rose around it.

"We can sit here," Kera informed them.

They all sat down. Kera sat opposite Yena, between Diyan and Paran. A small holo interface appeared before Kera. A moment later, Diyan's reality changed.

Chapter 13
Informing Confusion

Diyan looked around. The nostalgic feeling of entering a simulation had momentarily confused him. It was very dark, aside from a vaguely spherical ball of gentle, yellow light, the intensity of which increased the longer he stared at it. It seemed an arm's reach away, helping him focus his concentration. Something began to well up within him.

"A c-autom…are you a c-autom?" he almost sputtered. "I thought machine-lects couldn't survive here?"

The voice appeared all around him, just as Wiln's once had. "Machine life does not exist in this place. That is a mystery we still do not understand. I am an influx, and my role is to introduce you to Ringscape. You have been identified as Roranian and are permitted here. Identify yourself."

"I am Diyan, and my c-autom was Wiln—" he began, before correcting himself. "*Is* Wiln."

"Your identification has been successfully bio-referenced from the manifest. Your c-autom was recovered and is stored within the Administration's repository. How did you make your way here?"

Diyan spluttered, unsure of how to start his story. The influx inquired further, and he began to answer all its questions. Finally, when it was nearly satisfied, it moved the topic away from Diyan himself.

"The Roranian identified as Kera brought you to Fadin. Can you verify her identity?"

"What do you mean?"

"Is Kera who she purports to be, as far as you can ascertain?"

Diyan nodded. "Yes…"

The ball of light dissipated and a view that he recognised appeared.

The voice continued, all around him. "This is Upper-Fadin, situated on Ringscape's upperside, which, together with Under-Fadin, situated on Ringscape's underside, comprises the city Fadin, under the governance of the Administration. Fadin is the primary city of Ringscape."

From his vantage point, Diyan could see the bustling activity of life below. The shipyard was just off-centre, to his left, and the rest of the city was splayed out all around. Skimmers and individuals were visible, moving in between various structures. There were many, many Roranians, but also others that he did not recognise. His heart began beating faster as he rose higher in the simulation.

"Wait!" he cried. "Stop!" His ascent froze. The granular activity below him was still just about discernible. "What was that?"

In the simulated air, a figure appeared in front of him, rotating slowly. It appeared oddly familiar, and yet strange at the same time.

"Are you referring to this?"

"Yes."

The figure had three leg-like appendages, each thinner than a typical Roranian leg, and disappearing into a skirt-like piece of black clothing – which looked like it had the same texture as regwear – that wrapped around what he took to be its waist. Two additional arm-like appendages emerged mid-waist from its clothing, slightly lower than seemed correct. They waved about fluidly, as though unconstrained by skeletal mechanics, and ended with a mass of fibrous extensions. Diyan fingers twitched reflexively. The black clothing ended just above the creature's arm-like appendages, revealing about a third of its naked torso, which ended squarely and featured a long, sprouting neck in the middle. The neck curved a little forwards, and carried a large head, complete with two widely spaced black eyes and a circular aperture in the middle: its mouth. The creature's entire body was covered with fine white hair.

"These are the Vaesians. They are the predominant species we share Ringscape with."

Something touched Diyan's shoulder and he flinched.

"Come on," Kera's voice whispered, although he could not see her. "We'll finish up here, you can learn all about Ringscape later."

"But—"

"You'll be able to access another influx node later today." She was insistent. "Tell it I'll introduce you to Fadin."

Diyan nodded reticently. "Okay." He cleared his throat. "Is there anything I need to…know, before I can complete this registration later, if that's possible?"

The influx's voice sounded all around. "Preliminary registration has been completed. You have been allocated temporary accommodation." It then proceeded to offer a representative from the Administration to provide him with a physical tour of Fadin, which he politely declined; explained how to find his accommodation, which he confirmed he had memorised; related a list of rules he was expected to abide by, which he agreed to follow, and then informed him he had a certain number of days to become accustomed to life in Fadin before he would be expected to debrief his entire life story to the Administration and then work to support himself. The simulation dissipated.

He blinked as he acclimatised to the bright white lights of the shipyard's entry room again. Paran and Yena were doing the same. Kera was gesturing for them to stand.

"Come on," she said. "I'll show you about, then we'll go to where you're staying. There's a skimmer waiting for us outside."

They stood up and followed her to the far side of the room, where the wide entrance rippled open for them. A single skimmer waited. There were nearby buildings that were of a similar, simple style to the shipyard building they had just exited, albeit smaller and not as gleaming white. Most of the ground was covered in a green, familiar surface.

"It's like the mounds we used to have holo lessons on," Yena said, digging her heels in.

Kera nodded. "We managed to cultivate what made it through, and use it for our cities. It grows very well."

"Why?" Diyan asked.

Kera shrugged. "Maybe the first settlers wanted a reminder of home. It's what they knew." She gestured almost uninterestedly around them. "All of these are Administration buildings, and most of central Fadin is the same." There were a few other Roranians walking nearby, wearing loose-fitting, predominantly beige clothing, and no facepieces. "And no one flies during the main part of the day unless they need to, so it's often quiet around here." The skimmer's side folded up to allow them to enter. Diyan sat beside Yena, opposite Paran and Kera.

"Is the underside the same as the upperside?" Diyan asked.

"Pretty much. Roranians; Vaesians; a few others. Under-Fadin's a little newer though, so it isn't as built up as Upper-Fadin yet."

The skimmer set off, hovering just above the ground

as it glided along. Upon leaving the Administration-centric part of the city, the streets began to liven up. Kera pointed out various facets of Fadin more enthusiastically than before. It was clear that more resources had gone into the Administration buildings, as the others were less pristine and much more haphazardly constructed. They passed other skimmers and pedestrian Roranians as they journeyed.

"Who are the Vaesians?" Diyan asked. The others looked at him curiously, and then at Kera, waiting expectantly – it was clear they had also found out about the Vaesians from the influx node. "And where are they?"

"They aren't allowed to work for the Administration, so they tend to stay a little further out," Kera replied. "And they're stuck here, just like us."

Yena pointed to a white dome nearby. It was wider than all the other structures around it. "I saw one of those before, when we were in your ship, Kera. They're all over the city, what're they for?" The skimmer slowed to a halt.

"The backbone of the influx network. There are various hubs around the city like this. They're where the network processes our queries."

"What is the influx network?" Diyan asked. "The influx...it seemed like a c-autom."

Kera shook her head. "They're nothing like c-automs, otherwise they wouldn't function."

"Unless the Administration has figured out how to exploit a weakness in the probability wave..." Diyan mused.

"Are they smart algorithms?" Yena asked.

"Must be. The Administration is secretive about how they work, but they've enabled Fadin to thrive since before I arrived."

Shortly after the skimmer resumed its travel, a great, thick tether came into view. It was far more impressive when viewed from the ground than it had appeared from above, and far larger. The tether was affixed to the ground within a large planar structure, twice as tall as the nearby buildings. Drones circled the tether high up in the sky, with their small bloom fragments flicking about, wafting ethereal sparks of colour in their wake. Despite their small, black, spherical bodies – each only a little larger than a c-autom's – they looked powerful.

"And that leads up to a sky-factory?" Paran enquired.

"No, that's just a support tether."

An even thicker tether became visible in the distance, which the nearby supporting tether was joined to. Faint imprints of capsules could just about be seen moving up and down its length. Each looked to be at least the size of the skimmer.

"Strange aesthetic," Yena remarked, pointing to the slight undulations lining the top of the structure that fixed the support tether to the ground.

"Not aesthetic," Kera said, in a low voice. "Defences. The Administration's placing them all over the city's important infrastructure, making it almost impossible to attack them."

Diyan squinted and saw that Kera was right. The undulations were a row of turrets.

Paran laughed awkwardly. "Sounds like you've given it some thought."

"You always were the adventurous one," Diyan remarked.

The skimmer moved on again.

"There!" Paran shouted. "Over there!" He was pointing towards a strange figure that appeared to part-walk, part-swing in a strangely comical gait. The central leg moved in opposition to the outer two legs. A Vaesian. It was the same height as a Roranian. The skimmer maintained a respectful distance.

"What're they like?" Diyan asked.

"They were here before us," Kera replied. "They used to be the dominant species here. Later, you can ask the influxes all about them." She stuck her arm out, negating the conversation and pointing to a glowing building. It was entirely transparent, containing what appeared to be green mists, billowing about. Partitions levelled off the floors inside, which all looked far too low for a Roranian to stand upon. "Air terminal, for filtration," Kera explained. "The atmospheres of Ringscape and Barrenscape aren't optimal for most of us here. That's why we wear regwear with extra facepieces for salvaging – the regwear filters the air better than anything else we've managed to make. Too long unprotected and you'd start to get a headache. It's cumulative."

"Are we any closer to knowing why machine-lects can't exist here?" Yena asked, staring out of the skimmer.

Kera did not reply.

After a moment of silence, Yena continued. "Is anyone still trying to understand the reason we're here?"

"The meaning of life has changed for many of us." Kera pointed to a large building nearby. "There's a learning centre, and over there—"

"What's happening there?" Diyan asked, cutting her off, pointing towards the large group of Vaesians that had suddenly come into view. Immediately, the conversation ended as they stared out.

"Stop," Yena said sternly. The skimmer acquiesced, manoeuvring out of the sequence of skimmers it had formed a train with and halting by the side of the flow. None of the other skimmers had stopped, although some nearby pedestrian Roranians had also slowed down to watch from a distance.

A group of Vaesians had congregated, six of them. Although sounds did not permeate the walls of the skimmer, it appeared they were irritated. They were pushing each other, similarly to how Roranians might argue, and despite their strange movements, there was a familiarity to it.

"What's going on?" Diyan asked.

Kera sighed. "I presume one of them has become Silvered and they're concerned."

112

"Silvered?"

"Look," Paran said, pointing out one of the Vaesians. "The big one, it's shimmering…yes, it's a little silver, see? The others are completely white. That's the one they're arguing with."

The Silvered Vaesian was struggling against four of the others, who were attempting to grasp and restrain it, while the fifth appeared to be taking a more diplomatic approach, swivelling its neck about rapidly in an attempt to peer into the Silvered Vaesian's black eyes. It was not obvious who was winning the struggle since the non-Silvered Vaesians were being wildly swung around.

"Carry on," Kera said, and the skimmer began moving again. She spoke with less enthusiasm, and it was clear she did not want to broach the topic. "There is a plague affecting the Vaesians. It doesn't impact us."

"That Vaesian is carrying a disease?" Paran asked.

"Infection requires extended contact, but we can't be infected anyway. You can ask the influx network all about it. They're called the Silvereds."

"I saw two of ours – Roranians – laughing and jeering…" Yena trailed off.

"Anti-Vaesian fools," Kera replied. "The Silvereds just give them something to direct their hatred towards." It was obvious Kera wanted to end the conversation, but when none of them said anything, her speech softened. "I'm sorry, I'd forgotten how much there is to understand about Ringscape, it must be very overwhelming for you.

Maybe I should take you to your accommodation, there are influx nodes there that can give you all the answers you want. When I first came, I spent days just asking and asking."

Paran took her hand and looked her into her eyes. "We understand. It must be a shock for you too, us turning up together like this. Hardly any time has passed for us, but you never went to sleep."

Kera smiled gratefully and took her hand back, glancing briefly at Diyan. She directed the skimmer to their accommodation complex. Upon arriving, it was clear that their lodgings were near the bottom of the Administration's upgrade list. The outer walls were dark grey, with numerous gaps where panels had fallen off, exposing laughably archaic circuitries and infrastructure mechanics. The whole building looked as though it had been constructed as quickly as possible, from the remnants of whatever had been available, and appeared far less utilised than the surrounding buildings. A small group of Roranians stood nearby, giving them curious glances as they stepped out of the skimmer, before losing interest.

The entrance was a simple, sliding panel of wall that automatically moved to the side as they approached. They followed Kera inside. There was no reception area, just a cramped, noisy electro-boost platform for them to huddle onto, as it took them to their respective floors. Paran was on the second floor, Yena the third, and Diyan the fourth, at the top of the building.

"Once you find work, you'll be able to move somewhere nicer." Kera's tone was oddly distant. She remained standing on the platform as Diyan stepped off into the dimly lit corridor.

"Is everything okay, Kera?"

Her fingers were twitching. "Everything's fine, Diyan. It's been a long day, that's all."

He fumbled awkwardly. "There's a lot we still have to discuss when we're all ready. About what happened to you, and everything else since then." He chuckled. "I almost can't believe it. I'm glad we're all together." Her face was still impassive. "Is there something you want to tell me?"

She shook her head and looked into his eyes, with the hint of a smile. "Oh, Diyan, it is good to see you again. I'm happy to see you, all of you." She looked around, self-consciously. "And don't worry, I made sure you all got places with influxes. But, like I said before, if you do run into others around here, I wouldn't mention you're from our Great Ship. At least, not at first. There aren't many of us, you know. We're a curiosity."

"And Otherness?" Immediately, he knew he should not have asked after her c-autom. Her expression clamped up, and the electro-boost platform began to descend.

"I'm sorry, I need to go now. Goodbye, Diyan."

He waved, clumsily. "See you tomorrow, Kera."

A faint white light followed him along the top of the

dirty beige wall, stopping and pulsing at a doorway. It moved down and resolved into the image of a hand. He placed his own against it, and the door slid to the side in a rickety movement.

"Oh, Wiln, I miss you," he muttered, stepping in and looking around with apprehension.

Chapter 14
Updated Concerns

Diyan's accommodation was nothing like his annexe on the Great Ship, consisting of one small, shabby room with four bare walls, and a ceiling that was somehow even lower than the corridor. There were obvious areas for eating and sleeping, as well as a small side-room for washing. In addition to the essentials, there was an influx node, wedged in the space between the small table in the culinary area and the entrance to the side-room. It was a diminutive version of the cylindrical platform in the shipyard building, rising only a little taller than the table beside it.

Diyan strode over, grabbed the single chair from under the table, placed it in front of the influx node, and sat down. The chair made a concerning cracking sound, so he waited a few moments before shifting his weight and pulling it a little closer. He stared expectantly at the influx node.

"Err...hello?"

The node flashed brightly. The next thing he knew, Diyan was immersed in pre-simulation darkness, with the same indistinct ball of light rolling before him, and a voice echoing all around.

"I am an influx. This is your temporary connection to the influx network."

Diyan looked around the darkness, trying to think of where to start.

The voice continued. "What would you like to know?"

Diyan grabbed the first thought his mind offered. "The Vaesians, I've seen them. One of them was silver in colour, different to the others. I was told it is some kind of plague. Can you tell me about that?"

An image of a Vaesian appeared in front of him, levitating in the darkness. Its head faced slightly to the side and its mid-torso arms waved about fluidly. Round, black eyes gave the impression that it was looking both everywhere and nowhere at the same time. The Vaesian was identical to the image he had been shown by the previous influx. It began to expand in front of him and parts disappeared into his peripheral vision as his perspective zoomed in to a point on its upper torso. Under this magnification, individual white hairs became visible, then its dark grey skin, then the creases of the skin itself, then countless small, moving objects, squirming everywhere. Their bodies were lightly translucent, shimmering faintly silver. Each of the moving objects was diamond-shaped, with flexible edges that spurted out, latching onto nearby patches of skin, pulling themselves around. They moved about rapidly, occasionally seeming to sink into the skin and disappear.

"What are they?" Diyan asked, shifting his head back a little.

"Cell-scales. All Vaesians have them now."

The image zoomed back out. The same Vaesian he had been shown a moment ago was displayed next to another, almost identical-looking Vaesian, except the newcomer's triple legs were shorter and thicker, its body hunched over, and its neck drooped down.

"Before the introduction of the cell-scales, the Vaesians were ill-adapted to living on Ringscape, as the gravity is generally too strong for them. They are long-lived, as we are, but age takes a toll on their bodies. The cell-scales reversed that, making them strong again."

The hunched Vaesian disappeared, and the remaining Vaesian duplicated again, so that two identical images rotated side by side. Slowly, one of the Vaesians began to turn silver.

"Cell-scales are not completely understood. There are instances when the technology malfunctions and the cell-scales proliferate beyond their intended parameters. They draw too much energy from their hosts, who appear strong and healthy, but who consequentially have their lifespans significantly reduced. No cure exists."

"Why would they use something they didn't fully understand on themselves?" Diyan asked. "And where are they from, anyway? I mean, the Vaesians themselves?" His questions began to flow fast and freely. "And what is this place – the Source, what is…all of this?" His breathing was becoming heavy and erratic.

The influx was quiet for a few moments before offering an unexpected response. "Why don't we start at the beginning?"

Diyan nodded. "Yes, I want to know everything." He tried to calm his breathing as a spiral galaxy appeared before him. The image instantly spun around and Diyan was thrust towards one of the galaxy's tips. "Wait," he said. The simulation paused. "I've seen this before, many times. I know Tapache sent us on a mission to discover the cause of the probability wave that destroys machine-lects. You can skip this."

"You may not be wholly correct in your assumptions," came the influx's response, and the simulation continued.

The solar system at the edge of the galaxy came into view, then Tapache's leviathan ship. Diyan clenched his jaw in anticipation as the familiar shape of his own ship, the Great Ship, materialised. His jaw unclenched. He looked between Tapache's ship and the other ship.

"This isn't right," he muttered. "The scales are wrong. I've seen this a hundred times. Our ship was bigger, and it was positioned over there. Your simulation is incorrect."

"It is not our ship."

The small ship's bloom flicked to the side, propelling it around the planet and away, into the void.

"What was that? Tapache sent another ship after us?"

"Not after, before. Tapache sent many ships; we call them all Great Ships. Ours was not the first and it presumably will not be the last."

"How do we know all this?"

"The Vaesians, and other sources."

The simulation skipped forwards and other ships appeared beside Tapache's vessel as they were created. Some appeared almost identical to each other, others were noticeably different, with larger hulls, non-bloom propulsion units, and obvious external fortifications. Each ship left the solar system on the same trajectory, one by one.

"How many have there been?" Diyan asked.

"Hundreds, we estimate, each created many hundreds of standard years apart."

"But...that means Tapache's been waiting there for...thousands of years..." Diyan muttered weakly.

"Tens of thousands, possibly even hundreds of thousands." The influx waited for Diyan, but he did not respond. It carried on. "From what we know of the Wanderer civilisation and the abilities of their machine-lects, such as Tapache, experiments along such timescales are not uncommon."

The simulation changed. A ball of yellow-white light, somewhat like a dim star, was surrounded by a vast lattice of ships, in close orbit. Debris wafted in larger, eccentric orbits. Some of the ships with bloom units were clustered together, but many others had entirely different designs.

"That's what's outside, isn't it?" Diyan asked, breathlessly. "That's what we went through, before we came here."

"Yes. Aside from the ships Tapache sent, there are many others. Tapache's vessels make up a small contingent of all those you can see. We still do not know when the Source first came to be, how it came to be, why it came to be, or what its function is. But we do know that it is artificial, and that a large number of civilisations have sent investigatory expeditions over the course of its existence. Many remain. Few have succeeded in making it inside. We were fortunate in that regard."

"But...why would Tapache send so many? And all these different types—"

Uncharacteristically, the influx interrupted him, as though it were excited. "That's clear. Tapache is experimenting with different permutations of biological life, to see which might finally succeed and return to it. We believe it first sent unintelligent, automated drones, but they were likely discovered and repurposed by the ships already here. Then, it began to send sentients, starting with machine-lect variants, then hybrids, and then pure biologicals. No two ships seem to have carried the same type of sentient."

Diyan scrunched his fists. "Did Tapache promise each

the same – that it will help each and every one find their own civilisations when they return? Or has it made other promises?"

"As far as we know, yes. The Vaesians are amongst those Tapache sent before us; they were the main species in control of Ringscape when we made it into the Source. They were told the same as us by Tapache."

Diyan exhaled measuredly. "Was Tapache lying?"

The influx seemed to take its time in replying. Within the simulation, sparks of light around certain ships intermittently flared up as they moved about and conducted their activities. Occasionally, they appeared to send objects towards the Source without the means to attack, while other times they attacked with a variety of weapons: bright beams of radiation; physical projectiles; other bundles of matter; entire ships. Each time, the energy was dissipated, or the matter torn apart and flung back as debris.

"Whether Tapache lied to us or not is still debated, although the question is considered academic now – of less importance than it once was. No one can leave the Source. As you can see from the simulation—"

"But we entered!" Diyan almost shouted.

Diyan's vantage point in the simulation began to change again.

"Entering is different from leaving."

The bright sphere loomed closer. He passed through a gap in the lattice of ships and stopped right in front of the glowing ball. The surface looked incredibly smooth, perfect, with no contours to give the remotest hint of its underlying structure.

"We call the outer, spherical component of the Source the Haze Rings."

"Why rings?"

Suddenly, Diyan was on the other side of the Haze Rings, surrounded by the gentler light of day that immersed Barrenscape and Ringscape. He looked around. Nothing but open space and the solid, glowing Haze Rings were visible.

"The Haze Rings have been significantly dimmed within this simulation, to allow you to look directly at them."

A segment of the Haze Rings appeared to dim further. He squinted. Something large shot through, accompanied by smaller pieces of debris that scattered in random trajectories. The large object hurtled away. He quickly realised what it was. The mangled ends of two skimmers, which looked to have been fused together by prior impact. He looked back up. The dark patch of the Haze Rings had returned to normal.

"What was that?"

"There are rare incidences of entry permitted by the Haze Rings, of varying magnitude. That is how the majority of Vaesians entered, and then Roranians, through separate, massive entry incidents that appear to have been pure chance. You yourself entered more recently, during a smaller event—"

"You mean, we were just lucky?"

"That is one way of describing it. Currently, we do not know what triggers these entry events, but certainly the probability of you being destroyed upon impact with the Haze Rings was overwhelmingly high. So, yes. You were extremely lucky. While the entry events cannot be predicted, it is through these events that we can glean the structure of the Haze Rings. Aberrations of detected wavelengths around the entry events suggest many single, hyperfine loops, rotating extremely fast. Much of the Administration's research is directed towards understanding them, since the Haze Rings are what encompass and trap us here. They appear both indestructible and impenetrable from the inside. They generate light, which fluctuates between day and night, and during the daytime, they generate great winds that make it dangerous to fly safely above ground level. Beyond that, we can only speculate. We do not understand what it is within the confines of the Haze Rings that scatters light and other long-range signals, let alone what causes the probability wave affecting machine-lects."

Diyan ruminated on his thoughts for some time, watching the boundary of the Haze Rings with wide eyes. "How many of us made it through, at the start?"

The simulation changed again. He was looking high over Ringscape as parts of the Roranian Great Ship were falling from the sky. Most were burned, dark, and mangled. Some open caskets hurtled down, and many other parts of the ship he recognised. He turned instinctively as an enormous tendril whipped past him, leaving a sparkling trail of colour in its wake.

"Part of the bloom," the influx explained, as debris continued to impact against Ringscape, causing a multitude of explosions.

In the distance, Diyan could see the hazy outlines of structures.

"Some of the Vaesian cities were impacted too, though, thankfully, the parts of our Great Ship predominantly rained down on an uninhabited region of Ringscape."

The impacts faded away as time skipped in the simulation. A small settlement appeared.

"How many of us made it through?" Diyan whispered.

"Two hundred and three Roranian survivors, to start with. Their histories were cross-checked upon your introduction to the network. None were known to you."

"What do you mean 'to start with'?"

"When the Nesch took our Great Ship, they captured most of the Roranians who remained on the ship, training them to fight against the lattice fleet. There have been a few instances where captured Roranians have been found aboard wreckages that have entered the Haze Rings during entry events."

"I thought the entry events were highly improbable."

"We now know that the Haze Rings go through

periods where greater entry is allowed. Artefacts recovered from past civilisations established on Ringscape allude to this."

Diyan found himself looking down on Upper-Fadin. Time had skipped again, and the city appeared as it currently was. Skimmers moved rapidly about, gliding in trains, or filtering off on their own routes. All were stuck to the ground, no longer able to fly as they once had. He could just about make out individuals, both Roranian and Vaesian, strolling around as well.

"How many Roranians now?" he asked.

"Over eight hundred thousand. Fadin itself contains almost four hundred thousand; three quarters reside within Upper-Fadin. It is the first and largest of all Roranian cities. Harmend is the next largest, since the two smaller cities of Aesia and Harmend became one city—"

Diyan balked. "Eight hundred thousand!"

"The mechanism from the Great Ship preventing procreation no longer restricts us. We breed far more quickly than the Vaesians."

"Kera told me but...I never realised there could be so many."

"There has been a Roranian presence within the Source for almost three hundred years now."

"In Ringscape, not Barrenscape?"

"Barrenscape is too dangerous for us to attempt to occupy."

"Because of the Breaker?"

127

"Yes."

"What can you tell me about it?"

"Unfortunately, very little."

Chapter 15
Kera

She had been wandering around the Tug Field for some time now, irritated at the lack of anything forthcoming from the Tugs. Regretting not having brought a gravitometer with her, she walked aimlessly, quasi-lost in her own thoughts; quasi-vigilant for any sign of activity.

She wondered whether she had been wrong not to share her objectives with the others. Especially Diyan. She could lie and lie, but she would never forgive herself if anything happened to him. Was the burden really hers to shoulder alone? Of all of them, he would have been the most likely to understand. He had been with her since the very beginning, before Paran and Yena. Their c-automs had told them their caskets had been side-by-side, a long time ago, before Tapache had released them into the Great Ship.

Her hand tingled. It was the hand holding the device she had brought down with her, that she still spun between her fingers. Briefly, her hand had been drawn away from her. Pulled away. She followed the direction. Another tingle. She followed. Finally, the Tugs had noticed her.

Chapter 16
Misunderstood Danger

Diyan and Yena sat on the small wall that ran around the periphery of the air terminal building behind them, their backs glowing green from its light. Paran stood in front, the side of his face also glowing green whenever he turned to speak to them. His excitable mood had been brought about upon learning from the influx network that Loten had survived, and was safely stored alongside Rememox and Wiln. His smile was more energised than usual.

Each of them wore the loose-fitting, beige regwear that had been waiting for them in their accommodations. Though it was less comfortable than their combat regwear, at least it made them less conspicuous.

"They reprocessed it all." Yena sighed, pinching a clump of the beige regwear off her skin. "It's not as smooth, or as good."

Paran pointed rather animatedly to a nearby train of close-moving skimmers. "It's like they're still controlled by machine-lects, isn't it?"

The train steered elegantly about, somehow finding openings between other trains and pedestrians without significantly impacting the trajectories of either.

"Can't be," Diyan said.

"It's the influx network," Yena informed them. "What the Administration has managed to do since it came to power is impressive. Primitive, but impressive. Almost everything has been improved. Everyone gets along."

"The Administration didn't do all of this," Diyan argued. "The influxes yes, but—"

"But you can see why it's been as successful as it has, constantly improving and redeveloping Fadin's infrastructure."

"Has anyone spoken to Kera?" Diyan asked, slightly irritably. He looked apologetically at them. "Sorry. When I tried to reach her, the influx network said she was busy."

Paran nodded. "Same here. She'll find us when she can."

"Maybe she has to verify our identities, like we did hers," Yena added.

"Why was that?" Paran asked.

"Anyone who wasn't in the initial wreckage that made it through from the battle, when our Great Ship was destroyed, needs additional verification." Yena laughed at Paran's raised eyebrow. "I asked the influx."

"And Kera didn't know anyone else from the Great Ship who made it down here, until we arrived," Diyan murmured. "She was alone."

"She knows people here," Paran said. "She must do."

Paran stepped back and froze as a small group of Vaesians passed by. The strangest thing about the Vaesians was how they walked. Their three legs appeared far more flexible than Roranian legs, bending in different directions seemingly without preference. Yet, somehow, their movements carried a certain gracefulness. After some time watching them, it was clear they were not clumsy at all. Each bend of a leg was perfectly orchestrated, moving in perfect coordination with the other two.

Aside from their generally ganglier bodies, complete with long arms that ended in thin fibrous extensions; their stretched, bent necks, and their short white hair, the Vaesians were not unlike the Roranians. They talked to each other as they walked, in the Roranian language when in Roranian company and in a strange language that was deeply guttural when speaking to other Vaesians. They also laughed, frequently, constantly bursting into loud guffaws.

"Isn't it incredible," Paran murmured. "They're so similar to us. How they speak and what they say. I mean, they've got eyes, mouths, arms, and legs. And look at their mannerisms, how they shake their heads when they disagree, or they…"

He did not finish his sentence, staring eagerly a short distance away. The other two followed his gaze. There was something neither Roranian nor Vaesian. It moved quickly, too much so to fully distinguish, using its numerous sharp, pointed, white legs to tap its way across the floor. The rest of its body was hidden underneath a dark cloak. A moment later, it was gone.

"Don't stare, Paran. It may be rude," Yena reminded him.

"What *was* that?"

"I don't know. But don't forget, to everyone else here, this is all normal," Yena replied, sternly. "We've been in stasis for longer than many here have been alive."

"For them, it's a day like any other," Diyan concurred.

"Even Kera," Yena said. "She's been here for a hundred and twelve years."

"Did you ask the influx that too?" Paran asked, testily.

She nodded, almost guiltily. "I know, it's her story to tell. But I wanted to know. What's going on?"

Diyan and Paran looked out, their expressions becoming equally puzzled as they realised what she meant. The trains of skimmers were all gone, diverted away. Everything was suddenly quiet. Roranians and the occasional Vaesian still walked about, as did the species that were neither. None seemed the least perturbed by the change.

The large entrance to a nearby building rippled open, one of the buildings Kera had termed a learning centre.

While the building did not look particularly new, resources had clearly been poured into it. It was relatively featureless, simply rising vertically upwards, like a solid rectangular block growing towards the sky. Earlier, Yena had spotted some turreted shapes just about discernible at the perimeter of its roof.

Small forms began to wander out of the building, spilling awkwardly around a group of pedestrian Roranians, who were comically forced to take avoidance measures. Diyan, Paran, and Yena stood up, lost for words. The small forms ran around, some in groups, others alone, away from the building. High pitched, excited voices carried across to the three friends.

"I think they're…children," Diyan murmured.

The three of them stared for some time, transfixed, until the last of the children had disappeared. The sound of their chattering and laughter went with them, replaced by the sound of skimmers resuming their typical flow of traffic.

"Like Kera said, something stopped us from creating new life before, on the ship. It also prolonged our adolescence, but not anymore," Yena said. "Ringscape is our new home. We didn't know it existed before, but now, it's everything."

"Ringscape isn't just ours," Diyan added. "We share it. There are Vaesians in our cities, and Roranians in theirs."

"We do, but there are many more of us than the Vaesians already, and our cities outnumber theirs. Have you looked at projections of our population growth, especially in Fadin? The Administration is in talks with our other cities, possibly about taking control of them too. I think it will. Trading consignments have been halted while those talks are ongoing; everything's in a state of flux. That's why Fadin being a united presence on the upperside and underside is so powerful. The Administration represents cohesion."

"Why would they want to control the other cities?" Paran asked.

Yena shrugged. "The Administration controls the influx network and the sky-factories. It's clearly done something right." She pointed to one of the large tethers in the sky. "None of the other cities have them, Roranian or Vaesian. The Vaesian Union controls the Vaesian cities, but it's only a loose alliance; I don't think it has much influence. I wouldn't be surprised if the Administration eventually runs them too, in time. Plus, that would put a stop to the Anti-Vaesian Movement that's growing in some of the smaller Roranian settlements."

"Anti-Vaesian Movement?"

"Kera mentioned them, remember, and I asked the influx. The movement started as small groups of Roranians who believed the Vaesians were hiding things from us, things about Ringscape, though I'm not sure exactly what. Well, it grew to full-blown antipathy. For now, they appear to focus predominantly on the Silvereds. Fadin's the only Roranian city with Silvereds now. It can't be easy for them."

"You have been busy on the influx network, haven't you," Paran commented.

"We need to know what's going on," Yena replied matter-of-factly, pushing herself to her feet. She had just begun gesturing for them to start walking when crashing and shouting took their attention. Skimmers were bouncing off each other, haphazardly. The occupants inside were well protected, but they looked confused. Vaesians and Roranians were flailing their arms wildly. Screams followed, a mixture of high-pitched Roranian and deeper Vaesian. Pedestrians had been hit. Some lay on the floor, unmoving.

"Something's wrong," Yena shouted.

Someone was running towards them, fast. Reaching them, the runner pulled their facepiece down. It was Soji. She bent over slightly to catch her breath.

Paran went instantly to her side. "Are you alright?"

"You need to come with me," she said, standing up again. "Now."

They looked at her, bewildered. "Soji, where's Kera?" Diyan asked.

"Kera sent me. We need to go, now. The Administration's coming for you."

"Why?" Yena asked.

Soji pulled her facepiece back up. She looked at a device in her hand, then whipped her head up. A skimmer was hurtling towards them, the only one still moving on the street. No one was inside. It reached them.

"Come on! Let's—" The facepiece around the bottom part of Soji's head suddenly constricted. Her cheeks pressed inwards, sickeningly tight, more so than should have been possible, and her eyes turned red. She grabbed her head, nails digging into her skin as her mouth was forced agape. Dark red liquid oozed from her lips, and she slumped knees-first to the ground.

Out of nowhere, the four of them were surrounded. Ordinary-looking Roranians weaved around the fleeing pedestrians, holding devices that looked like the thermal ejection rifles they had used in the competitions aboard the ship, long ago. Diyan and Yena fell to their knees, retching. Paran was shouting, although his fierce defiance was abruptly stopped and he fell heavily to the ground, with a wide, fresh gash bleeding freely from his cheek. A group of thick-set Roranians stood over them. The world went dark.

*

Sounds of screaming accompanied Diyan's return to consciousness. Groggily, he opened his eyes. Four blank, beige walls. Was he back in his accommodation? The screaming continued; the memories returned. No. This was different. A prison.

He shook his head and rose to his feet, stumbling a little, waiting for his head to clear. There was nothing there. Just the walls around him. He walked the room from end to end. The floor was square, no more than a few long strides across. He brought his hands up to his face, feeling for signs of injury. Aside from the bleariness, he was fine.

A holo flickered into existence in the centre of the room, uncomfortably close. He fell back against one of the walls, still unsteady. The holo was an image of Irido, Kera's other companion, identifiable by the small patch of white skin on her cheek. Not Soji, who had just been killed right in front of him. Diyan had never seen a dead Roranian before, or even considered that possibility.

Irido was lying horizontally with her arms by her sides, unable to move anything but her head. She was terrified, frantically looking one way then the other. As she opened her mouth, a piercing scream resounded around Diyan's four walls. He slapped his hands to cover his ears and closed his eyes. Nothing drowned it out. It vibrated through his hands, shaking his bones. When it finally stopped, he opened his eyes. Irido was whimpering.

"I don't know anything," she said, in a pitiful, hoarse whisper.

"How can we be certain?" a voice replied, calmly. It was medium pitched. Its owner, a dim figure, materialised into existence beside the horizontal Irido, standing by her head.

"I would tell you if I knew, I promise!"

"But how can we be sure?" The voice was measured.

Something happened again, Diyan did not see exactly what, and Irido's screams returned. When they finally died down, she was being asked questions.

"Where is Kera?"

"I don't know!" Her entire body quivered.

"Where has Kera gone?"

"I would tell you!"

"Then tell me."

"Please, no, no!"

More screams.

The calm voice spoke as though Irido's screams were nothing, ignoring her torment. "You'll heal, over and over. Tapache made us to be strong, after all. I can melt parts of you as much as it pleases me, from the inside. You won't die, but you'll wish you could."

"I don't know anything," she whimpered.

The figure kneeled beside her, whispering into her ear. "Perhaps, I'll make you part of the influx network. We need to repair it, after what Kera did. You'll still exist, but you won't be you anymore. You won't be anything."

Irido began to shake her head again, staring forwards. "Please, I don't know anything. I just work with Kera, nothing more. I don't know anything! I don't know how she—"

"I know *how* she did what she did," the voice said, cheerily, as the figure rose up again. "She was validated, by *friends* she just happened to find in Barrenscape, and you helped her. From there, she was eligible to apply for work in the Administration. She entered a recruitment centre and...well, you know what happened, don't you? She revealed just how augmented she was and attempted to decimate a great swathe of the network, almost reaching its core, before fleeing. She nearly succeeded too, but the network is more resilient than that. The effect won't be noticed. She failed. Tell me, just how long were you planning this?"

"I didn't plan anything..."

"What was she looking for?"

"Please, I don't know!"

"Did she find it?"

"No, please..."

"Is she working with the Silvereds? We know about her affiliation with them. We're going to move in on Sunsprit. That's where she's gone, isn't it?"

"I don't know!"

The figure continued. "The Vaesian Union can't stop us, it's too weak. They don't care for Sunsprit and its seditious principles anyway. They hate it more than we do! We should never have let the Silvereds congregate like that. They're jealous of what we've achieved." The voice was no longer as calm, not quite rambling, but there was a frenzied fervour about it.

Despite her obvious pain, Diyan could see Irido's face forming a shallow frown. "I know nothing about the Silvereds, or Kera, or anything about what she was doing with them. Please, I don't know anything!"

"The Silvereds have been plotting to overthrow us. We know this." The voice was calm again. "Kera is helping them, that much is clear."

The holo sharpened and the shadowy figure resolved more clearly into the form of a Roranian man. He leaned forward again so that his mouth was right beside Irido's ear. She stared ahead, quaking, the muscles in her neck spasming.

"Would you like to know what I'm going to do next?"

Although talking to Irido, the man was glaring out of the holo, looking directly at Diyan.

Chapter 17
Hollowed Mind

Diyan stared despondently at the far corner of his prison. He sat in the opposite corner, shivering, with his arms wrapped around his knees. A holo flickered into existence in the centre of the room. He clenched his arms tighter. It was the man from before, the man who had tortured Irido.

"Diyan."

Diyan stared at the floor, clutching at his knees.

"Diyan," the man repeated. "I'd prefer not to use a neural conjoiner to speak with you. Once implemented, sadly, some of the damage isn't reversible."

"What do you care?" Diyan spat.

"In honesty, very little."

"What do you want?"

The man's face was impassive. If the holo was to scale, he was a little shorter than average; nondescript. His clothing was equally unexceptional: beige, well-fitting, and suited to most occasions. His crop of hair, the same length as Diyan's, was neat and styled well. Cultivated unremarkability. Once their gazes met, Diyan found it difficult to look away.

"What do I want?" The man's nose wrinkled, as though he was genuinely thinking about Diyan's question, giving it careful consideration. His tone was genial. "I want to know what you know, Diyan. I want to know why you came here. I want to know why you helped Kera, and, most of all, I want to know where Kera is." He smiled, completely changing his face. His features fleetingly complemented each other perfectly, and he looked surprisingly handsome. "And you're going to tell me."

"I don't know what you mean," Diyan said, gesticulating hopelessly. "I told the influx everything already, there's nothing else."

"Not quite like the annexe you're used to, is it?" The man paused for a few moments, achieving a patronising glare despite his face's impassive look, occasionally flicking his eyes around the room. "Do you really think your story about being in stasis for all that time is believable? Quite the story, isn't it? That, somehow, we missed you in Barrenscape, all this time. Not even the Breaker could get through to you, but Kera found you. You expect me to believe you slept for hundreds of years while we made Fadin what it is today?"

"It's the truth."

The man blinked in condescending irritation. "Down

here, on Ringscape, we Roranians are a new civilisation. Barbaric, you might say. Especially at the start. In fact, I'm sure future generations will say that. But they will also thank us." He paused, as though thinking to himself, then shrugged. "On the Great Ship, I'm told all Roranians were trained thoroughly, especially in the areas they showed aptitudes for, but nothing prepared them for what was down here. We were like children again. We needed order." He smiled as though he had made a joke. "I'm going to be honest with you, Diyan. I suspect you're lying, and that means we're going to have to...extract the truth from you. I really had hoped it wouldn't come to this." He took a step back.

"Wait!" Diyan shouted, rising to his feet and stumbling, waving an arm as he steadied himself against the wall. "Is Kera okay? And the others? Yena? Paran? Please, tell me."

The man chuckled, shaking his head superciliously. "Kera. We need to find her, you know. We really do. The damage she has caused...some of our projects have been set back years, I'm told." He tsked. "And you helped her, with your cloying, misplaced devotion. You helped her attack the influx network, Diyan. The influx network is the staple of our society—"

"I don't know what you're talking about! I don't know anything! Kera can't have done this, and I haven't helped anyone! You're wrong!"

"Kera has been working with the Silvereds to bring the Administration down. Don't take me for a fool, Diyan."

"Why would the Silvereds want to bring you down?"

The man sneered. "Why wouldn't they? We've achieved what the Vaesians and their pathetic union never could. These cities, everything on Ringscape, is because of us. Even the union cities rely on our technologies. The fragments they recovered from their own Great Ship long ago gave them nothing, and they've done little with the debris that's made its way through the Haze Rings since then. Now, it's our turn. We changed everything. It was us. Not Tapache. Us. We even gave them the cell-scales to try to raise them up with us, and the Silvereds blame us for that. The Silvereds are angry that the cell-scales don't work correctly for them; they're jealous of the other Vaesians and hate us for helping them. It's why many Roranians hate the Silvereds in return – a natural response. So, we're going to move on Sunsprit, the Vaesian city where all the pathetic Silvereds flock. It's leaderless; fractious. They think we can't control it like the others. Well, it's about time we changed that. The Vaesian Union will thank us."

Diyan looked about the room aimlessly. "None of this makes any sense. I don't understand anything you're saying. Kera would never help the Silvereds. She's a Roranian."

The man's smirk dissipated as quickly as it had come, and he was calm again, utterly in control. "I was born here, Diyan. First generation, and one of the first amongst them. My parents told me of their c-automs, and how they helped you, abiding by your every whim." His eyes briefly lit up. "I must admit, I was a little jealous. Still am. Life was quite easy for you. Perhaps Tapache really does still wait for us. But they also told me something else interesting about your c-automs. About their names." The man was staring into Diyan's eyes, unflinching. "Yours was called Wiln, you named it that. Why?"

Diyan shrugged, confused. "It was one of the first words I uttered. When I was old enough, I decided it was fitting. Many do the same."

"And you never changed its name?"

"It suited," Diyan answered, almost petulantly.

The man looked serious. "In many ways, the chosen names reflected the Roranian companions. You named yours Wiln because you shared a bond, and you were naming that bond. Identifying it. Kera named hers Otherness because that is a reflection of herself. She is different. Alone."

Diyan began shaking his head. "No, you're twisting it—"

"Who knows what the Silvereds offered her. Power? Control at the helm of a new Administration? They may have lied, but it doesn't matter. We know what she did. Her actions speak for themselves. We have stopped Silvered attacks against the influx network before, but we never expected such an attack from one of our own. And you validated her, you helped grant her access to the Administration."

"No!" Diyan shouted, taking a step towards the holo. "Look, if I could just speak to her, I know she'd be able to explain everything. She hasn't done what you think she has!"

"She must answer for what she's done. You all must."

Diyan took another step closer, raising his hands gently. "Let me speak to her. She needs the chance to explain. Look, if you think she's in this place...Sunsprit, let me go there. Don't attack, just give me the chance to find her. I'll talk to her, and she'll come back, she'll explain everything. Just let me try."

"You?" The man smirked, contemptuously. "You think you could find her in Sunsprit? You say you've only been awake for a few days. You're a relic of our past."

"I know Kera," Diyan replied. "I've known her my entire life. If anyone can convince her, it's me. If she's there, I'll find her."

"You love her, don't you?" The man's cold sneer caught Diyan off-guard. "And so does Paran. It's obvious. But she didn't choose you, did she? She chose him." Before Diyan could respond, the man's expression changed. "Fine. And don't forget that Yena and Paran are still guests of the Administration, here in Fadin, along with your berthed c-automs. I expect you to return."

Chapter 18
Redeeming Quest

The last of Fadin's built-up streets were some way back, as were most of its inhabitants, as Diyan made his way through the outskirts of the city. The skimmer passed structures here and there, but the main things that caught Diyan's attention were the intermittent rows of weaponry, similar to the turrets that had appeared on the tops of buildings around the city. They rose up around the skimmer's path, descending back into the ground as it moved away. Up close, Diyan could see that they were coloured a combination of dark reds and blacks, as though they had been frozen upon partial mixing, and were similarly shaped to closed caskets, rising no higher than the skimmer, set side by side, each a few strides apart. Multiple barrels stuck out of each turret, pointing in all directions. Whereas before they had appeared a mere curiosity, now they were imposing; deadly.

Ringscape was almost completely flat, and whichever way Diyan looked, the only thing obscuring his line of sight was the thick atmosphere. Just after the last of the turrets, the green foundation of Fadin, which covered the open ground of the entire city, ended, revealing Ringscape's natural dark brown surface. The skimmer rose a little higher into the air.

Only a few other skimmers moved about nearby. Diyan counted five. Four of them were empty, returning to Fadin. One was filled with four Roranians who looked to be excited, talking animatedly and barely casting a single external glance. He saw only one lone walker, another Roranian, wearing something clunky across his back.

Diyan turned to face movement in his peripheral vision. Ahead, something tall was resolving into view. He squinted, peering forwards. It was a long, thin pole, spearing high into the sky. As the skimmer hurtled closer, he counted ten Roranians and two Vaesians congregated around the bottom. Each wore a bulky pack across their backs, the same as he had seen on the lone Roranian just before. They also wore black regwear, the same as his current outfit, given to him before leaving his confinement. It was the same regwear that had been worn by Kera, Soji, and Irido. Something was circling, high up in the sky; the form was just about recognisable as either Roranian or Vaesian, but something large protruded from the sides of its pack…something that looked an awful lot like a pair of great, unfurled wings.

As the skimmer moved closer, Diyan watched as one of the Roranians attached herself to a small capsule at the base of the pole, a bit like the capsules that moved up and down the tethers to the sky-factories. The capsule was embedded into a long groove that ran the length of the pole. The Roranian pulled her facepiece up from her neck and over her entire head; a moment later, her body was shot up and launched into the sky. A pair of large wings extended from her pack and she began to glide about, gracefully, circling the pole. Next, one of the Vaesians began to attach themselves to the capsule, which had returned to the bottom of the pole. None of the group paid Diyan's skimmer any attention as he passed them by.

There were other small blots in the distance that looked like groups partaking in similar activities, but Diyan never drew close enough to see them. The skimmer continued travelling, and soon they had journeyed far enough from Fadin that Diyan had not spotted any other skimmers, Roranians, or Vaesians for quite some time. The skimmer slowed to a stop and sunk to the ground.

The holo of the man from the Administration appeared beside Diyan, projected by the skimmer. It flickered occasionally.

"What do I say if anyone asks?"

The man shrugged, nonchalantly. "The truth is always the most convincing."

"What if I tell them you're coming for them? That you're planning to attack Sunsprit if I don't find her."

The man laughed. "It changes nothing. They're Silvereds, no one will listen to them anyway. You're our spy, Diyan. Just find Kera and bring her back."

Diyan's cheeks reddened and he clenched his jaw. "How do I get to Sunsprit?"

The man gestured lazily to a small point resolving in the distance. It was becoming larger. It looked like another skimmer.

"Who *are* you?" Diyan asked.

"I represent the Administration," he said, before disappearing.

The side of the skimmer folded up and Diyan duly exited. It moved off immediately, back in the direction of Fadin, and he was left alone, waiting. Ringscape's brown surface was not unpleasant to stand on and was only slightly springier than Fadin's green underlayer. He drew his facepiece over his head, finding that his eyes saw perfectly well through it, before deciding to draw it down to just above his nose. The effect was subtle, but the air became a little easier to breathe.

The other skimmer drew closer. It appeared older than the skimmer he had just exited, and very battered. Its opaque grey surfaces were scratched, and the transparent sections were all tinted slightly different hues – obvious replacements. It was also thinner than a standard skimmer, as though it had been sliced in half down the middle, only comfortably allowing for two occupants. It travelled close to the ground, just about keeping clear of Ringscape's brown surface.

Diyan tipped his head back as the skimmer stopped just a few paces away from him. He was less surprised that the front seat appeared to face in the same direction as the back seat – with a raft of controls spread out before it – than he was to see that the occupant of the front seat was a Vaesian, wearing similar black regwear to his own, pulled up over its mouth. The front part of the skimmer's side folded up smoothly, revealing the Vaesian's body. White hair, longer than that of the other Vaesians he had seen, was visible along the length of its limbs, spilling out between gaps in the creature's black clothing, and its three legs were neatly bent forwards, with the lower halves tucked under the seat. As its head swung to face Diyan, he saw the tight fabric move over its circular mouth.

"Take your time!" its deep voice bellowed.

Dumbly, Diyan walked to the side of the skimmer and waited for the back half to fold up.

"Something wrong with you?" the Vaesian asked, rhetorically. "Pull it up!"

"But—"

"Not a fancy new skimmer from Fadin. Just yank it up and get in."

Diyan bent down to feel for the edge of the skimmer's side and pulled. Something gave, disconcertingly quickly, and it crumpled up, instead of folding smoothly, with a high-pitched, mechanical screech.

The skimmer now appeared more comically battered

than before. The inside was cluttered, and the seat's fabric had long since worn away, leaving only a metallic frame, like on Kera's ship. Diyan pulled his facepiece down and looked enviously at the Vaesian's seat, which was overlaid with thick cushioning. He bent down and slid in, slouching back. The compartment smelled faintly of sweat, which unfortunately seemed to be coming more from Diyan's seat than the rest of the vehicle.

"Pull the fold down," the Vaesian instructed, as its own slid down automatically.

Diyan glimpsed rows of dark yellow strips at the top and bottom of the Vaesian's mouth, in a similar position to his own teeth. They were chipped and worn in places but looked sharp, and somehow older than the rest of the Vaesian's body. Diyan gripped the bottom of the fold awkwardly and yanked it down again. It did not quite meet the bottom. He waited while the Vaesian fiddled noisily with the controls in the front. When the fiddling stopped, the Vaesian grabbed the fabric around its head and pulled it right up to the top. Diyan pulled his own a little higher, almost reaching his eyes. They began to move off, away from Fadin.

Diyan cleared his throat. "Your skimmer's different to the others in Fadin."

"Skimmer?" The Vaesian sounded genuinely confused for a moment. "This isn't a skimmer."

"Oh, I—"

"And we aren't in Fadin anymore, look around you.

Skimmer! You lot like to think you gave us everything, don't you? Skimmer!"

"Oh, sorry. What is it then?"

"What is it?" The Vaesian guffawed incredulously. "A glazer, obviously."

"It looks almost like a skimmer—"

"From our Great Ship, not yours." The Vaesian hesitated. "You've really never heard of a glazer before?"

Diyan shook his head. "No, I haven't," he admitted. "And you're actually the first Vaesian I've spoken to, and…it's a complicated story, but I've not travelled out of Fadin before."

"The first…and you're going…" Again, the Vaesian's incredulity was loud and immediate. "You're in for quite something, headed to Sunsprit. You'll be surrounded by all the Vaesians you can get, and they'll be Silvereds too. Sunsprit is the city of the Silvereds. Most of our own kind give it a wide berth, and it's even rarer to see one of yours. Quite some trip you've planned for yourself."

It swivelled its head back and stared at Diyan with its black orbs. Murky structures were just about visible within the orbs, coalescing like nebulous clouds in the direction it was looking – him.

"You've *never* heard of a glazer before, and you've *never* spoken to a Vaesian before?"

"There are a lot of things I haven't done yet."

"Well, you'll get used to it pretty quick. Glazers are dependable. Although bumpier than you'll be used to, I'm told. Never actually been in a skimmer, but at least I've heard of them! Anyway, there's nothing we can do about that now, your lot should have checked beforehand."

"What do you mean they're dependable?" Diyan asked. "Skimmers are completely dependable."

"Completely!" The Vaesian's loud guffaw filled the glazer, causing Diyan to wince. "Dependable, out here? You must be joking. Take a look around you. Pure Ringscape, no Fadin. Your city's skimmers are probably all influx-controlled now, you must know that. But the influx network's signals can't penetrate far through the thick atmosphere, no matter how intelligent it appears to be, and intermediary signal relays are highly power consumptive too, probably for the same mystifying reason. That's why most systems for almost everything you can imagine are short-range, whether in Fadin or anywhere else. And hardly any Roranians have bothered to learn how to take manual control over the skimmers. Anyway, the Administration seems to find it humorous to send you lot through in our transports. They might as well just fly you over in one of their ships!" The Vaesian paused, as though it had just considered something. "Unless the Administration have solved the power dissipation problem?" It silently waited for an answer.

"I, err, I see what you mean." When the Vaesian said nothing further, Diyan elaborated. "And no, I don't know if the Administration have discovered how to deal with the power dissipation issues. I know nothing about that."

155

The Vaesian did not immediately reply. When it did, its tone was more distant. "Well, that's why I'm here anyway, ferrying you with my trusty glazer."

"Are you Silvered?"

"Do I look Silvered to you?" It sounded perturbed.

"How long till we arrive?"

"The better part of a day."

"I'm Diyan, what's your name?"

Another pause, before an indignant response. "Why would I tell you that? The less we know about each other the better. I don't want the Administration to send me to one of its centres!" Its body became more rigid whilst the ends of its arms began twitching more, as though it were suddenly busier.

Diyan turned to look out at Ringscape. There was little for his eyes to latch on to. Just the monochrome, flat ground, and the unending, infinite sky.

"Do all of you speak our language?"

"All of us?" The Vaesian replied, more wearily than before. "Almost everyone on Ringscape does, now. How couldn't they if they want the chance to deal with you? Apparently, the Administration's planning on creating fixed trading routes between the major cities on the ground. Specious or not, it makes no sense not to prepare ourselves. Most of us speak Roranian, all the smaller groups too. Except the Alpuri, but they're way across on the opposite side of Ringscape and they don't talk to anyone. You ask a lot of odd questions, don't you?"

"The Alpuri?" Diyan sighed. "I'm just trying to understand how everything fits together, this is all new to me. I need to find someone...she's called Kera...I need to piece it all together. There was an attack...I was told she's augmented, somehow." He hesitated. "She's in Sunsprit. Do you know where I should start?"

The Vaesian's reply was stern. "What are you doing? Didn't I tell you the less we know about each other, the better?" Its body tightened up again and its arms became busier. "Whatever the business between you and the Administration, it stays between you and the Administration. I'm just here to take you from one place to the next, nothing more."

Another uneasy silence settled between them, and Diyan resumed staring at the bland scenery, which was, in many ways, just as barren as Barrenscape. Maybe even more. At least Barrenscape had sediment that wafted into the air. A few times, he saw what appeared to be glazers or skimmers in the distance, but none came close.

"What's that?" Diyan pointed out, suddenly alarmed. At the limit of his sight, the land simply dropped away.

"You must have seen the edge of Ringscape before?" the Vaesian replied, sounding bored.

"Not from the ground."

"Don't you know anything?"

Chapter 19
Silvered Landscape

Diyan was transfixed by Ringscape's edge, which ran adjacent to them. It was close enough that he could definitively see the discrete end to Ringscape, but far enough that it would still take some time to reach, even travelling at the glazer's current speed. The edge did not become any less strange the longer he stared. There was nothing else that complemented the oddness of the sudden drop, no discernible change to Ringscape's surface or barrier running alongside it. The glazer ride was still a little bumpier than a skimmer, as the Vaesian had rightly told him to expect, but aside from that, everything else was normal – except the edge of everything that loomed nearby.

"Will we go closer?" he asked.

The Vaesian sighed. "And kill ourselves? Have you heard of the Vaesian concept *tetibat*?"

"No?"

"It's the process of acting to increase your stability in life, in all measures. Very often, it's literal. Anything to improve your position. Going over the edge would be going against tetibat in the strongest sense."

"I didn't mean right up and over, just closer."

"Gravity doesn't work correctly, or as you'd expect, when you're close to the edge. It's unpredictable. Currently, this surface is unsafe. There's nothing sticking us down. The closer you get, the more unpredictable gravity becomes. You must know that? It's how most cities in Ringscape generate their power. They exploit changes in the gravitational gradient—"

"So those are the structures along the edge that lead to Fadin," Diyan interrupted, interested.

"Ah! You *have* been to the edge before!" the Vaesian shouted, indignantly. "You've even seen the gradient transducers!"

Diyan shook his head. "It's complicated." He offered no further explanation and the Vaesian asked for none. Casting an eye to the other side of the glazer, away from the edge, he saw two vehicles moving in the same direction as them, albeit much faster. Somehow, the Vaesian seemed to know which direction Diyan was now facing.

"Probably Silvereds," it said more seriously. "No one else tends to travel to Sunsprit unless absolutely necessary."

"Why're we closer to the edge than them?"

"Because I don't exactly operate in typically allowed parameters, as you might have guessed, so it's better for both of us if we're seen by as few others as possible. Wouldn't help for my fellow Vaesians to ask questions about the spy in my glazer." It guffawed, unexpectedly, and Diyan flinched. "So, let's keep this journey to ourselves."

"I'm not a spy." Diyan expected the Vaesian to reply, but it did not. "Why do you do it?"

"Why do I do what?"

"Why are you taking me to Sunsprit for the Administration?"

"The Administration's changing things fast, and we live long, Roranians and Vaesians. I'd like to be included." The Vaesian spoke as though it were bored.

Their conversation dwindled as the daylight dissipated. Evening crept up on them, and it became difficult to discern where the sky ended and the surface of Ringscape began. A few other glazers crossed Ringscape in the distance – identified by the Vaesian – but all too far off to properly distinguish, and there was nothing else to break the monotony of the journey. Diyan leaned against the side of the glazer, lulled by its rhythmic undulations into sleep.

A thud jolted him back into consciousness. He opened his eyes, immediately sensing something was different. It was dark, clearly, although the inside of the glazer was lit a gloomy white, and it no longer rumbled, but travelled smoothly, more like a skimmer. Looking outside, he saw they were now travelling along a flat, somewhat metallic surface that radiated a dim white glow, wide enough for ten or more adjacent glazers. The surface started a little way back; he could just about make out where it began. The glazer also seemed lower, as though it were on the surface instead of hovering above. The edge of Ringscape still loomed to the side, albeit closer than before, just about visible in the glow coming from the metallic surface. Nothing else seemed to have changed, although with the darkness around them, it was difficult to be sure.

"What's going on?" he asked, groggily.

"Someone's woken up."

"Where are we?"

"Welcome to the magnetic paths of Sunsprit. Not like the gravity emulators you might be used to, but just as effective. Unless you'd rather be at the mercy of a flip."

"A flip?"

"Gravitational fluctuation, small reversal. Well, not a reversal, more of a sudden decrease, sometimes a complete absence. Like what happens right at the edge, but less frequent. You can thank whoever it was that built Ringscape."

"But why are we…" He smacked his head and sat up, fully alert. "Sunsprit's built on the edge?"

The Vaesian's head flicked back. Diyan glimpsed a shiny blue substance pressed against the lower yellow strips of its mouth. The substance emitted a faint, misty haze.

"Now you're just pretending. You *must* have known that. Why else did you think we were travelling so close to the edge? For fun?"

"You said it was so we weren't seen by anyone else!"

The Vaesian shook its head in a recognisable gesture of disbelief, before facing forwards again. "That's just why we moved closer to the edge earlier than we might have. You really don't know anything about Sunsprit…you haven't been joking."

"I know it's a Vaesian city, and it's where your Silvereds live, mainly."

"Well, you'll find out more soon enough anyway, but you should know that it's a city of two parts, like Fadin. A dual city. They are the only two cities like it on Ringscape, and they happen to be close to each other."

"Is the main part on this side of Ringscape?"

"There is no main part. It's much older than Fadin, fully joined. That's why it straddles Ringscape's edge. From above, it looks like a great sphere that's been wedged against Ringscape's side."

"I thought travel wasn't possible during the day. The haze winds—"

"You don't need to fly from one end to the other! Fully joined, like I said. And even if you did fly, the haze winds are only really dangerous between Barrenscape and Ringscape. Not at these lower levels."

"But…why build a city right on the edge?"

"It's a good thing we did, from the Silvereds' point of view. Even though Sunsprit's close to Fadin, the Administration haven't influenced it as much as our other cities. Initially, they weren't interested, since Roranians have a hard time adapting to the gravity effects, and now they can't, because the Silvereds have congregated there and don't trust them like the rest of the Vaesians do. So, the Administration now resorts to sending spies like you over to find out what's going on. The Administration would probably rather Sunsprit didn't exist, and the Vaesian Union doesn't want to be affiliated with the city either, but unfortunately for them, they can't be seen to let the Administration do what they want with a Vaesian city. It's quite a mess. Do I really have to explain Ringscape politics to you?"

Diyan was frowning. "If Sunsprit's such a dangerous place, why would Kera be working with the Silvereds to destroy Fadin's influx network, and then hide there, and so close—"

"Don't!" the Vaesian shouted, clearly alarmed. "No names, nothing absolute. I don't want to know about any associates you may or may not be looking for. How many times do I need to tell you? The less specifics, the better."

Diyan huffed. The magnetic path was straight, though there was a slight diagonal tilt towards the edge. They were moving closer and closer. His eyes drifted away as he looked back across Ringscape on the glazer's other side, searching for signs of life.

Turning back a little while later, he gasped in surprise. The edge had snuck up on them. They had closed the distance by quite some way, almost half. There was nothing past the edge, just endless, dark, empty sky. Fortunately, the path looked to have straightened out, and was no longer tilting them dangerously close to oblivion.

"Fun, eh?" the Vaesian remarked, sounding happier than before. "Not long now."

"I don't feel any different yet. What was it you were saying about flips?" Diyan commented, a moment too soon. His stomach suddenly lurched as though he was freefalling. Thankfully, his body did not actually move since his lower half was wedged into the seat's depression and his feet were latched onto a footrail beneath the Vaesian's seat. The glazer itself stayed rooted to Ringscape and carried on moving as before. The flip dissipated almost as quickly as it had come, and gravity returned to normal. Diyan was pushed down with unexpected force into his seat, as though he had just dropped from high up.

"Felt that, didn't you?" the Vaesian smirked. "They're unpredictable. You'll get used to them. Complete dissipation; no gentle phasing in or out. We're fine here. That's what the path's for, to keep glazers grounded."

One of the Vaesian's hairy, flexible arms lunged back and Diyan impulsively moved his body away. Thin, wavy protrusions, sticking out from the bulbous end of the creature's arm like a miniature, stubbier version of a bloom propulsion unit, wiggled in the same direction.

"Relax, check that compartment there. It's a gift from the Administration."

Diyan tore his eyes from the Vaesian's arm and pulled the compartment casing aside. There was a pair of battered-looking boots inside.

"Put them on before you leave. They'll stop you floating off…hopefully."

Diyan inspected them. "They're not very heavy," he said. "How do they work?"

"Same as these, but better," the Vaesian replied, again thrusting the same arm back to display its wavy protrusions. "You have fingers, we have these. Tensirs. Ours are better for low and zero-gravity environments; we can grip most surfaces. It is said that when my species lived aboard our own Great Ship, we were forbidden from touching our c-autom helpers in case they became stuck. I don't think there's much truth in that, but it's interesting to think about. Anyway, those boots are highly adhesive, but easy to step off at an angle. You'll find most wear them in Sunsprit." The Vaesian's arm returned to the front. "We did manage to develop a few things before you came along."

Diyan opened his mouth to reply when sparkles of light ahead captured his attention. They were unobtrusive, complementing the gloom rather than extinguishing it. There were faint outlines of towers, tall and thin – they looked to be covered in the same brown matter as the uncultivated and unprocessed surface of Ringscape. Interspersed between the sparse, tall towers were shorter, stubbier constructs, and ringed structures, rising perpendicularly from the ground and with the uppermost sky-facing segments of their rings missing. The towers and other constructions were densely packed in a thin perimeter around a great dome that rose high into the sky, dwarfing everything else. The dome's lattice structure was covered with the same brown matter as the towers. Other glowing magnetic paths weaved towards the city from different directions, none as close to the edge as theirs. The paths joined together, pooling into a bright, silver underlayer, upon which the entire city appeared to float.

"That's Sunsprit?" Diyan asked.

"It is," the Vaesian murmured.

"It looks…permanent," Diyan replied.

"We did make them well. We worked with this place, not against it."

"What was it like?" Diyan asked.

A guffawing sound emanated from the front of the glazer. "You think I was around then?"

Diyan strained his neck to the side. "Is it a dome?"

"Yes and no. You can't see from here, but it's a stretched dome, as I told you before. Most of the city lies within it. At the edge, the dome stretches right across and down to the underside, joining up with its other part. So, it's not really a dome, but let's not be pedantic."

"What for?"

"No one likes a pedant."

"I mean, what's the dome for?"

"Oh, that," the Vaesian said, entirely unconvincingly. "Couldn't get the air purification systems to work." The Vaesian guffawed loudly.

"It must be enormous!"

"Many of our old cities were like this. We were never able to create so many ships, like you, and most of them failed in time anyway. Our cities needed to be like this if we wanted to join both sides of Ringscape."

"And Sunsprit is the only one left?"

"Like this, yes. Before you came along, we also had our own issues on Ringscape. Many cities were destroyed..." The Vaesian's voice softened. "But life goes on. We even tried to build on Barrenscape, but the Breaker put an end to that."

"What is the Breaker?"

"Wouldn't everyone like to know."

"Does no one know?"

"No one alive."

Diyan's eyes flickered to the Vaesian. "Just how long have you been here? Vaesians, I mean."

"We think we were amongst Tapache's first, but we can't prove it. Just ask your influxes." Its speech became more rapid. "Anyway, Sunsprit belongs to the Silvereds now. Your Anti-Vaesian Movement should be happy about that, at least some of the Vaesian population is nicely congregated away from them. Something for them to hate from afar." The glazer began to slow down, swerving gently to the side of the metallic path. "And this is as far as I go."

"You're not taking me all the way in?"

"That place? No. This is your journey, not mine. Don't forget to put on your boots, I want to get paid."

Diyan sighed and unhurriedly put the boots on, leaving his old footwear behind in the compartment as the Vaesian dictated. At one point, the back of his hand brushed against the thin, black extensions protruding from the soles of the boot, and he had to slowly peel it off at the corners to release himself. Once he was done, he pulled his facepiece tightly over his head, yanked the glazer's back fold upwards, and stepped out. Looking at the vessel as it touched the ground, Diyan realised how different it was to a skimmer. The bottom appeared to be made from the same solid material as the rest of the glazer's external bulk, but upon closer inspection, its edges could be seen rippling faintly against the ground, as though restless, perpetually searching for something. From a distance, the movement was unnoticeable.

The glazer's front side folded up automatically and the Vaesian stuck its arm out. The blue substance in its mouth was gone. "There." It pointed ahead to one of the open rings. "You see that old docking ring? Next to the tall thin tower? On its other side is an entrance. You'll be stopped on the other side, but they won't question you much, probably just scan you. If they do, I'm sure they'll find nothing on you, they never do. You can tell them whatever you like, they know the Administration sends its spies. Word's also spread about the attack on Fadin's influx network, so all the Vaesian cities will be expecting an increase in Roranian spies. No one's going to challenge you above the perfunctory requirements – appearances and all that."

"And once I'm inside—"

"You'll be watched, so don't do anything suspicious."

"But I'm looking for—"

"No names! And pull the fold down. This is where my help ends. I hope your path from here contributes towards your tetibat, and mine for that matter."

Diyan did as he was told, shivering a little. It was slightly cooler than was comfortable, although he could already feel the threading of his regwear tightening in response, closing off routes for his body-heat to escape.

"So, what now?"

The Vaesian simply looked forwards as the front fold of the glazer closed, then the vehicle turned around and sped off, back the way they had come. Diyan waited in disbelief. He was alone in the darkness, standing upon a structure within the Source – a situation he could never even have dreamed of whilst on the Great Ship – about to search for Kera within a city filled with a strange species, all carrying a technological plague, while his fellow Roranians from the Administration presumably decided whether or not to retaliate against the recent attack on

169

their information network. Tapache was an unfathomably advanced machine-lect, with abilities Diyan could never comprehend…and yet, at this moment in time, Diyan knew more about the Source than it did, despite understanding very little, if anything.

He raised his feet one by one and placed them back against the magnetic surface a few times, testing the boots. Although not affected by the surface's magnetism itself – as the glazer had been – they stuck down remarkably firmly. He tested wriggling his feet free, needing to angle them slightly inwards when pushing off so that the soles were not faced perpendicularly downwards. He began to walk along the path, at first very slowly, wrenching his legs up as hard as he could, and then more fluidly. Surprisingly, it did not take long before his body adapted, and he was able to walk with an almost normal gait. He took a curious step off the path, onto the brown ground of Ringscape. The boots stuck firmly, but not as firmly as on the magnetic path, to which he quickly retreated, not wanting to be caught out during a flip.

As he drew closer to Sunsprit, reaching the point where his path merged with other paths to become part of the glowing underlayer of the city, he made sure to stray no closer to the edge than he already was. The place the Vaesian had told him to head towards, next to the old docking ring, was not far off. A lone glazer came into view, moving about some way off, along another magnetic path towards a different part of the city. Moments later, it had circled far enough around the city's outskirts that it disappeared from view, behind the towers.

As Diyan walked closer, the outer towers loomed even more imposingly than before. They were dark. The sparkling lights only came from the inner towers, further in than he would be walking. There was an eerie silence as he trudged along, the towers appearing to grow taller as he drew nearer.

He stopped a few paces before the docking ring, which stood just to the right of a tower, with barely a finger's width gap in between. The docking ring was thick and bulky, with a diameter a few multiples of his own height. Grooves in its surface hinted at the underlying structure — it was constructed of conjoined segments, each at least an arm's length long. One of the segments had a large crack running down almost to its midpoint. The crack's innards were the same brown as Ringscape.

Diyan took a few more steps back, gazing leftwards at the other nearby towers, not yet wanting to look right, towards the entrance to the city. All the towers were coated in brown matter, and were mostly square-based, rising straight upwards out of the ground. The space between some of them was sufficient that Diyan could have walked all the way around them, and some were thin enough that he could probably have done so in one breath each.

Eventually, his eyes wandered to the entrance, beside the docking ring. It was small, on a different scale to everything else, and long, clearly extending backwards. It was like an entrance encased within the stub of a wall of towers. It formed an archway, just about large enough for him to walk through comfortably. Despite being dissimilar to its surroundings, it was also unremarkable. If he had not known it was there, he would probably have missed it. The glow from the ground dissipated above knee-height within the passage that the archway opened out into, making it almost pitch-black inside. Diyan took a deep breath, then walked through.

Chapter 20
Innocence of Sunsprit

Unnerving whirring noises emanated from the walls of the passage around him, and light from the ground intermittently flashed with a high intensity, too rapidly for him to make out the wall's features. After the first few flashes, he fumbled around while his eyes readjusted, but he soon took to stopping and waiting for his vision to return. The regwear threading loosened, allowing a pleasantly warm breeze to waft against his body.

"Hello?" he called out, with all the confidence he could muster. There was no response.

He carried on walking, waiting for the passage to end. With no warning, his stomach lurched. A flip. He gasped in terror. The disappearance of gravity rippled through him like a shock of force upwards. He had been mid-stride, so his free leg waved awkwardly about, harder to control. His arms flailed and he struggled to correct his position. Only the other foot, which was firmly stuck to the ground by his boot, held him roughly in position. Normal gravity returned. His attached leg had been unprepared, causing him to fall clumsily into a kneeling position.

His head throbbed and he pressed his hands against both sides of his temple, still kneeling and breathing heavily, disoriented. Once his breathing steadied, he stood up and continued. The light from the floor dimly showed the passage curving sharply to the right – he had long since lost all sense of the original direction he had been travelling in. Upon turning the corner, a bright, blue wall of light seared into his vision, blinding him.

"Pull down your facepiece!" a deep voice sounded.

Diyan stumbled to the side, waiting for his vision to return while attempting to acquiesce. He pulled down his facepiece to expose his eyes, attempting to gather his bearings as his sight came back.

He was in a small, simple, well-lit room, with the same glowing magnetic floor as the passageway and the outskirts of the city. Looking around, the brown substance he expected to see was gone, replaced by sterile, white walls, not unlike the Administration room at Fadin's shipyard. Directly in front of him, three very silver-looking, serious-looking Vaesians – Silvereds – were standing side-by-side, staring keenly back at him. The two at the ends were the same height as Diyan, and appeared stockier than the central Silvered, who was a little taller and thinner. All three wore the same black regwear garments as the Vaesians in Fadin, and stood with their middle legs protruding in front of the side two. The Silvered to the far left was fiddling with a long device that extended from the wall: a mechanical arm with a small screen attached to the end. Its long neck was stretched almost completely straight as it looked at the screen. The arms of the other two Silvereds were hidden behind their bodies, making it appear as though they were intermingling their tensirs in the same manner that Roranians clasped their hands.

"Are you from Fadin?" Diyan mumbled, his face reddening as he looked around nervously.

"Roranian, pull down your facepiece completely and identify yourself," the Silvered in the middle reiterated, more loudly this time. As with the Vaesian who had taken him to Sunsprit, the middle Silvered also had a shiny blue substance in its mouth. As it spoke, wisps of blue escaped. Diyan cautiously pulled his facepiece all the way down, below his chin. Despite the regwear's temperature regulation capabilities, a fresh glean of sweat revealed itself.

The Silvered tapping the wall-mounted mechanical arm took a few steps towards Diyan, swinging its middle leg and then its side legs twice each. The mechanical arm moved smoothly alongside it, elongating from its fixed point in the wall to keep up. A dark blue holo square appeared just beyond its tip, and the arm receded a little.

Although largely obscured behind the holo, the Silvered appeared to be manipulating certain controls through it. Once finished, the holo vanished, and both the Silvered and mechanical arm moved back to their original positions.

Diyan looked at the Silvereds uncomfortably. "I'm Diyan."

The Silvered to the left spoke to the central Silvered. "That flip was probably confusing. This one looks inexperienced. Still, politer than the last one."

"Are you confused?" the central Silvered asked, still streaming blue wisps from its mouth. Its black eyes fixated upon Diyan's own. "When you speak, do speak up." The blue substance it chewed was diminishing, exposing the rows of dark yellow strips along the top and bottom of its mouth – uncracked, unlike the Vaesian who had ferried Diyan to Fadin. "Have you never seen a Silvered before?"

Diyan nodded, eagerly. "Yes, I have. I've come from Fadin."

The middle Silvered turned to the Silvered on the right. "You're right. Fifty-ninth today. We've even had the occasional one protesting they're not a spy. They're sending in all calibres now!" It emitted a brief guffaw.

"At least they're not sending soldiers."

"Maybe this one'll surprise us."

All three guffawed in unison.

"You *were* sent by the Administration, weren't you?" The blue substance had gone, the last of the wisps dissipating to nothing.

Diyan nodded.

"Everyone has their first time," the one on the left said. It shuffled towards the wall with the mechanical arm. The central Silvered moved in the same direction, slowly, stepping with each of its three legs, one-by-one, and the right Silvered shuffled in the opposite direction.

"You won't find anything here related to the attack against Fadin," the central Silvered assured Diyan. "That was nothing to do with us." It then proceeded to give him a rapid, almost prosaic explanation of some very clear things he was allowed and not allowed to do within Sunsprit. "And of course, you are free to enter and stay until you are satisfied. Accommodation can be provided if you require." It gestured to the wall behind it, which slid smoothly across. A throng of Silvered bodies rushed about on the other side, and an immediate barrage of noise filled the small room. "Welcome to Sunsprit." Its black eyes followed him as Diyan walked forwards. "Go on then, we haven't got all day!"

As Diyan stepped out, trying to make sense of the bustle of activity all around, he was faintly aware of the wall sliding back into place behind him. Silvereds strode about in all directions on a large flat concourse, unsurprisingly made of the same shining material as the magnetic paths. Many walked, although just as many ran, with an elegant swagger he had not seen from the Vaesians in Fadin. They all wore boots that looked similar to his own, and which did not appear to impede the fluid process of their curious gait – central leg first, then outer legs in unison. The smaller, ostensibly younger Silvereds, with shorter hair, were a little less steady. They jumped and ran about with each of their three legs moving one by one, causing them to dip deeply from side to side. In general, their outer legs completed the sequence, lifting and propelling their bodies forward, just about stopping them from crashing to the ground, although some of the smallest did still fall, laughing with their high-pitched, goofy guffaws when they did.

Small versions of the towers he had seen outside the dome circled the other side of the concourse. High steps and stairways led to other platforms and concourses, and the towers densified and increased in height towards the centre of the city. Nothing was covered with the brown substance of Ringscape other than the protective dome above them. Instead, everything was a light, solid grey, as though a reflection of the Silvered's own bodies. The air was bright, though there was no obvious source of light. It was nothing like the dark, gloomy city he had assumed it would be, based on the outside of the dome.

A flash of motion drew his attention. Near the end of the concourse, the back end of a glazer disappeared into a thin lane between two towers. Although almost everything was structurally grey, there was a spectrum of colour. There were iridescences about certain Silvereds that made them shimmer beautifully, alongside the blue wisps coming from some of their mouths. Items they carried and certain unique clothes – that did not appear to be purely regwear-derived – added further dashes of colour. The brown domed ceiling; the clear air; the glowing floor…Sunsprit seemed more vibrant, colourful, and full of life than anywhere Diyan could remember. Diyan spotted occasional non-Silvereds, some shockingly white, and a few other Roranians walking about, rather more assertively than he was. Most ignored him, although some looked back, curiously.

Diyan took a deep breath, preparing to make his way to the other side of the concourse and the short sequence of tall steps he had spotted, which appeared to lead to a quieter platform from which he hoped to gain a better vantage point, and figure out where to go next.

"Not as awful as you were expecting, eh?" a low voice hummed at his side.

Surprised, he turned to see a Silvered, almost a head taller than he was and very sturdily built, standing beside him. Its eyes were a little closer together than most other Vaesians, almost approaching that of a Roranian.

"It reminds me of my annexe, in a way," Diyan replied, frowning as he said it. "I mean, the stairways and platforms…" He dwindled off. "You probably have no idea what I'm talking about."

The Silvered guffawed. It appeared to find his comment genuinely humorous. "We've heard of the annexes from your Great Ship. But…forgive me…you weren't on the Roranian Great Ship yourself, were you, Diyan? You don't seem...like you've been around long enough."

"I was in stasis," Diyan replied. "You know my name, who are you?"

"I was once new here, myself," the Silvered replied.

"Who are you?" he repeated, flinching as one of the small Silvereds bumped into him. Its hair was smoother than he had expected.

"My name's Hespinr. I'm here to show you around, Diyan. You can be straight with me."

"I'm not here to cause any trouble."

"No one is." Again, the guffawing. "But we both know about the recent attack against your influx network. We're innocent and cooperating as best we can, but the Administration is certainly sending a lot of you over all of a sudden. Anti-Vaesian rhetoric is picking up, I'm told. Not good for us. Tell me, where do you intend to go?"

"I'm not anti-anything," Diyan muttered. "And I don't really know where I need to go. I'm just trying to understand where I am. I..." He noticed a non-Silvered walking slowly. One of the Vaesian's arms was shaved, from midway right up to where it joined at the body, revealing dark grey skin. He pointed. "What happened there?"

"That's a *Veiler.*"

"A what?"

"They belong to a group of Vaesians called *Behind the*

Veil. They believe there's something in Ringscape that no one else can see." Hespinr guffawed. "Removing hair supposedly represents that. They visit here, from time to time, but they're harmless. Anyway, come, I'll show you around," Hespinr replied, motioning with one of its thick arms. "This way."

It moved off with the triple-legged gait Diyan was becoming accustomed to. Silvereds in its path moved out of the way.

Diyan hurried to keep up beside it. "Where are we going?"

Hespinr pointed to the same quiet area at the perimeter of the concourse that Diyan had been about to target, with the high steps leading up to it. "There."

"What's there?"

"You're about to find out."

Diyan froze, closing his eyes and clenching his jaw as a ripple of change spread about his body. His hair fluttered as though a strong wind had suddenly buffeted against him, and his arms raised comically high. His legs wobbled, though he thankfully managed to remain upright. He reached up and pressed his palms against the sides of his head. By the sounds of it, no one else had been noticeably affected by the flip. Diyan opened his eyes to see several Silvereds patting their hairs down as they wandered along, but no one else paid the flip any further attention.

"We're getting nowhere fast if you do that each time there's a flip," Hespinr said. "Walk through them and don't panic."

"Easy for you to say."

"Your body will adjust, and you'll stop noticing. I've seen plenty of Roranians adjust before, it won't take long. It'll count for your tetibat. Just make sure you've always got one leg on the ground."

Diyan glared at Hespinr and patted his hair down. "Like I said, easy for you to say."

"Come on."

They reached the high steps and moved to the smaller platform, just big enough to accommodate both of them. Diyan looked up – the dome was already curved high enough that the sight made him dizzy. Hespinr urged him on again. Small towers surrounded their narrow path, and the frequent steps were thankfully not all too steep. They walked for quite some time. Occasionally, they passed other Silvereds, many uttering low greetings to Hespinr. They spoke a mixture of Roranian and their own, incomprehensible language.

"Hespinr," Diyan said, slowing down.

The Silvered turned around. "Yes?"

Diyan pointed up. "It's brighter than before. How?"

"Daylight. The dome emits light to reflect the brightness of the Haze Rings. The light is generated by excitations in the air just below the dome's surface, technology from our ancient Great Ship."

"Our c-automs could do that too. They had auras."

"I know."

They carried on. Turning up a new set of steps, two small Silvereds rushed down past them, moving so fast that Diyan could barely see their legs. He almost fell over trying to move aside in time, to Hespinr's guffawing delight.

"They were…" Diyan stared after them. "I barely saw them."

"Children run whenever they can," Hespinr said.

"But they were so fast. The others I saw—"

"At the entrance?" Hespinr resumed walking, forcing Diyan to hurry after. "They weren't running."

"I saw them, there were—"

"Diyan, did you know that some Vaesians choose to be Silvered?" Hespinr asked, although it did not appear to want an answer. "Some are born Silvered and some later become Silvered through no choice of their own. Yet others choose it. This way." Still walking, it pointed a long arm to another set of steps, bordered by thin towers. "It seems there is very little you know of us. But don't worry, you're no different to most other Roranians I've met."

Diyan wiped the sweat from his forehead and groaned. "Another…Hespinr, I can't keep doing this." He stopped, forcing Hespinr to do likewise while he leaned against a tower. "This city, all these steps, it's…" He trailed off upon spotting a broad concourse through the gap between the two towers beside him. It lay quite some way below them, although he could easily tell it was far larger than others he had seen. He moved over for a better look and leaned against one of the towers. More Silvereds than he could count littered the concourse. "I thought being Silvered was a plague. That's what I was told."

Hespinr guffawed. "A plague?" It strode over to Diyan and pointed a wavy cluster of its tensirs towards a group of young Silvereds playing in the concourse. "Do they look afflicted to you?"

Diyan shook his head.

A docking ring sat at the centre of the concourse, like the one Diyan had seen outside Sunsprit's entrance. Even though Diyan had to squint to make it out, it was obviously heavily battered and cracked. Young Silvereds were climbing it. They swung around, using their three legs more than their arms. The ends of their limbs appeared to stick to the docking ring with ease, allowing them to move like a Roranian never could.

"What're those for?" Diyan asked.

"The docking rings are relics, from when we still used ships. This one's been taken in from outside the dome, as a reminder for our young, a curiosity."

"Where are your ships now?"

"We used their parts to improve our cities long before you came."

"What is that?" Diyan exclaimed, pointing to a wide, squat figure that was scuttling rapidly from one side of the concourse to the other. It appeared to be half the height of a Vaesian adult. A black cloak was draped across its top, and short spikes jutted up through the cloak's folds like miniature towers. Six white legs, ending in points, were visible underneath the cloak. There were also four other appendages amongst the white legs – dark, chunky extensions that moved less fluidly. They reminded Diyan of how his boots functioned, sticking him to the ground.

Hespinr guffawed. "A Prietman. They are few and far between, but we have some in our cities. Most are with the Alpuri."

"What are they? I think I saw one in Fadin."

"Sent by Tapache, like us. A few made it through not long after you, but not in the same numbers. They waited in their ship outside the Source for some time, and now that they're here, they haven't shown themselves to be very resourceful. Anyway, come on."

Diyan tore his gaze from the concourse and the Prietman, and sluggishly followed behind Hespinr, trudging up the steps.

"Hespinr…"

The Silvered carried on walking up the steps without looking back. "Learn to walk through the flips, Diyan."

Diyan climbed after Hespinr with his fists clenched and slightly raised.

"Better."

Sounds of distant guffaws from behind let Diyan know his distress had been seen. "Hespinr!" he shouted, irately. "What are we doing? We're talking about nothing of substance, and you're leading me around like a fool! What's going on?"

Hespinr turned around. "I don't think you are a fool."

"Then why lead me around like this."

"It's what we do," Hespinr replied as though it were obvious, disguise lifted. "The Administration sends its spies, and we lead them around the city. It's a show of your power that we have to do this, nothing more. Why don't you tell me what it is that you came here for?"

"I'm looking for someone."

"A Silvered?"

Diyan shook his head. "No, a Roranian, like me. Her name's Kera."

Hespinr's head flinched. Diyan could see the internal mechanics of its neck pulsating as though it were suddenly on high alert.

"Diyan, why don't you let me show you the divide within our city."

Chapter 21
Vaesian Divide

Upon reaching the top of the final staircase, having waded through increasingly frequent, protracted flips and with a consistent ringing in his ears, Diyan sighed with relief through his facepiece, which Hespinr had recently advised he pull up. He moved politely to the side, as much as he could manage, as a Veiler walked slowly past without acknowledging him. Straightening out his legs, Diyan leaned against the side of a tall, thin tower, taking deep breaths while waiting for his exhausted limbs to recover. Despite the howling winds that now battered against him, their walking was finally over. He was just a few strides away from the edge of Ringscape, which had been obscured by the heights of the steps only moments before, and he could see Sunsprit's great dome high above them, curving down over the edge.

"Don't mind them," Hespinr shouted, referring to the Veiler. "They're absorbed in their own thoughts most of the time. They see veils everywhere: conspiracies; covers; camouflage. They're harmless."

Diyan did not reply. Only recently, the mere thought of standing right at the edge would have terrified him, but now, he was almost thankful for the reprieve it gave his tired body. The flips continued, but they no longer disturbed him to the same extent. Judging the correct amount of effort for each action in the presence of a varying gravitational field was not an easy skill to master, but at least his movements were less jerky now, more economical. The main problem was his internal response: the ringing in his ears, the headache, and the blurry sight.

Hespinr waited next to the railing, right at the edge. The Silvered did not appear to be under any stress as far as Diyan could tell. Diyan sluggishly pushed himself up from the tower, stumbling a little as he overdid the force required mid-flip, and carefully made his way over. He could see other Silvereds further down the railing, on either side, apparently taking in the same view he was there to see. He also spotted two Roranians, one of them relatively close by, both with their facepieces up and standing beside Silvered companions. The Roranian furthest away seemed equally interested in looking back over at Diyan. He waved awkwardly towards the stranger, receiving an awkward wave in return.

"It's like being back on the ship," Diyan shouted over

loud winds, as he grabbed the railing tightly with both hands, wincing. "I could use some more of your tetibat right now."

Hespinr guffawed. Both of its arms were by its sides, tensirs wafting passively in the wind, as Diyan looked out, enthralled. Sunsprit's dome disappeared over the ridge, obscured by the thick atmosphere – something which still seemed to apply within the Vaesian city. The space encompassed by the dome was staggering. Directly below Diyan's feet, quite some way down, the natural surface of Ringscape stuck out one long stride further than his current position. Sunsprit's layout was not flat like Fadin's, and the steps they had steadily climbed had taken them high above ground level.

Large, cylindrical tubes of widely varying sizes jutted out beneath them, taking up much of the space along Ringscape's edge. The tubes straddled the edge, curving over it and disappearing down. Through their translucent exteriors, dim shapes could be seen intermittently whizzing back and forth within them. The tubes were segmented with thick, white, glowing frameworks holding them together, each no more than the length of a few skimmers joined in a train. The framework looked to be of the same magnetic material as Sunsprit's paths.

"What do you mean it's like being back on your ship?" Hespinr asked. Its deep voice cut surprisingly well through the strong winds.

"On our Great Ship, we had a chamber where we could

look down at these caskets…the caskets in which we were made. Where Tapache made us. This platform…this view…it was a little like this. I don't mean it looked the same, not at all. But the feeling…"

"Was it as loud?"

Diyan laughed. "No. And not as windy either." He paused and pointed down. "We're very high from the surface."

"Sunsprit was built over a long time, and nothing sinks in Ringscape."

Flips occurred constantly, sometimes between each breath, but mostly lasting longer. Even from just the short distance between the top of the steps and the railing, Diyan could feel the increase in the gravitational phenomenon enormously. He began to lose sense of precisely when they were under the influence of gravity and when they were not. His eyesight was uncomfortably blurry; he shook his head repeatedly to try to correct it. He tested his feet constantly, ensuring they were planted firmly against the ground, and further tightened his grip of the railing.

"Don't you need a mask or a facepiece too?" Diyan shouted, still looking down.

"I'm used to it, and my cell-scales also help. You're doing well, though. Many have asked to leave by now."

"Used to it?" Diyan forced a hearty laugh. "If I stay long enough, will I become used to it?"

"Perhaps."

"What're those?" He pointed to some of the smaller railed structures lining the edge, dropping down in between the tubes. They looked like the ones he had seen back when they had flown over Ringscape's edge, near Fadin. "Your gradient transducers?"

"Yes, they power the city, same technology as Fadin's and all other cities in Ringscape. Our technology. The flips increase in magnitude the further down from the edge you go. They're strongest right at the mid-point between the underside and the upperside. The gradient transducers provide us with the power we need." Hespinr pointed to one of the larger tubes beneath them. "And those are how we travel from one side of our city to the other, from Upper-Sunsprit to Under-Sunsprit and back. But our physiologies are different to yours, we deal with the gravitational stresses very well." Hespinr sounded almost bored, as though reciting something it was expected to say. "I don't think the same system would work quite so well for your cities. The engineering required…it's simpler for you to use your ships, but it means Fadin isn't quite connected. It's not truly one city." Hespinr turned its body to Diyan, its piercing black eyes staring into his. Diyan gazed back.

"Why did you bring me here, Hespinr? So that we won't be overheard?"

"Diyan, I want to ask you something."

"What?"

"Let's put talk of tetibat and other inconsequential

things aside. Administration spies come and go. We take them around the city, but it's always the same. We respect your power; you know that; the Administration knows that. It is a formality. But you are different, Diyan. You aren't a typical Administration spy. You don't seem to know much about us at all, and you appear to have come to our city with a specific purpose. I need to understand why. That's my purpose."

"I told you, I'm looking for Kera, nothing else."

Diyan brought a hand to his temple – the howling winds, flips, and blurry vision were making his head throb, and he was cold, as though blood was draining away from his skin. He looked over to the other Roranians. The one furthest away, who had waved back, was now gone, but the nearer Roranian was still there, looking over the edge. There were more Silvereds than before. On Diyan's other side, behind Hespinr, there were also more Silvereds. Some cast brief glances in his direction.

"Should we stay here for so long?" Diyan asked. "I don't feel right."

"You'll need to be more specific, Diyan. There are many Roranians called Kera."

"Here, in Sunsprit?"

"There are Roranians here too, living amongst us. Just as in Fadin."

"What can I tell you? On the ship, we all had our own names. She was the only Kera." Diyan scrunched his eyes, trying to concentrate. "She's beautiful, and she's..."

"Why are you looking for her?"

"The Administration thinks she has something to do with the attack on the influx network."

"Did she?"

"Of course not," he snapped, squinting so hard his eyes closed. "But I need to help her explain. I need her to come back with me."

"Diyan, you need to be sure who it is that you are searching for. Sunsprit can be a dangerous place."

"It's possible there's another name associated with her. Her c-autom, Otherness—"

"Otherness."

Diyan opened his stinging eyes and saw that Hespinr's body had stiffened. "You know where she is, don't you? She's in Sunsprit, isn't she?" He stood up straight, pulled down his facepiece and spoke more loudly, "Why aren't you answering any of my questions?"

The nebulous clouds within Hespinr's black eyes had coalesced, focusing on something behind Diyan's shoulder. Diyan turned around. All of the Silvereds between him and the other oblivious Roranian were staring straight back.

"Hespinr…what's going on?" Diyan released a hand from the railing, looking askance as the other Silvereds also began to release their own grips, stepping back from the railing with their middle legs, as though daring him to make another move. The other Roranian was just beginning to notice, turning in interest. Diyan looked back to Hespinr, and then to the Silvereds on the other side. They were glaring at him. They were also moving closer. "Hespinr—"

Before Diyan realised what was happening, Hespinr had moved in front of him and was firmly holding onto the sides of the railing, pinning Diyan in. "Diyan, prepare yourself!" Hespinr was shouting, sounding worried.

Diyan squirmed, trying to free himself. The Silvereds on either side were approaching with intent, all pretence gone. Behind them, other Silvereds and the Roranian were frozen in apparent confusion, simply watching. Diyan shouted, trying to signal to the other Roranian for help, but his voice was lost in the wind.

"What's going on Hespinr?"

Some of the Silvereds rushed away from the railing, hurrying down the steps leading away from the edge, as the menacing gang of remaining Silvereds approached. Slowly. First, middle leg forwards, then, outer two legs catching up. Diyan's stomach lurched, independent of a flip.

"Steady yourself," Hespinr said quietly, just loud enough to be heard over the wind.

"For what?"

The last thing he saw was the rush of figures hurtling towards him before he instinctively closed his eyes. Then, the sensation of falling. Opening his eyes again, his vision was even more blurred than before. Everything was spinning. It was like one long, prolonged flip, except he knew it was quite different – he really was falling. A flip occurred, but did little to impact his trajectory. Diyan reached out, briefly catching sight of Hespinr's outstretched arms and flailing tensirs reaching back, struggling amid an angry throng of Silvered bodies. Diyan spun uncontrollably. The Silvereds' deep shouts died down as the ferocious noise of the wind took over. The large pipes that straddled the edge were coming towards Diyan worryingly fast. All he could think to do was to cross his arms over his chest and curl up, bracing for impact.

His body was impacted. However, it was not the crash or pain he had been expecting, far less violent. The winds still roared, and upon gathering his senses, Diyan realised he was still moving through the air, but he had somehow missed the pipes and was instead falling between them, face first, towards Under-Sunsprit. The side of Ringscape, the region between the upperside and the underside, was speeding past him, almost within arm's reach. He stretched towards some of the tubes that ran along it, his movements awkward, the gravitational fluctuations almost seeming to draw him closer before forcing him back.

"Careful there, you don't want to touch them at the speed we're going, Diyan. Hard enough navigating the air currents without you sabotaging my efforts."

Diyan looked down. A pair of extremely silver, hairy arms were locked around his waist, tightly gripping him.

195

He stopped struggling and tried to catch his breath, unable to reply. His vision was becoming worse and the strange sensations in his body were becoming more evident. Twisting towards the large tube to his right, intermittent reflective segments of its glowing framework flashed images of who was behind him. It was a Silvered, with great unfurled wings like the Roranians who propelled themselves from poles and glided above the outskirts of Fadin. The Silvered wore black, skirt-like regwear, the same as most other Vaesians he had seen, as well as a pack from which the wings extended, and a dark, bulky device across its face. Its three legs were joined together, moving about fluidly like a tail in the water. Diyan reached for his facepiece and pulled it over his head. His breathing improved, though it was still strained. He tried to speak, but his voice was not strong enough.

Alarmingly, one of the Silvered's arms loosened, and the other one tightened in response. Diyan reached for the free arm, but the Silvered moved it away, out of reach.

"Relax, Diyan. Everything's going to be okay."

The Silvered's free arm then wrapped itself around one of Diyan's own arms, surprisingly flexibly, and proceeded to move roughly up and down, as though wanting to gain an impression of every part of his body. It then replaced its arm around Diyan's waist, removed its other arm, and completed the same manoeuvre on the other side. Gradually, it moved its limbs all over Diyan's body, including his face, which Diyan unsuccessfully tried to protect. He was forced to bear the examination, staring at the side of Ringscape only a short distance away as they sped along. His vision was becoming hazier and hazier. Finally, he felt the Silvered's body relax.

"All done," the Silvered said. A moment later, something was plastered over his face, attached securely at the back of his head, completely obscuring his vision. Fortunately, he was now able to breathe as normal.

"This one isn't designed for Roranian features, I'm afraid," the Silvered told Diyan as he drifted into unconsciousness. "You've got strange eyes."

Chapter 22
Kera

She was taken. No longer in control, a calm washed over her. The strange nature of the Tugs was revealed, though she was still none-the-wiser. Sleep descended as her horizontal body glided down, beneath the surface. Her hand vibrated rhythmically – not from the internal machinations of the device she held, but due to the external forces acting against it. Gravitational forces. The Tugs were excited to finally export their data.

There was some overlap, some spill-over, from the senses of the Tugs and her own. She was no longer quite sure whose was whose. Somehow, Kera knew that Diyan was near, searching for her. His imprint was seared throughout Sunsprit. The Tugs identified him with ease, although they did not know his importance to her. What did he think of the betrayal? He would never understand that she had other concerns, all joined by one destiny. He had not lived her life. There was one path that would satisfy them all. Tapache and the rest.

Chapter 23
Imperfect Resistance

Diyan woke up naked, surrounded by almost complete darkness, the remnants of a headache still festering. Fortunately, the ringing in his ears had mostly dissipated and his vision was no longer blurry, as far as he could tell. Immediately, a flip occurred. A moment later, there was another flip, and another, and another, and another – irregularly timed but consistent all the same. He waited for them to pass, realising with frustration that they would not. Curiously, his body seemed better able to tolerate them than before. The roaring winds were also gone, replaced by complete silence.

He rolled slowly onto his knees and looked around. As his eyes adjusted, he could see he was surrounded by four equidistant walls that tapered into a thin point high above, perhaps five times his own height. A cold, white light emanated from the pinnacle. He could not tell whether the light came from within the room, or if it was an opening in the ceiling that exposed the room to Sunsprit's dome, Ringscape's skies, or something else.

"Where am I?" he asked, loudly, crawling over to one of the corners where his clothes and boots lay in a messy heap. Pulling them on, he sat back down to look at his new prison. "Hello?" he said, to no response. He tried a few more times, then banged his fist against the floor. "You're just the same as the Administration!"

The walls were featureless. Nothing gave him any indication as to where he was, aside from the constant flips. After some time, an idea struck him. He moved to stand at the centre of the room, kicked off his boots, bent his legs, and jumped in time with the next flip. While he rose higher than without the assistance of the flip, it had not been high enough to reach anywhere near the top of the room. He landed awkwardly, bashing a knee. He tried several more times before giving up, miserable, having gained several knocks for his efforts, and put his boots back on.

"Are you hoping to burst through the ceiling, Diyan?" a rich, deep voice growled.

Diyan turned around. An even darker void had replaced one of the walls, and the dim shape of a Vaesian stood in the middle.

"That won't count for your tetibat."

"What's going on? What am I doing here?"

"Here," the Vaesian repeated.

Diyan took a step closer. "Obviously, I'm in Under-Sunsprit, that's where I was taken before I blacked out, and these flips mean I'm near the edge...very near. And you...you must be a Silvered. What do you want with me?"

"Kera."

"Where is she?"

The Vaesian guffawed. "You're not a typical spy, are you?"

"I'm not a spy at all."

"We may not countenance techniques like the Administration's neural conjoiners, but we do have ways of making you more amenable to speaking the truth."

"I'm not lying!"

"The Administration sent you."

"I had no choice."

"Explain what you mean."

Diyan took a step closer, reaching out and feeling a cold hard surface between them. The walls of his prison were still there. "How do I know this isn't a test from the Administration?"

"You don't. But it isn't."

"What if I tell the Administration what I've seen?" he threatened. "I'll tell them about you and—"

The Vaesian guffawed. "The Administration know we interrogate some of their spies, that is a part of the game. Sometimes we feed them information, it's an exchange. They like to believe they know which faction is in charge.

So, tell me the truth. I'll know if you're lying. Otherwise, assuming we allow you to leave, you will return to Fadin with nothing. For some reason, I sense this would be very bad for you. You are highly...motivated."

Diyan gritted his teeth. "Look, the Administration suspect Kera has something to do with the attack on their influx network. I know Kera, she wouldn't have...but you; the other Vaesians; the Administration, none of you are my concern. I'm not lying. I only care about Kera, I've got nothing to hide, and..." He faltered.

"And?"

"There were four of us. Kera, me, and the other two, who are with the Administration. Being held by the Administration. They also have our c-automs. If Kera doesn't come back with me, I don't know what's going to happen to them. She'll be able to explain everything." He expected the Vaesian to guffaw, but it did not. The silhouette rippled. It was just a holo, or some other type of projection, but the ripple briefly gave a clearer image – light silver, not as pronounced as many of the other Silvereds he had seen. Diyan frowned. "Have we met before?"

"What if I tell you that Kera did attack the influx network?"

Diyan's eyes bulged. "I...I don't believe you."

"But if she did?"

"Then there must have been a reason!"

"You were in stasis."

The statement took Diyan by surprise. "I was, but I never told you that."

"We've been watching you. Tell me about it."

Given his predicament and seeing no point in lying, Diyan told the Silvered his story – about what had happened on the Roranian Great Ship; his journey in the casket-ship; ending up in Barrenscape.

"Who are you?" Diyan asked afterwards.

The silhouette disappeared.

*

Diyan was sitting in a corner of the dark room, tapping his feet against the floor. The rhythmic tapping was the only sound he could hear. For a while, he fancied there was a deep, low humming coming from somewhere nearby, although he could not be sure it was not just his imagination. He paid little attention to the constant flips, letting his hair become as unruly as it liked. Finally, breaking the monotony, one of the walls adjacent to the opposite corner shimmered and disappeared, replaced with a black void, as before. The silhouette returned.

"We want you to help us, Diyan."

He scoffed. "Help you?" He rose to his feet. "How? I have nothing you want."

"You may be able to help us reach Kera."

"Reach Kera?" he repeated. "What do you mean? Don't you know where she is either?"

"If you don't help us, you will never see Yena or Paran again, you can be sure about that. The Administration is brutal. Dissent isn't tolerated. Those who disagree with the Administration disappear, we have strong evidence that—"

"But if *you* don't even know where she is, what can I do?" He looked about helplessly. "I came to Sunsprit to find her. If she's not here, then, where is she?"

"I said reach, not find. We believe we know where she is, in Sunsprit, but we cannot reach her."

"Why not?" He glared at the silhouette but the Silvered did not reply. "What have you done to her? What did you make her do?"

"As attractive as that may be for you to want to believe, your assumptions are mistaken." The Silvered took a step closer and the silhouette expanded. "Do you think Kera does anything she doesn't want to?"

Diyan shuddered. "So, you do know her."

"Yes."

"Then…what do I do?" he asked feebly.

The Silvered moved forwards again, and its image moved into the room. It was bathed in a curious new light – still clearly a holo – with long, pale silver hair.

"You!" Diyan exclaimed, staring at the same Vaesian who had ferried him in the glazer from Fadin to Sunsprit. The same Vaesian who had been utterly disinterested in his reasons for being sent by the Administration. The same Vaesian who had forced him to enter Sunsprit alone.

"What are you doing here? You're not even... you weren't Silvered before!"

"There are many things you don't know about us, Diyan. And you were wrong, you aren't in Under-Sunsprit."

Before Diyan could reply, his captor disappeared. He became disoriented, as though a particularly strong flip were occurring. His vision seemed to stretch and the prison he was in elongated – the floor was descending. He bent his legs to lower his body, finding it increasingly difficult to remain steady. Noise began to reverberate all around – verbal, unmistakeably Vaesian. Diyan continued to descend, down the dark walls, the light at the top becoming smaller and dimmer. The flips were increasing yet again in intensity and frequency. Soon, his legs tired, and he sat down, resting his chin on his knees, and keeping his feet firmly anchored to the floor. His thoughts became sluggish and his prior confidence was eroded as the headaches returned, stronger than ever. His eyesight blurred to the point of uselessness. He became faintly aware of something approaching him. He barely cared. He weakly slouched back, lying face up, eyes closed.

"Flips play havoc down here, more than anywhere else. You'll adjust soon enough."

Chapter 24
Tug of Gravity

Light filtered through his eyelids. Many voices, speaking mostly in the unfamiliar Vaesian language, flitted around as Diyan regained consciousness. Warm air blew across his face. The wind was audible, though thankfully quieter than at Ringscape's edge. He focused on two of the more easily distinguishable voices – not as deep as the Vaesians', and both close.

"He's not going to be able to do it, Lellara."

"Depends if he was lying or not, but why would he have lied to Osr? Perhaps he really does know her, from before. It's possible. She didn't tell us much."

"I don't mean that. I mean…she might not even be here."

"She must be."

"What about what he sees? He might escape—"

"They don't think that's likely. He wants to find her.

She's with us. He's staying."

Diyan opened his eyes. Directly above him, the ceiling was a dark, smooth grey, darker than any of the other greys he had seen before in Sunsprit, but not quite black. He tilted his head up, noting his prone position on a raised rectangular platform, just wide enough to accommodate his outstretched body, which was thankfully clothed this time. Thin, loose holds were fastened across his legs, waist, and upper torso. The two who were speaking – both female Roranians – were almost within reaching distance.

"He's a spy!"

"Bomera, the Administration's just using him, he said he didn't even know—"

"Taking him was dangerous."

The sides of their faces moved about animatedly. Both were taller than average, with slim builds, although Bomera – who sounded more critical of his presence there – was a little more muscular. Her skin was lighter than Diyan's own, and her hair was tied into a neat bun at the back. Her pretty face was punctuated by a quizzical frown. The other, Lellara, had skin the same dark shade as Diyan's, and her angular, more defined features, made her strikingly beautiful, almost as beautiful as Kera. Her hair was longer, coming some way down her back, ruffled by the winds. Both Bomera and Lellara wore similar regwear to the Roranians in Fadin, but theirs was far more revealing, leaving most of their limbs and mid-sections exposed. Diyan understood why – he could see the sweat glistening off their bodies. It was almost uncomfortably hot.

The ground they stood on was the same colour as the ceiling, but rough and uneven, with many spikes jutting upwards to waist-height. Only the immediate area they were standing in was well-lit, everywhere else was dark, receding to pitch black. Others moved about slowly in the gloom, barely casting second glances at him, not caring that he was clearly awake, nor alerting the two next to him, who had not yet realised. They all wore chunky masks, despite breathing seeming to be perfectly manageable. The majority were Silvereds – wearing small skirt-pieces around their mid-sections, just about covering where their three legs joined their torsos. Blue wisps escaped from some of their masks. Like the two Roranians next to him, the other Roranians wore little to no regwear at all. All the Roranians and Silvereds held devices which they repeatedly looked at as they walked between the spikes.

Lellara continued. "Kera was certain she was onto something."

"If she was right—"

"Exactly – *if* she was right. We need to understand what it was she found out. Everything depends on it, all our work, everything. We could finally understand this place."

"Apparently, he said she was augmented. What did he mean?"

"I don't know."

Diyan tried to push himself up. As soon as his body struggled against the restraints, they receded into the sides of the platform and he was free. The two women paused and turned to face him, waiting expectantly.

"Strange, but not too strange, right?" Lellara said, breaking the awkward silence with a friendly smile.

Diyan frowned. "It's all strange…" he muttered, trailing off. He suddenly noticed the flips, having barely paid them any attention since waking. They did not bother him anymore. "I don't feel like I used to." He wiped the beads of sweat from his forehead and swung his legs carefully over the platform, seated upright. "I feel…alright."

The smile remained. "We've given you certain physiological treatments, they'll all count for your tetibat—"

"What treatments?"

"Derived from Vaesian treatments. You should be good for a few days, then you'll need a boost." She chuckled. "Don't worry, nothing we don't take ourselves. But they really help with the flips, which are extremely consistent down here. Otherwise, you'd be a mess. The winds are also nowhere near as bad as you'd expect, given the flips, but this is a closed system, so we can control them better. Can't help with the heat though, you'll just have to get used to it." She had rattled off the last part quickly, as though unsure he would be interested.

"The Tugs don't like it too cool," Bomera added

matter-of-factly, with a less cordial expression.

"No, they don't," Lellara agreed.

"Where are we?" he asked.

Lellara spread her arms wide. "Welcome to the side of Ringscape."

"Which side."

Both Lellara and Bomera frowned. "*The* side. Didn't Osr tell you?"

"So Osr is…you mean my interrogator, the Vaesian who took me from Fadin to Sunsprit?"

"Yes." Lellara nodded.

"Osr told me very little."

"You're on neither the upperside nor the underside," Bomera said, seriously. "You're between them, along the side that runs from one to the other. Still in Sunsprit."

"The city continues on Ringscape's side…" Diyan nodded. "Ah, yes."

Bomera scowled and looked at Lellara. "Perhaps the treatments altered his mind, or the heat's affected him."

"Why am I here? And where is Kera?"

"This is the Tug Field," Lellara said, gesturing all around them. Her arm stopped at the nearest group of spikes, pointing to them in turn. Silvereds and Vaesians continued carefully walking around, their gazes flicking between the spikes and their devices – it was unclear whether their carefulness was due to the flips and the spikes, or whatever it was they were studying. Nearby, there was an open, circular area, with no spikes, where two smooth recessed surfaces had been cut into the ground. Above them, on the ceiling, were two rectangular voids. As he watched, a platform descended through one of the voids in a similar manner to the electro-boost platform from his accommodation in Fadin. It carried three Vaesians, all wearing the same chunky black masks as the others. Upon reaching the ground, the Vaesians stepped off and dispersed into the darkness. The platform disappeared into the ground, then rose into the air gently from the other rectangular surface, before disappearing into the void above.

"That's what takes us up and down," Lellara said, having followed his gaze.

"Where are we?" he asked. "What's the Tug Field? I came here to find Kera. Where is she?"

"It'll help if we show you."

He clenched his jaw, moving cautiously to his feet. "Where is she?"

Bomera passed something to Lellara, who held it up to Diyan – a mask, the same as those worn by the others.

"Put this on."

"Why? I can breathe fine."

Lellara shook her head. "Tug Masks let you see. They also cool your head a little – unfortunately, regwear isn't designed to deal with the extreme flips down here."

He took it and looked at it suspiciously. "I can see just fine too."

Bomera sighed exasperatedly, mumbling about his

tetibat, and took something out of her pocket – a small capsule, the size and length of a finger.

"The Tug Masks allow you to see the Tugs' gravity strings. The Vaesians have used other methods, but none work as well as these masks." Bomera pointed at the spikes all around them. "They're the Tugs, and they emit gravity strings. These capsules provide the masks with the fuel to allow you to see them." She spoke slowly and deliberately, shaking the capsule in her hand. "Vaesian technology, given to them by Tapache, long ago. In the same way that Tapache fitted our Great Ship with technologies our own civilisation once had, this is something it presumably found amongst the ruins of the Vaesians' ancestors. The fuel is divided into a sequence of compartments, only half is expelled into the mask." She pointed to the front of the mask that Lellara had given him. "Some of it comes out the front, there, directed by your sight. Fortunately, the visual tracking works as well for us as for the Vaesians." She scowled at his bemused expression. "Anyway, you put the Tug Mask on, you can see the gravity strings."

"I can see gravity strings," Diyan repeated, simply. "How—"

"The particles in the fuel are entangled, so only half-pairs are expelled by the masks," Lellara explained, smiling enthusiastically. "Even the Vaesians don't know what the fuel is, they use their old Great Ship's generation units. It's some type of matter that's attuned to gravity field vectors and affected by them, or something like that. In a strong enough field, the particles are destroyed. The particles back in the helmet react and a visual representation of the gravity field is displayed within the mask. Visible light tends to ruin the process, hence the darkness around us. More importantly, the process requires conscious activation. Essentially, if no one's there to observe it, nothing happens."

"That wasn't what I was going to ask. I was going to ask how any of this relates to me being able to find Kera," Diyan replied, impatiently. "Unless she's a gravity string, this won't help!"

Bomera smirked, shaking her head. Lellara raised her mask and placed it against her face. Thin straps, like those that had restrained him when he had awoken, crossed around the back of her head and locked the mask in place.

"See, you can still hear me just fine." Her voice was a little louder. "There are visual holos projected inside, so your vision is pretty much normal, except you can also see gravitational fluctuations. Down here—"

"You keep saying *down here*," Diyan said. "But you said we're on the side of Ringscape."

"It's both," Lellara replied, patiently, taking the mask back off with a gentle tug from the front. "It's not the underside or the upperside. We're at the side of Ringscape, but there's a recess within the side, and that's our precise location. Sunsprit is built over the only recess that exists in all of Ringscape, the only indentation into Ringscape itself. The Administration knows nothing about it. Osr's allowed us to tell you."

"We're currently standing perpendicular to anyone in Upper-Sunsprit or Under-Sunsprit," Bomera added.

"The influxes told me mining Ringscape was impossible? It's too hard after—"

"The Vaesians don't mine, and they never have," Lellara explained. "They found the recess. It was here before they arrived. Probably created by Ringscape's original architects, who knows."

"Or maybe the Tugs did it," Bomera shrugged.

Diyan looked critically at the spikes sticking up from the ground. "You think they did it? What are they?"

"Just put the mask on," Bomera said exasperatedly. "She'll explain soon enough."

"You?" Diyan looked at Lellara, puzzled. She smiled and shook her head.

"Not me. Someone else you'll recognise."

"Who—"

"Finally, you're awake!" a deep voice boomed from behind him.

"There she is," Lellara grinned.

Diyan turned around, alarmed. A mask-less Silvered was rushing towards him – one that he recognised. Sturdily built, tall, and with eyes a little closer together than most other Vaesians. Hespinr. Despite the flips, it – *she* – moved as though gravity were completely normal and behaving itself. She seemed excited, forgoing the usual one-and-two gait in favour of each leg moving forwards quickly in turn. Diyan took a hesitant step back, frowning as Hespinr came to an abrupt halt in front of him.

"You!"

"I'm glad you're here, Diyan," Hespinr replied, as though oblivious to Diyan's accusatory stare.

"You're with them! These…whoever they are…" He gestured to Lellara and Bomera, and then the Vaesians and Roranians around them. "And this *Osr*?"

Hespinr guffawed. "I'm afraid so. You've been under observation from the moment you left Fadin. Osr doesn't do much glazer work anymore, you know. Still, she likes to delve back in every now and then. In a way, you should be honoured, you might have got—"

"Honoured?"

"Osr is well respected, a high—"

"She told me *not* to tell her about my mission!" Diyan shouted. "She didn't want to know any of it."

Another polite guffaw. "We spy on the spies sent to us by the Administration. It's only natural. And she wouldn't have been a particularly good spy if you'd suspected anything. We're extremely careful. But you actually told her quite a lot, freely, and she believed it warranted further investigation. No offence Diyan, but you're a bad spy. You're too honest. Anyway, I tested your story and agreed with her assessment of you, especially when you verified you were indeed looking for the same Kera as us. You're different to the other spies the Administration sent to look for her. We decided to intervene more…significantly, which is something we rarely do."

"But why did she, or you, imprison me again. I woke up without my clothes on!"

Lellara and Bomera giggled. "Osr wanted to be absolutely sure," Hespinr said. "We had to conduct a more thorough check for Administration tracking technologies before you were allowed down here."

Diyan smacked his forehead. "That was why we were at the ridge, wasn't it? Not for the sights, not for privacy, but so you could take me. But…why? Why not just ask me to come with you. I would have. I need to find Kera, I'd have done anything."

"They had to be seen taking you," Lellara interjected. "It had to look real so that news would spread back to Fadin that one of the factions had decided to abduct a spy. The Administration thinks Sunsprit is far more fractious than it really is, and that's a cultivated image that needs to be kept. Most of the Silvereds here think their leadership is fractious too, although it doesn't bother their daily lives."

"But you were never in any danger," Hespinr reassured him. "Although the abduction was certainly very believable. The other Administration spy who saw was suitably impressed, I'm told, scurrying off back to Fadin immediately to relate what happened."

"What happens now?"

"They'll send other spies to find you. Failing that, the

Administration will send word to Sunsprit demanding your release. We can put them off for a while."

"Why're you telling me all this? What if I return, and they ask me—"

"I believe we can trust you, Diyan," Hespinr replied, seriously. "As does Osr. And you represent an opportunity we cannot ignore. Finding Kera is too important."

"How can I find her?"

"We're not sure."

Diyan curled his fists. "Why can't I get a straight answer from anyone? Either she's here or she isn't!"

Hespinr turned to Lellara and Bomera. "I'll take over now."

They nodded curtly. Bomera turned away immediately. Lellara passed Hespinr a spare Tug Mask, casting Diyan a curiously lingering glance as she walked away. They both placed their masks over their heads and disappeared into the darkness.

"Where are they going?" Diyan asked.

"To make their observations," Hespinr replied. "There's always work to do here."

"Observations of what?"

"The Tugs. Put your mask on."

Chapter 25
Necessary Pursuit

Diyan wandered around the Tug Field with Hespinr, as the Vaesian patiently explained what he was seeing through the mask. Whenever Diyan looked directly at a spike – or Tug – fine strings of light green appeared, extending up from the tip, reaching up to just a hand's width from the ceiling, before ending. The gravity strings. Hespinr informed him that all the spikes and their strings were precisely the same lengths.

Initially, upon putting the mask on, its sensors had been overwhelmed with the constant flips – a dense green fog of compressions and rarefactions had clouded his view, depicting the flips and their gravitational eddies. Hespinr had fiddled with some controls on the mask's side, altering its sensitivities to ignore the flips and focus on the Tugs. Occasionally, particularly strong flips seeped into the mask's sensor range, but Diyan learned to ignore them.

A faint blue wisp escaped from the edges of Hespinr's mask, from the chewed substance Diyan had now learned was called *muvaeyt*. It had a gentle, sweet smell.

"I told you before, my species is well-adapted to low gravity, and without assistance, we cope far better with the side of Ringscape's conditions than you Roranians. It's speculated that our ancestors used tools like these," she pointed with a clump of tensirs to her mask, "to explore exotic gravitational habitats. That's why Tapache gave us these technologies aboard our Great Ship: it found them amongst our remnants. They were probably commonplace. On our Great Ship, we used them as part of a gaming system. We've yet to rediscover exactly how they work, but we know enough to manufacture small quantities of the fuel they require."

"And the Tugs?"

"They were here before us, before any of the Vaesian cities."

"Did Tapache send them here too?"

"We don't know. Our work down here is dedicated to attempting to communicate with them, but we've been mostly unsuccessful so far."

"Are they sentient?"

"We think so," Hespinr said. "They know we're here. We take gravimetric readings about them, but we don't have access to the influx network or any other technologies with significant computational power, it's just us."

"Can't you build something to help?"

Hespinr guffawed. "Before the Administration developed the influx network, there was nothing like it on Ringscape. Nothing approaching that level of intelligence is supposed to exist here. You know what happens to machine-lects: they die, immediately. And we're not going to tell the Administration about the Tugs, they're too important. So, it's up to us. We can't even put relatively simple automated machines down here – the Tugs don't like them. We've tried. We've attempted to observe and record them through many different methods, but the strings vanish. They only show themselves for us when we're physically present."

"That's what Kera was in Fadin for, isn't it? She was trying to find out about the influx network, to help you build your own, to understand the Tugs?"

Hespinr did not reply immediately. She walked to another Tug and began circling it, with Diyan following. Her tensirs were twitching. "She always thought it might be possible, yes. She understood their importance. They were here long before us; they must understand Ringscape in a way we cannot. Tapache's mission, the secrets of this place…everything relies upon them."

"Then why did she try to destroy the network, and how? Did you augment her?"

Hespinr's tensirs twitched even more. "We don't know," she admitted. "And no, we did not augment her –

we knew nothing about that, she explained very little when she returned to Sunsprit, and news of the attack did not immediately follow. We were unaware. Since then, our own spies have been trying to ascertain the details of the attack, but the Administration is keeping a tight control on the flow of information."

"But you must have known something?"

"I wish we did. In fact, we only know about her augmentation from what *you* told us."

"What?" Diyan blurted. "So, she was trying to help you figure out how to create your own influx network, then she tried to destroy Fadin's to…To what? To cover her tracks? That makes no sense!"

"There are many answers we don't have, Diyan. That's where you come in."

Diyan took a step closer to Hespinr, who was staring at the Tug's gravity string, as though transfixed. "Where is she?"

"The Tugs have her."

Diyan looked at the gravity string and frowned. "What do you mean?"

"After returning to Sunsprit, she had a device with her – a prototype related to the influxes – that could store and transfer large quantities of information. Monumental quantities, and with network permissions from the highest level of Administration access. The Administration wants to extend its influx network and is looking for ways to solve the thick atmosphere problem. She called the device a *dummy node*. She thought the Tugs might understand the purpose of the dummy node and impart their knowledge into it. She believed they might know the secrets of Ringscape...of everything, even the Source itself. She was down here for many days. We should have watched her more closely, but there's only one way in and out. No one had any idea that she might just...well, vanish. Shortly after, you arrived in Sunsprit looking for her, and you know the rest."

Diyan spluttered, ripping his mask off. "You must have some surveillance?"

"The Tugs don't—"

"The Tugs don't allow it," Diyan mimicked, angrily. "They don't seem to allow much!" An uneasy silence descended. Others had given them a wide berth, and the Tugs around them were free of observation. "When she did what she did, did she know we would be taken by the Administration? Yena, Paran, me...did she know?"

"She used our network in Fadin to alert you. We understand she tried to arrange for you all to—"

"But she could have waited, couldn't she? She could have explained to us...given us time to...to prevent what happened. Why didn't she just wait?" Diyan turned away. Without the mask on, he was engulfed in near-complete darkness. A tear started to form in the corner of his eye, threatening to roll down his cheek. Hespinr moved beside him. "What do I do now? How do I find her? Even though she betrayed us."

"We're hoping you can figure it out. She's down here, somewhere, waiting for you." Hespinr's arms flapped to the side in a surprisingly Roranian-like gesture. "Kera always seemed to know what she was doing. I hope you find her, for all our sakes."

*

Diyan walked alone in the strange darkness, his thoughts a maelstrom of chaos. He barely had to think about the flips anymore; his body reflexively did most of the work for him. The Tug field was enormous, and he had been able to venture in the same direction without stopping for quite some time. There were others some way off, but he had long since become accustomed to their little-to-no regwear appearance, and barely paid them any attention. They seemed even quieter and more disparate than before. It was as though there was a reverence for the Tugs. Sometimes, he fancied he heard a low hum from nearby – the same hum he thought he had heard when being questioned by the Silvereds, in the small room with the light at the top.

Hespinr had long since left him to wander, and he had been glad to do so. The burning questions he had were not those that could be answered by anyone but Kera. He knew he was being watched from afar, but the observers were discrete, and he barely noticed them. Every now and then, he looked at the portable gravitometer Hespinr had given him, the settings of which had been adjusted for Roranian use. It was an old, battered device with a small handhold at the bottom and a screen at the top – not a holo display, but a physical, solid display, that seemed more fitting down here. It registered the gravity strings, displaying simple analytics.

Diyan stared at the Tug before him. The thin, green gravity string was perfect – unwavering and consistent. He glanced at the gravitometer in his hand before shifting his focus to the gravity string again, moving the hand that held the device back to his side. Without thinking, he cut through the gravity string with a finger, feeling nothing. The string was too thin and weak to register with his senses. He flicked the gravitometer screen up again – a minute change had registered, a decrease in intensity, nothing useful.

"Kera?" he whispered. Something brushed against his arm. He looked around but there was no one close enough. His hand spasmed and the gravitometer jerked away as though it had been pulled. He frowned and looked at it, but nothing additional registered as having been recorded. "Kera?" he whispered again.

After standing still for some time, he gave up and moved to another Tug. The mask was mildly cooling, though he was still sweating more than he was used to. The warm winds did little to help. Diyan looked around. There were some others nearby now. Mostly Silvereds, aside from one lone Roranian, wearing regwear around his waist. Diyan walked over and raised an arm in greeting, taking his mask off.

The other Roranian spoke first. "You must be Diyan." He also took his mask off. He had long, scruffy hair that was being gently buffeted by the constant flips and the omnipresent winds, and a wide, friendly smile. "Nice to meet you, again."

"Again?" Diyan looked at his gravitometer. The Tug's readings were like all the others.

The man's smile became a cheeky grin. "It's why I've been reassigned to Tug duty now. I was a little too…conspicuous."

Diyan nodded. "Ah, you waved at me, on the ridge. It was you, before I fell."

The man chuckled. "The name's Ilouden. And you're right. You caught me watching you, and when you waved…" He shook his head, tsking. "Well, that was the end of my first time trailing a spy. I wasn't even there for you; I should never have become distracted. There was another spy closer to you with a Silvered chaperone, I was there to observe them! No hard feelings, I hope?"

Diyan shook his head. "None." He smiled.

"You're not boiling down here?" Ilouden asked, gesturing to Diyan's whole-body black regwear.

"I'm managing." Diyan looked around them and lowered his voice. "Why are you working with them?"

Ilouden's eyes widened in honest surprise. "The Silvereds? Because I live here. Same as Lellara, Bomera, and the others. Sunsprit, that is, not the Tug Field!"

"But this is their city. What about our own?"

"Ah." Ilouden nodded. "I understand you've not been here for long. You must think it's Fadin against Sunsprit, Roranians against Vaesians, the Administration against the Vaesian Union." He rattled off the comparisons. "No doubt that's what the Administration wants you to think, but that's not true, it never has been. Roranians are in the minority here, and in the other Vaesian cities, but we're still citizens of these cities every bit as much as the Vaesians."

"Then it's the same in Fadin, there are Vaesians there too."

Ilouden shook his head. "Not exactly. I've heard the reports. Vaesians don't have the same permissions as Roranians, can't work for the Administration, and there are Roranians who don't want them there..." He heaved a sigh. "It's not us against them *here*, that's what I'm trying to say."

"How come *you* are here?"

Ilouden shrugged and the cheery smile reappeared. "I don't know any different, if I'm honest." He curled one of his hands into a fist. "When parts of our Great Ship somehow made it through the Haze Rings, all that time ago, not everyone landed in the same place. Most did, but some didn't." He uncurled his fist and wriggled his fingers as he deposited imaginary pieces of debris around the air between them. "Some of the Roranians who made it down were taken in by the cities that already existed on Ringscape. My own early family members found themselves in Aenoun and Uthrit – both Vaesian cities – and ever since then…well, we've been a part of the Vaesian Union."

"Your own family…are they here, in Sunsprit, now?"

Ilouden laughed. "No! Sunsprit does have quite a few Roranians, but no, none of my family. They think it's too dangerous. It has something of a reputation, you could say, probably because the Administration hates it so much. They think I'll come to my senses and return to Aenoun soon enough, but they don't know what I'm doing here. If they did, they'd understand. They'd be worried, but they'd understand."

"Why do the Silvereds trust you?" Diyan hesitated. "Or the Vaesian Union…"

"Because they have no reason not to. I'm one of them."

"I…" Diyan faltered. "I'm not sure where to start. It's all been so quick for me. Your family from our Great Ship…what are they doing now?"

"Living their lives. A few have died." He whistled nonchalantly. "A lot can happen in three hundred years."

"How old are you?"

"Almost forty."

"Standard years?"

"Of course."

"You're older than me!" Diyan said, and they both

laughed.

"You've existed for a little longer, from what I've heard," Ilouden said. "You were just asleep."

"If there are so many Roranians, where are they?" Diyan asked. "I barely saw any in Sunsprit."

Ilouden gestured above them. "Sunsprit is huge, much larger than the Administration realises, with layers upon layers. The Administration's never going to be able to peel them all back, even if it wanted to. It doesn't have the understanding or the ability. It's too conceited to think the Silvereds and their city are anything more than a plague."

"What do you mean, the ability? I thought the Administration's military presence was the most powerful on Ringscape."

Ilouden scoffed. "Sunsprit has its secrets."

"Like what?"

A brief look of hesitation flitted across Ilouden's face. He looked at his device, then showed it to Diyan, as though he could understand the readings from a glance. "Well, this one's bored already."

"Bored?"

"It's one reason we believe the Tugs are sentient, like us – they get bored. Well, I think they do, anyway. See, here," he showed Diyan the device again. "Gravitational readings attenuate to almost nothing, past the detection threshold. If we move over to this Tug…" He put his mask back on, motioning for Diyan to do the same and then follow him. "See, the readings spike again. This one's more curious, it's already taking longer to attenuate, but you can see...there! Same magnitude, before the decay. Bored."

"Are you sure?" Diyan asked, trying not to sound unconvinced.

"Another way of looking at it is that the Tugs are trying to communicate with us, just like we're trying to communicate with them, but neither of us knows how. That's what I mean by bored." He pointed at the tip of the Tug's gravity string. "They're composed of pure gravity – just streams of gravitons – but if you want to know what I think...I think they're something else. Look at their tips, the graviton stream just disappears. It makes no sense. They're something more. Perhaps they're not even made of gravity, that's just how they appear." He tipped his head pensively to the side. "I like to think we'll find out, someday."

Diyan sighed. "There's a lot to understand."

Ilouden hesitated, then spoke quietly, as though he did not want to be overheard. "When you're done here today, I'd like to show you something. And after that, I'll take you to where you're staying – you're in the same accommodation as me."

Chapter 26
Gravity's Whisper

Diyan looked critically at Ilouden. They had left the Tug Field only moments earlier on a rectangular platform, which appeared to lift them up and out of the Tug Field's depths…except, the platform had stopped, at an equally dark, seemingly empty level. Diyan suspected that their exit journey had been somewhat cut short.

Ilouden instructed Diyan to step off the platform, and they walked along a thin, straight passageway. Eventually, they came to a small, featureless room, shaped like a cube, only a little larger than the room where Diyan had been trapped before he had been taken to the Tug Field.

"What now?" Diyan asked, suspiciously. He was slouched over, tired after the intensity of the long day.

"I'll leave you for a few moments."

"Why?"

"You'll see."

As the sound of Ilouden's steps faded away, Diyan looked around, wondering what was supposed to happen. He half-expected the entrance to disappear, replaced by a hard, impenetrable wall, trapping him again. Turning to face the entrance, he paused. Something was there, in the room with him. His gaze shifted; he felt momentarily off-balance, a feeling not attributable to the flips. It was the same sensation as pressing a finger against a closed eyelid; starry figures of white appeared, swirling in the peripheries, not quite there. Like a galaxy of stars, all around, yet wherever he looked directly, the stars disappeared. There was no one else in the room, but it did not feel empty.

What am I doing here?

He frowned. The question had entered his mind like a thought of his own, except it almost seemed like a communication from Wiln – c-automs were capable of directly communicating with the mind. But c-automs always 'spoke' politely, with obvious intent. This was different, in-between a thought and a communication. Even though his body could still feel the flips, his thoughts were dissociated from them.

I don't know what the Tugs are. I'm not a Tug.

He cleared his throat, attempting to take control of his wandering mind. It was as though certain strands were being selected, isolated, and strengthened.

Who are you?

Thoughts of his life flooded his mind. He tried to focus

231

on a different question. It was impossible to be precise.

I don't know.

The response was less than fruitful. As before, Diyan found it difficult to discern whether he was answering his own question or someone else's. He attempted again, pushing his questions by brute force to the front of his mind.

I cannot be Tapache. Tapache isn't here. Tapache didn't send me. I am three.

His eyes widened. Three? He was getting closer. This was not him. It was something else.

The Wanderers are an advanced civilisation of machine intelligences who are embroiled in a galactic quest to defeat their enemy, the Sensespace. They scour the galaxy for instances of the Sensespace in their attempts to destroy it. Tapache is a member of the Wanderers but has temporarily engaged itself in a different quest – to investigate what it calls the Source. Tapache has been shielding itself, using the remnants of civilisations it has collected to probe that which it does not understand. The Roranians are one such probe. You. It has promised, conditional upon your successful return, to seek out what became of your civilisation. That is the bargain chosen for you, Diyan, and the reason you are here.

Diyan's thoughts continued to unravel, although less disconcertingly than before. More akin to letting everything fall into its correct place.

Why have the Wanderers engaged in their quest to destroy the Sensespace? Don't they have worlds enough to conquer? Why did Tapache embroil itself in this new task? The promises it made were not just to the Roranians; there were many other Great Ships, probably more still to come. Was it lying? Did the Roranian civilisation ever exist? Is it even wise to look for what remains?

The questions were unmistakably Diyan's own, although separate components were pulled and strung together, forming complex sequences he had never consciously concerned himself with.

Why does no one care about Tapache's mission anymore? Perhaps it would not matter if they did. Even if they had not stopped caring long ago, would it have made a difference? Can anything change?

He staggered to the centre of the room, his legs suddenly feeling heavy. The flips were less than an afterthought.

Kera is the same, but she is changed. She has evolved.

Everything he had ever known or thought about Kera was laid out before him.

Kera cares about Ringscape. It isn't clear how, but she does. Everyone sees it, but they also don't. Perhaps she's the only one. She's crucial, she always has been. And you are the bait to draw her back.

He began to feel guilty.

You are being used by Fadin and Sunsprit. Tapache's quest still draws you. Your friends need you. You have unbreakable bonds of duty that bind you. Like Kera, you have too many masters. Tapache made you to be strong, but are you strong enough? We know that Roranians can die. Nothing lasts forever. We are all finite.

It was as though parallel parts of Diyan's mind were operating all at once, and he was experiencing a clarity he had never imagined possible. New connections were explored and laid bare.

Whom do you trust? The Vaesians hide things too. They are hiding me.

Before Diyan had the chance to form a new sequence of views and further shape his strange internal dialogue, other topics arose.

Ringscape contains layers upon layers. Perhaps the Veilers have it right.

"Diyan?"

Ilouden was staring down at him. Disconcerted, Diyan looked around. He was still in the dark room, although he had fallen to his knees at its centre. His head was slumped down, facing the floor. He had been utterly engrossed in his thoughts. Ilouden extended a hand and helped him up.

"Well, that was…"

"Quite something?" Ilouden grinned.

"How long did you leave me for?"

"I just walked back to the platform and came right here again."

"That was it? It felt like—"

"I know." Ilouden's grin remained. "Did it help you?"

"I think so. I know I need to find Kera, desperately. She's important."

Ilouden nodded, apparently satisfied. "Good. Once is usually enough. I heard a rumour that Kera came here first, upon returning to Sunsprit. I thought it might be useful."

"What's in here? What is it, some Vaesian technology?"

Ilouden shook his head and shrugged. "It's even harder to detect than the Tugs. Something, clearly, but we don't know what. It was discovered long ago. We call it Echoes of Gravity. All we really know is that it somehow helps widen your understanding. When the Vaesians first found it, they venerated it. Now, it's more of a curiosity. It's a local legend that the muvaeyt they sometimes chew on was created after a Vaesian was inspired by this place." Ilouden led Diyan out of the room and they walked slowly back to the platform. "I wanted to take you here because with everything that's happened...you needed to order your thoughts and orient yourself."

Diyan looked back. The room appeared innocuous. "Can it escape?"

"It stays there. It likes the dark, same as the Tugs, apparently. The Vaesians think it generates energy from the shadows. Or maybe it's the flips." Ilouden's tone became more serious. "There is one thing you can do for me, Diyan. Please don't mention to anyone that I took you here."

Diyan nodded. "I won't." He thought for a moment. "It wasn't sent by Tapache, it told me."

"Are you sure?"

"I'm..." Diyan stumbled over his words. "I'm not sure exactly what it meant. It mentioned something about being *three*, if that makes any sense?"

"No, but I've heard that mentioned before. There are

lots of theories about what it might mean. Perhaps we're not ready for what it has to say." Ilouden laughed as they reached the place where the platform would appear. "That's the one problem with Echoes of Gravity. You're never quite sure if it's all you or not. Some things seem just different enough, but you always second guess yourself afterwards. Having said that, it certainly helps. I'm sure you've heard of the concept of tetibat by now." Ilouden chuckled. "It can seem rather abstract, unnecessary sometimes, but…in a genuine way, I hope this has counted for your tetibat."

"Thanks." Diyan nodded, surprising himself at his own agreement, as the platform appeared from the darkness. They stepped forwards.

Chapter 27
Nameless Reading

Diyan awoke, shaking his dreams of Kera aside. Over the past few days, he had seen her as he slept, wandering alone in the Tug Field, whispering his name. She always looked the same – wearing the Gronwenthian cloth from the last time he had seen her aboard their Great Ship, with a sad, downturned face, and slow, shuffling footsteps. Despite her pace, try as he might, he was never able to reach her. She always faded into the darkness.

He stretched and yawned loudly, nodding to Ilouden who was already up and getting ready for the day. Unlike where he had stayed in Fadin, his new accommodation was sparser and far smaller, and in no way private. There was no boundary between his accommodation and the next. Ilouden's was beside his, a few strides away. A Silvered, who did not appear to be interested in communicating beyond the perfunctory, was settled on the other side. Diyan was in the middle. A tall staircase was accessible at the end of Ilouden's segment of the accommodation, from where they could walk down to the next three-set below. There were communal facilities available for their other needs a few levels down. The accommodation structure was a tower, similar to those which Diyan had previously seen all over Sunsprit, though far larger and wider.

Most of the time, Diyan's routine consisted of moving only between the Tug Field and the accommodation tower, but occasionally he would venture outside, looking about at their chasm within the side of Ringscape. It was like a microcosm of what he had seen of the rest of Sunsprit; while a large number of towers rose out from the base of the cavern, he could still see the cavern boundaries all around, coloured Ringscape's natural brown. The Vaesians had found it, an enclave hollowed out into the side of Ringscape, and built their towers inside. The tallest towers were capped in height, stopping just short of reaching the chasm's end and the enormous flat cover that was built across the chasm's opening. Beyond the cover, on the other side, the great tubes ran across, leading from Upper-Sunsprit to Under-Sunsprit and back. The chasm was completely hidden, and on the outside, most of the inhabitants of Sunsprit went about their daily lives oblivious to its existence.

The towers behind the chasm were connected by various open and enclosed walkways, which layered up on top of each other repeatedly; it was impossible to see the whole way down. The Tug Field was beneath the foundations of the lowest towers, hidden completely from sight. This hidden part of Sunsprit was used purely for the study of the Tugs, and the exotic gravitational anomalies that were present within the chasm. Diyan's initial captive pen had been pointed out to him – one of the closest towers, narrowed at the top, at the centre of the chasm. He had not returned to Echoes of Gravity, nor had he felt inclined.

"Where's Hespinr?" Diyan asked.

Ilouden was tapping away lazily at his gravitometer, waiting politely for Diyan to get ready for the day. "Her accommodation is lower down, very close to the Tug Field. Different tower. And Lellara and Bomera are both in a tower over that way." Ilouden pointed in the direction of one of the walkways stemming from their tower.

"Is the rest of Sunsprit like this?"

Ilouden shrugged. "Similar, not quite so bare. I understand it's not what you're used to, from the Great Ship or Fadin, but it works for us."

"Does Sunsprit have any other secrets?"

Ilouden laughed. "Most, I don't know about, I'm sure. The Vaesians are old. They've been here a lot longer than us, Diyan. They have legends stretching back thousands of years. Many events occurred since their time with Tapache. Talk to a Veiler if you can. Most Vaesians, Silvered or non-Silvered, dismiss them, but I find their stories and theories interesting."

"Perhaps the Veilers have it right."

Ilouden looked surprised. "What?"

"Something that came to me when…" Diyan lowered his voice. "Echoes of Gravity."

"Ah. Well, who really knows?"

Diyan took Ilouden's cue to stop and changed the subject. "What are the Vaesian legends?"

"Battles, adventures, meetings with other civilisations and species. And the Veilers think other species live among us. Not the ones we know, but others. Maybe even Ringscape's true creators."

"What happened to these other civilisations?"

"I don't know. Perhaps some of the stories are just that, stories. But in some of the legends, the Vaesians seem a little like the Administration, if you ask me. They fought others here." He shrugged, then said with a conspiratorial smile, "It's possible some of the old civilisations are in hiding. Maybe that's the reason the Alpuri are so reticent to communicate with anyone."

"What do you know of the Alpuri?"

"Other than to leave them alone? Not much. You might as well ask me about the Breaker." He laughed.

Diyan pursed his lips. "What's the name of this place?"

Ilouden frowned. "Name?"

"This cavern, all these towers, the Tug Field. What's it all called?"

Ilouden nodded slowly. "It doesn't have one."

"You must refer to it as something."

"We don't. If you name it, it becomes identifiable. With no name, it's easier to remain hidden." He turned back to his gravitometer while Diyan pulled his regwear on. Once ready, they picked up their Tug Masks and descended the stairs to the other levels, making their way towards an exit point of the tower. Ilouden led, as always.

"I'm surprised they're not watching me, making sure I'm doing what they want, searching for Kera," Diyan said.

Ilouden laughed. "They? What do you think I'm here for? We're not like the Administration; you're not going to be forced into doing anything. But you're still being monitored, Diyan. The Vaesian Union has managed to keep this place hidden for far longer than you and I have been alive, they're not going to risk its discovery through complacency now."

"I'm not going anywhere, not until I find Kera. I felt her, Ilouden. She's there."

"I'm glad to hear it. She could be vital for our future. The Administration is creeping across Ringscape, it wants to control everything and answers to no one. We can't let that happen to Sunsprit. They can't ever know what we have here."

They reached the exit level and walked out of the tower. The route was covered on all sides with translucent tubing.

"Ilouden, I want you to know, I'm not taking a side in

this power struggle between the Silvereds or the Vaesian Union and the Administration. I just want to find Kera. The Administration have my friends, she's the only one who can save them."

"It seems Kera's quite important for everyone, then."

They approached the end of the walkway. Other walkways also joined at the same point, funnelling into the entry point of another thin tower, where platforms could be accessed that would take them down to the Tug Field below. A queue, predominantly comprised of Vaesians, waited in line. The few Roranians there were all dressed respectably in regwear, though most of them would strip off various items once they reached the Tug Field. Diyan had yet to partake in that particular activity.

Ilouden motioned for them to move further up and push in, but Diyan stopped him.

"It's fine, they won't mind," Ilouden reassured him. "Most of them know why you're here."

"It's not that. I wanted to ask about Kera."

"What is it?"

None of the others in the queue were quite close enough to hear them, but Diyan lowered his voice anyway. "The Administration told me that she was augmented. That's what enabled her to attack the influx network, and then to escape. What do you think that could mean?"

Ilouden shrugged. "I really don't know, and I don't think Hespinr or anyone else in Sunsprit would know either." He looked seriously at Diyan's expression of disbelief. "I'm not lying to you, Diyan. When she was here, with us, she never mentioned anything about it. Aside from the cell-scales, augmentations aren't that common amongst Vaesians, let alone Roranians, so it's a question that would never have been asked. The mention of augmentation came as a surprise to us too."

"Why did she come here? I don't understand."

The queue was moving forwards, slowly bringing them closer to the entrance.

"When she first passed through the Haze Rings, she landed near the city and was taken in, given a life. Then she left for Fadin and falsified her story, so that it appeared she had just arrived on Ringscape. She was a part of our spy network there, although we did not realise her value. Because she was unable to verify her credentials, she couldn't get close to the Administration, but then you came, adding your verification to her story, and she took the opportunity. It wasn't planned."

Diyan looked around, hopelessly. "So, she must have been augmented before she arrived. That's what you're saying."

"In my opinion, yes. Whatever that means. It's most likely she received these augmentations when she was a soldier for the Nesch, before she came through the Haze Rings and the Vaesian Union found her. Although I know that other Roranians who live within Vaesian cities, and were soldiers for the Nesch, all deny any augmentations." He paused. "Try not to be upset that she didn't tell you, it's something that she kept from everyone. And this is all assuming the Administration didn't lie to you about her and the attack."

Diyan still found it hard to look at Ilouden. "It's just...it's different now."

"What is?" Ilouden's face softened. "Diyan, Kera has lived a long life, and most of that time was not spent with you. I am sorry to tell you this, but she has undoubtedly changed. You should never have expected otherwise. She fought in many battles for the Nesch, she joined the Vaesian Union, and then she became a citizen of Fadin, all while you slept——"

"Then what am I doing here?"

"Because, while she is more than she once was, you're still a part of her past. An important part. You have that connection with her. Don't forget, she tried to save you in Fadin. She cares for you."

"She failed. It was a betrayal."

"But she tried."

"Soji was killed. Irido too, I think. Were they both part of your spy network in Fadin?"

Ilouden tsked loudly, shaking his head. "Soji was. I met her a few times, she had potential. A lot." He looked away for a few moments.

The last group waiting in front of them stepped onto the platform and descended away from view, into the dark depths of the Tug Field. Three of the six had been chewing the muvaeyt substance, and its sweet smell and faint blue trails were left in the air behind them. Diyan and Ilouden waited for another platform to arrive, then stepped onto it, steadying themselves as it descended.

"I'm sorry about Soji," Diyan said.

"Thank you. If we find Kera, it'll all be worth it, I hope."

"I just don't know how."

"She's there, somewhere."

"Maybe she's only going to be found if the Tugs let her?"

"Or if she wants to be found."

"Could she be anywhere else?"

Ilouden sighed. "I really don't see how."

They stood in companionable silence for the rest of their descent. Upon reaching the Tug Field, they stepped off the platform and moved to the side.

Ilouden patted Diyan on the arm. "I'm going to give you a bit more space today, everyone who's been watching you will. It's possible nothing's happened because the Tugs know we're watching." He put on his mask and began to walk off, checking his gravitometer, then paused, seeing Diyan's confused expression. "Is everything alright?"

"It's gone," Diyan said.

"What's gone?"

"There's normally a low...hum, down here. But I can't hear it anymore."

Ilouden laughed. "Well, I can't hear anything." He

continued walking away. "Anyway, I hope you have more success today."

Diyan put on his mask and cursorily checked his gravitometer. Nothing beyond the usual showed. Wiln would have been proud of his efficiency. He picked a direction and began walking.

After some time, he found a patch of spikes devoid of other Roranians or Vaesians and began investigating. He moved from one Tug to the next and paused. Although he had not been intentionally looking at it, from the corner of his eye he noticed that the gravitometer had registered something, a brief flurry of unexpected gravitational excitement. The excitement did not appear related to any of the Tugs. He stared at the screen, watching as the excitement attenuated rapidly to nothing. The hairs on the back of his neck stood up. He waved the gravitometer towards the nearest Tug, holding his breath.

Something brushed against his arm. It was the same sensation he had felt before, during his first visit to the Tug Field. There was no one else around him, he was alone. He looked at the gravitometer's screen. A second excitement had registered – a gravitational peak that was attenuating more slowly than before. His heart began to race.

"Kera?" he whispered. "Is that you?" He waited, completely still. "I'm here to find you, Kera. I want to bring you back."

The spike stopped attenuating. It flat-lined, then rose

even higher. He looked at the Tug's gravity string. It appeared the same as usual, just a thin green line stopping a hand's width from the ceiling. But the gravitometer told a different story. The reading soon dwarfed all other readings he had taken of any Tugs previously, by many orders of magnitude. Warnings began to display – thresholds of the device's capabilities were being reached. Diyan did not know which thresholds they referred to. Despite the mask's cooling abilities, he was sweating unbearably. Water dripped from his forehead into his eyes. He took the mask off to wipe his face with his arm, then put it back on. The Tug's gravity string was gone. Bewildered, he looked around. Something pulled against his arm. There was no one there, although the Tug in the direction he had been pulled also had no gravity string emanating from the spike. All the other Tugs had their gravity strings, as normal, except the Tug he was standing in front of and the one he was being beckoned towards. He took a step closer, suddenly aware of the flips again, feeling unsteady. His vision was becoming blurry. He shook his head, scrunched his eyes, and calmed his breathing. Once he had regained control, he opened his eyes again. Nothing had changed. Clenching his jaw, he walked over to the empty Tug.

As soon as he had reached it, he felt another pull, this time on his fingertips. He pulled his hand back and shook it instinctively, dropping the gravitometer, which landed face-up, displaying an internal diagnostics test. The Tug in the direction his fingers had been pulled also had no gravity string. He moved over, leaving the gravitometer, and was pulled again. Over and over, he was drawn into a zigzagging maze, clueless as to which direction was which.

Eventually, upon reaching a Tug and closing his eyes, waiting for the familiar pull, nothing happened. Confused, he looked around. Some way ahead, there was a wall that extended to the ceiling – the end of the Tug Field.

"Kera?"

It was possible to make any manner of shapes out of the field's Tug distributions, and Ilouden had described many of the theories to him. Potential symbols had been identified, attempts at deciphering visual languages codified, but they were just rudimentary theories, nothing more. Still, it did appear that he stood at the perimeter of a ring of Tugs. The neighbours of the Tug he stood at all curved equidistantly around. The gravity string reappeared at his Tug, as though it had always been there. He looked at his hand, realising with irritation that he no longer had the gravitometer. The gravity string looked thicker. In fact, all the Tugs' gravity strings in the ring did.

The ground encircled by the ring began to ripple and Diyan felt a gentle wind blowing up against his toes. He took a step back, planting his feet firmly onto the ground. A layer of dust and dirt began to rise at the centre of the ring and a fine cylindrical mist spread upwards, all the way to the ceiling. Strangely, aside from the light wind, he felt almost nothing unusual. The gravitational effects of whatever was happening in the ring were localised. The Tugs lining the ring changed – their physical bases dissociated into dust that also drifted up to the ceiling, leaving behind pure strings of gravity that rose from the ground.

The mist began to thicken at the ceiling as more layers of dirt ascended upwards, as though a large clump of muvaeyt was being reassembled from its blue wisps. The mist rarefied from the bottom, leaving the area near the ground mostly transparent. Something dark was being exposed, where the ground had previously been. Diyan stooped low, crossing the threshold of the ring to look more closely, ignoring the ripple of upwards force coursing through his body. It was more than a wind. He felt lighter; if he relaxed, he was convinced that his body would just float up with the dirt.

A final layer of debris flew up and Diyan gasped. Below him, suspended within a sea of writhing dark green, so dark it was almost black, was Kera. Despite the mask and black regwear that covered most of her body, her shape was unmistakable. She floated at the top of the sea, which began to rise terrifyingly all around her, threatening to swallow her whole. The dark green surface flickered repeatedly, unusually, some of it rising through the material mist in thin extensions the size of Diyan's arm, like giant gravity strings, stopping near the ceiling. Around the periphery of the hole, thin green lines rose through the blackness – the gravity strings of the Tugs. The strings and the sea were all part of the same structure.

Diyan fell flat to the floor, ignoring the disturbances and the chaos around him, and reached down to grab Kera. She was facing upwards now, lying horizontally, her hand clasped around a mysterious object. Pushing himself to the limits of his reach, he managed to grasp her shoulder and pull her limp body towards him. She was so light; it felt as though she really was floating. He pulled her completely out of the hole, dragging her away from the ring, and lay her down on the solid ground, ripping off her mask before tearing off his own. It was a relief to finally see her face again.

"Kera!"

Nothing. Her eyes remained closed. Diyan lowered his ear – her breathing was shallow and slow. She was alive. Suddenly, he became aware of being pulled back, by a mass of Silvereds. They were far too strong for him, and Kera disappeared behind a wall of their bodies. There was noise all around, but he could not make sense of it. The flips filtered through his body, like the beats of his heart. Ilouden was nearby, shouting something at him, wide-eyed and mask-less, pulling at the Silvereds, trying to calm them down. Diyan was still being held back – he realised he had been struggling. Most of the Silvereds rushed off, taking Kera with them. The remaining Silvereds hurried after them, leaving him with Ilouden. Lellara also stood nearby, looking confused.

"He found her," she said, quietly.

Diyan stood up, disoriented. His legs were barely able to function. It was like he was back in the dream; there was nothing he could do to reach her.

"Where have they taken her?" Diyan asked in a dazed voice.

Ilouden shook his head and glanced at Lellara, who also appeared to be at a loss. "We need to find Hespinr," he said calmly. "She'll know."

Someone came out of the darkness, ripping off their mask, panting. It was Bomera. Her movements were jerky, her haste having made it difficult to compensate for flips.

She started speaking, breathlessly. "They're taking her to Osr, and Osr's already sent word back. She wants to know how Diyan found her."

Diyan frowned. His strength was returning. "The ring—" His voice faltered as he looked to where the ring of Tugs was, where the dirt had lifted from the floor and Kera had appeared. Everything was back to normal, calm. It was as though nothing had happened. He pointed towards the ring. "She was beneath there."

Chapter 28
Domed Alliance

Diyan stared up at the grand structure, across the open concourse. It stuck out ostentatiously, like a beacon. Whilst it stood as high as the tallest tower Diyan had seen in Fadin, unlike almost everything else in Sunsprit, it was not a tower, but a dome, like a miniature replica of Sunsprit itself. There was space between it and the nearby towers – again quite unusual for anything other than the city's concourses – with motionless Silvered guards stood in a perimeter, wearing all black regwear that covered their entire bodies. Each held identical, heavy-looking weapons, resembling Roranian thermal ejection rifles.

The dome was held up by tall, grey-white pillars, and occasionally, Silvereds could be seen entering or leaving between the pillars. Bulbous, concentric rings, made from the same luminous material as Sunsprit's magnetic paths, wrapped around the dome from the tops of the pillars to the structure's apex.

"Right in the centre of Upper-Sunsprit. Looks

important," Diyan muttered, cocking his head to the side. "A little different, though." He looked around the rest of the concourse.

"Still, it must be nicer to be back here, where gravity's more stable," Ilouden said, with a chuckle.

Diyan nodded. "The flips are far easier to deal with."

Ilouden's tone was less than serious. "The *Great Dome*. It's where the quarrelling factions meet. Many come from other cities just to glimpse it – it's an odd architectural style the Vaesians rarely use in Sunsprit. Come on, no point waiting."

There were groups of Silvereds dotted about the concourse, but it was far less busy than any of the other concourses he had seen. A few non-Silvered Vaesians also wandered about, sporadically stopping to look at the Great Dome.

"The factions the Administration believes to exist?" Diyan asked.

"Exactly."

"Why didn't Hespinr take me here the first time?" From the corner of his eye, Diyan spotted a large group of Silvereds sauntering across the concourse. They were all engrossed in their own conversations; none seemed too interested in the Great Dome. Curiously, there were a few Roranians on the concourse too, in groups of two or three. Despite being dressed in relatively colourful attire – none wore the dark regwear Diyan had become accustomed to seeing them in – they all looked a little stiff, presumably still acclimatising to the flips.

"She would have, if we hadn't taken a liking to you." Ilouden slapped Diyan on the back.

"That's one way of putting it." Diyan's countenance became more serious. "But it's the Vaesian Union that's there right now, isn't it? It's not a gathering of the faction leaders of Sunsprit – there are no real factions, right?"

"You catch on fast," Ilouden teased, looking about to make sure they could not be overheard. "The Administration believes Sunsprit is mostly cut off from the Vaesian Union, but it couldn't be more wrong. The union is directed by a council, and that is who truly governs us."

"And Kera's there right now – with the council?"

"She is, and she's asked for you to be brought before them."

"What for? I explained everything over and over. They know what happened."

Ilouden shrugged. "Kera has a way of getting what she wants."

"Where is Hespinr?"

"I don't know," Ilouden admitted. "She's often tasked with guiding new Administration spies through the city. She's good at confusing and tiring them out."

Suddenly, Diyan was buffeted to the side. He stumbled, attempting to regain his balance. It was the large group of Silvereds he had spotted sauntering across the concourse. Evidently, they had been sauntering faster than he had realised and had bumped into him.

"Watch where you're going!" Diyan glared at them. One of the Silvereds stooped over to help, its tensirs attaching to his arm to help stabilise him. He waved the help off. "I'm fine." He patted down his clothes. Mutters of apology followed, and the group quickly continued on its way. "Second time today!" he said, rubbing his shoulder. He spotted a group of three Roranians nearby, shaking their heads in the direction of the Silvereds.

Ilouden laughed. "Perhaps you should watch where you're going, Diyan. Come on, we're nearly there." He pointed up ahead, to a high-stepped path that was just visible from where they were standing, its first steps jutting out from behind the curvature of the Great Dome. The path was nearer to the closest, bland tower than it was to the Great Dome itself, though it appeared to wind around the shape of the Great Dome.

"Why don't we just walk in?" Diyan pointed to a nearby gap between two of the pillars. "Everyone else is."

Ilouden shook his head. "Just follow."

They made their way along the path as it climbed steadily higher. Once they were directly behind the Great Dome, hidden from all those on the concourse, and high enough that Diyan's feet were now aligned with the heads of the Silvered guards who stood around the dome, the path levelled out. The back of the Great Dome looked exactly like the front, though the public concourse did not extend around to this side, and there was only space for the guards.

"We're not going to get there from here," Diyan said hesitantly, looking at the Great Dome, which they were no closer to. The path carried on around, presumably returning them to the concourse on the other side of the Great Dome, though it also split off ahead into two branches, both directed away from the concourse into the midst of the tall towers around them.

"We're going that way." Ilouden pointed to the first of the two branches.

Diyan frowned but said nothing, following Ilouden as they took the branch and walked away from both the concourse and the Great Dome. The narrow path meandered confusingly. Finally, they came to a halt – two large Silvereds stood in their way. They were unarmed. Three separate sets of steps were behind the two Silvereds, all leading in different directions. Ilouden nodded to them, and the Silvereds moved to the side. Ilouden and Diyan took the middle set of steps, leading them to an even narrower, more meandering route.

"The Great Dome's not where anything really happens, is it?" Diyan said. "You're just supposed to think it is."

Ilouden's head shook from side to side, bemused. "And you've figured it out."

"The guards, the size…that's what you'd expect. It's what the Administration expects. That's why so many of their spies were on the concourse."

"There were quite a lot, I must admit. Usually, they're more subtle about the game." He carried on walking but turned back to look at Diyan. "Consider yourself lucky to be learning Sunsprit's secrets, and so quickly. Kera's request to have you come here wasn't granted lightly." He turned back, taking them around another corner. "That's why we had to wait for so long. The Vaesian Union has never let an Administration spy into a council meeting before – not a real one. Ever."

Diyan began to protest. "I'm not an Administration spy—"

"Your special circumstances are understood. And Kera insisted on you bearing witness to their discussions, where they concerned you."

"You mean, discussions about us returning to Fadin?"

Ilouden did not reply. The path continued to twist around, taking them further and further from the Great Dome. The towers at their sides became increasingly tightly packed. Soon, they could not have walked side by side, even if they had chosen to. Turning a final corner, they reached a dead end.

"We've gone wrong somewhere," Diyan muttered, irritated. "And what's that sound? Can you hear it?" A low rumble reverberated around them. There was also the faint, sweet smell of muvaeyt. The hairs on the back of Diyan's neck prickled. The rumble became louder, sounding like the echoes of many Vaesians speaking together, from somewhere close by, although the source was nowhere to be seen. He looked back the way they had come.

"Diyan," Ilouden called.

Diyan turned around. The tower blocking their path was gone. There was now a small stretch of the path left, leading to another tower at the end, with a dark, black entrance – it was open, unguarded. The tower rose as high as those around it, but was far wider.

"That wasn't there before," Diyan said suspiciously. "None of it. It was a holo, wasn't it?" The tower was not as obviously impressive as the Great Dome, but there was something different about it, somehow separating it from the other tower structures in Sunsprit. Diyan whipped his head around, sensing something beside him. "And what's that humming?"

"Come on," Ilouden said patiently. "Let's go." They walked to the end of the path and entered the dark void.

The darkness was extinguished as soon as they entered. A bright, cavernous, circular room was revealed, clad in the same brown substance as the natural surface of Ringscape. Diyan looked back through the entrance – the path outside was now obscured by a dark void. Diyan moved his eyes across the room's brown coating.

"Natural protection against prying sensors," Ilouden explained, following Diyan's gaze. "That's why we use it all over the city's dome too. Makes the thick atmosphere that little bit thicker. Did you know it's actually believed to come from an ancient war that happened here, long ago? All that remains is this organic, brown detritus. It has odd properties, becoming denser the deeper you go. That's the real reason no one can excavate beneath the surface of Ringscape. Anyway, come on."

The humming was still present, as was the smell of muvaeyt. Diyan shivered, despite the warmth, drawing his facepiece a little further up. Ilouden had moved to the centre of the room and was gesturing for Diyan to join him.

"What now?" Diyan asked quietly, standing in front of Ilouden, looking around for a hint of what was to come. Ilouden did not need to answer. Diyan's knees buckled momentarily as a circular patch of the ground began to ascend into the air, with the two of them at the centre. The flips had hardened Diyan's body to sudden shocks of force – had they not, he would have fallen to the side. The circular platform ascended slowly. Diyan looked up. The ceiling remained very much present.

"It's a holo, isn't it?" he asked.

Ilouden shrugged. "Hope so. This is a first for me too. My instructions end here."

Diyan looked over the side of the rising, circular patch they stood on. "Doesn't this seem a little unsafe to you?"

Ilouden laughed. "Vaesians have three legs. They're a lot more stable than us."

They both steeled themselves as the tips of their heads reached the ceiling, unable to resist the temptation to duck a little. Diyan's jaw remained clenched and he closed his eyes. Immediately, he heard deep voices booming all around. He opened his eyes again. The two of them were emerging from the floor, at the centre of a wide circular space, many times the size of the room below. There were no obvious entrances or exits, or other apertures of any kind. The humming was louder than before and the muvaeyt smell more intense, despite there being no hint of the blue wisps. Vaesians, mostly non-Silvereds, stood around at regularly spaced intervals, behind simple grey plinths that came to mid-chest height, talking loudly. They spoke and shouted over one another, barely taking breaths between sentences, and giving no indication that they had noticed, or cared about, the two new arrivals. Some wore black regwear – of Roranian style – while others wore more colourful clothing, of completely different styles to those that Diyan had encountered before.

Ilouden and Diyan continued to rise, the floor of the room – luminous white – now level with their knees. The empty space with them at the centre was ringed by two steep, circular steps. The Vaesians all towered above them, strong and determined; not the typical Vaesians from Fadin, nor the ordinary Silvered Vaesians from Sunsprit. These Vaesians possessed a clear stature and confidence. Diyan was reminded, unpleasantly, of the man from the Administration who had set him on the journey to Sunsprit.

"The whole council is here: all thirty representatives from all the different regions," Ilouden whispered. He sounded excited. "I've never seen all of them in the same place before. Whatever's being discussed, it must be important."

"What regions?"

They stopped ascending – their feet were finally level with the floor, and the circular patch around them vanished, as though it had never been there.

"The twelve major Vaesian cities. Some have more than one representative, based on size. Sunsprit has three, for example, all Silvereds." As he spoke, some of the representatives wandered from their plinths to speak with their neighbours, before returning. There were many loud guffaws. "There's Osr."

Diyan turned in the direction Ilouden was gesturing. Osr was there – the gruff Vaesian who had ferried Diyan from Fadin to Sunsprit, and then interrogated him. Osr's long hair was still a pale shade of grey, instead of pure white from when Diyan had first encountered her.

"How does she do that?" Diyan asked.

"What?"

"Her colour."

"Oh, that," Ilouden said, innocently. "She's special in that way."

Diyan was about to question Ilouden further when his mind froze. Kera came into view. He sucked in sharply. She had been animatedly discussing something with another Vaesian, but now walked up to stand beside Osr. Kera still wore the same regwear as when Diyan had found her, and was looking distractingly alluring. Her thick black hair was no longer in a tight bun, instead wafting loosely against her shoulders. Their gazes met, briefly. She then glanced and nodded at Ilouden, before turning to speak with Osr.

"Osr's our main representative," Ilouden said. "She's the true authority behind the factions. The other two," he gestured to the two other Silvereds who stood on plinths nearby, "defer mostly to her."

Diyan stared at Kera, waiting for something, some further spark of recognition, but she was busy. While her exact words could not be heard above the general commotion, she was now clearly shouting at Osr, presumably arguing. Osr was shouting back.

"This…is the Vaesian Union."

"The ruling council, yes." Ilouden grinned. "Don't sound so disappointed."

"I thought it would be more…"

"Orderly? Me too. Well, at least everyone's getting their say."

A wave of quiet began to spread throughout the room, and they could hear one of the Vaesians speaking, softly.

"We must decide, and we must decide to act now," the Vaesian's voice rumbled. "I propose we attack the Administration."

"I agree," a Vaesian beside the initial speaker said, also quietly. "They have sent more spies than ever before; they are growing restless."

The original Vaesian resumed speaking. "They want Kera back; they want to know what secrets of the network she stole. They know we harbour her. We have no choice."

"You are simply restless!" a different Vaesian, from the opposite side of the circle, near to Kera and Osr, growled back, although still with a low voice. "You are young, you are brash—"

"And you are old and slow!"

Diyan looked between them. They both looked the same age…then again, all of them did. Every single Vaesian in the room, aside from Osr, with her longer, slightly matted hair.

Another Vaesian spoke out, gesturing to Diyan. "This Roranian was a test, a test sent by the Administration that took too long. They will not wait. Kera is an excuse and they will use her presence here to lay waste to Sunsprit. And do not think they will stop there. Next, they will turn their attentions to our other cities that have yet to succumb to their rule."

"It's true," another said. "We all know of their plans."

The exchange continued; despite the quiet nature of the debate, there was a powerful force behind their words.

"See what you've done!" an angry Vaesian hissed at Kera, who looked defiantly and unwaveringly back into the Vaesian's black eyes. "You don't even know what it is you stole. This device, this *dummy node* that you claim now holds the secrets of the Tugs, might be worthless! And now, the Administration will attack – the Vaesian Union could fall, all for nothing!"

"Gelirn's right," another Vaesian added. "You claim the dummy node holds all the answers – to Ringscape, to everything – but you have no proof. You don't even know whether the Tugs recognised the dummy node as an information storage device, let alone whether they were able to implant their information into it!"

"You admitted you don't remember what happened after the Tugs took you!"

"And what if the Tugs have different aims to ours? What if they don't know *anything*?"

"They're new, and things that are new are dangerous."

"No, they are vital! And who are you to call the Tugs new?"

"I am referring to their aims. Whatever they really—"

"And why do you think their aims are new?"

Kera cleared her throat. The discussion died down. Diyan saw her jaw clench – she was controlling herself. Attention was upon her.

She spoke quietly, with a measured tone. "I have explained, but now I shall do so again. The Administration cannot be stopped by you. It cannot be stopped by the Vaesian Union as it is." She paused for effect. "The dummy node can change all that. It holds the answers. The Tugs understood the device's potential, I am certain of it. The dummy node contains the information we seek. The meaning everyone on Ringscape has sought for so long.

The meaning of all this." She spread her arms wide. "Ringscape, the Haze Rings, Barrenscape. Everything. If there is the slightest chance I am correct, you must give the dummy node to me, and you must allow me to return to Fadin. Our own efforts to understand it haven't worked. There is no time. The dummy node will still connect with the influx network, and that is the only equipment on Ringscape we know of with the computational abilities to read it. I destroyed all traces of its—"

One of the Vaesians interrupted her, and she immediately stopped speaking. "Ah yes, your actions, that you did not see fit to inform us of upon your own return here. A curious oversight. We still have many questions for you, Roranian. Forgetting what you want us to think, Kera, tell us, how did you attack the influx network? And what augmentations do you have, *precisely*?"

She frowned innocently – Diyan had seen that look before. "I'm stronger than you thought I would be. What did you expect? I was a soldier for the Nesch, I have never pretended otherwise. And I am not the only one with secrets. I'm the same as you with your cell-scales, only—"

Another Vaesian spoke up. "You're missing the point, Aivinr. Kera is right. We need the answers that only the Tugs can give us, we cannot afford for the Administration to have them. Can we risk inaction?"

"You sound like a Veiler!"

Various other Vaesians began to interrupt each other again, still using their curiously quiet method of debate, speaking one by one.

"Our own spies in Fadin heard rumours of the Administration's attempts to increase the range of the influx—"

"Impossible! Ringscape doesn't allow it!"

"That doesn't negate the fact that they will be coming. We all know this."

Kera cleared her throat again. "Let me try. Give me the dummy node. What do you have to lose?"

"What do we have to lose?"

"Everything!" one of the Vaesians replied, indignantly. "If you are captured, they may learn absolutely everything. All of our secrets, all—"

Kera interrupted the Vaesian. "But I won't be captured."

"You cannot possibly guarantee that."

"What would you do?" Osr asked, speaking for the first time. She turned to the side, staring into Kera's steely eyes. "Were we to release the dummy node back to you, what comes next?"

"I would go to Fadin." Kera flicked her head towards Diyan and Ilouden, still facing Osr. "The easiest way to do that is to let Diyan complete his mission. He can take me back. Once I'm there...well, leave that to me. They don't know the dummy node survived my attack on the influx network, and they don't know that I took it."

"Leave it to you?"

Multiple Vaesians attempted to speak at the same time, immediately interrupting each other, resulting in a sea of staccato outbursts. Osr raised her arm, flexing her tensirs, silencing them all.

"Would you be asking us permission if the dummy node was in your possession?"

Kera turned away, despite Osr's proximity. She looked slowly and pointedly from Vaesian to Vaesian as she spoke. "I understand the risks, believe me, and I understand why you don't trust me. I took an opportunity. I was verified. I finally had the ability to access Administration facilities. Before, I was only able to salvage—"

She was interrupted. Diyan saw her clench her fists.

"You still haven't fully explained your augmentations. Don't think we've forgotten that. You're skilled at deflection, Kera, we all know that. What exactly happened to you beyond the Haze Rings? What did the Nesch do to you?"

"It's not important," another said dismissively.

"She's never explained what the Nesch did to her! And, if they ever pass through in significant numbers, they'll make the Administration seem like good friends!"

Again, others joined in, and the room descended into restrained clamour, as before.

"What's important is that now they send spies after spies. We're having trouble identifying half of them, there are so many. Some appear to be genuine travellers—"

"The safety of Vaesians is our priority."

"Citizens of the Vaesian Union…they aren't all Vaesian, as you well know."

"Can we trust Kera?"

"She is a citizen of the Vaesian—"

"She's lived with *them* longer than with *us*! She's Roranian!"

"No, she—"

"You need your mind straightened. Go see Echoes—"

"Go yourself!"

"That's not—"

"You know why I help you!" Kera shouted. The Vaesians were stunned into silence. Kera appeared not to care about whatever unspoken rule she had broken. "You found me, you rescued me. I am one of you! It does not matter that my species is Roranian, there are many Roranians within the Vaesian Union – look at Ilouden, he is here with me, yet he is of the Vaesian Union too! I am one of you. I act to save us against the inevitable onslaught and corruption of the Administration."

"Well," one of the Vaesians muttered after some silence. "We've all heard the rumours about the influx network and how the Administration created it with their enhanced cognition experiments. If even half of it is true, we cannot abide by it. I vote in Kera's favour."

Chapter 29
Altered Fated

Diyan strode back across the open concourse with Ilouden at his side. Around them, there were more groups of Roranians than before, all watching the Great Dome.

"Travel to Sunsprit certainly seems to be picking up," Ilouden muttered. "They can't all be spies." Ilouden looked at Diyan. "Are you okay?"

Diyan was glaring at the end of the concourse, where they were headed. "She only brought us there because she needed a route back into Fadin," he hissed. "She doesn't care anymore."

"About what?"

"Anything!" Diyan shook his head. "About Paran, Yena...me." He stumbled over his words. "You saw her – she barely looked at me!"

"Diyan!"

The shout from behind caused Diyan's step to falter.

Ilouden cast an awkward glance towards the source. It was Kera, rushing after them.

"Should we…" Ilouden decided not to finish his sentence.

"Wait, Diyan – can you slow down?" Kera begged, drawing closer. Ilouden walked further to the side, away from Diyan, as Kera reached Diyan and grabbed his shoulder. "What's the matter? I thought you'd be happy to see me." Diyan slowed, only stopping when she tugged him even harder. "Diyan, what is it?" She looked genuinely puzzled.

He clenched his fists. "What do you want?"

A hurt look spread across her face. "Diyan, don't be like this. We need to talk."

"Now you want to talk? But in there you…you wouldn't even look at me! You said nothing about Paran, or Yena, or anything. All you care about is this stupid dummy node!"

"Diyan," she said, sternly. "What difference would it have made if I spoke of Paran and Yena in there. If anything—"

"What difference?" Diyan asked scornfully. "Have you even asked? Do you realise why I'm here – and why I need to go back to Fadin? I'm not just some Administration spy, Kera. They have Paran, and they have Yena. Our friends! And they have our c-automs!"

Kera held Diyan's arm and gently pushed him so that they resumed walking, avoiding the perplexed stares from around them. "Diyan, you need to understand, I couldn't tell you anything in Fadin. It risked too much. I tried to warn you—"

"They killed your friends, and then they took us," he hissed. "Paran, Yena, and me. And…and Wiln, Loten, Rememox, and now…now, I don't know what to do! Because if…" He was almost unable to continue. "If I do take you back…if I do take you back, they might kill you, Kera."

They stopped walking. "You need to take me back," she whispered. "It's the only way."

"But it's not for them, is it?" Diyan asked. "Why don't you care about us anymore?"

She placed her hands on either side of his head. "On the mounds we have our answers."

"What?"

"Remember when I used to say that to you?"

"Yes, on our ship, when our c-automs taught us everything."

Her hands held him there. "Now, the Tugs are the mounds. And they have given us their answers, through the dummy node. We need to know what answers it holds for us."

"But what do you want, Kera?" Diyan asked quietly. "I don't understand."

She looked into his eyes. "When we opened your ship, in Barrenscape, and I looked inside…when I finally found you, all I wanted to do was hold you, Diyan."

"What do you really want?"

"I want to destroy the Administration." Her eyes lit up. "I want to destroy it all." She leaned forwards and pushed her lips against his. He held her by the waist as her hands moved down to his shoulders.

Loud, deep Vaesian screams and higher-pitched Roranian shouts caused Diyan's eyes to reopen. Kera looked startled too. They turned around. The groups of Roranians were advancing close to the Great Dome, some were running inside. Many of them held small weapons that appeared to be miniature versions of thermal ejection rifles. Dozens of Silvereds lay on the floor, motionless, with dark black trails of liquid seeping from their bodies, forming pools beside them. Others were twitching, some groaning, trying to move out of the way. The Silvered guards were mostly on the ground, wounded, although some were rushing towards the Roranians – batting them to the side with apparent ease before being picked off by thermal blasts and falling down, parts of their bodies caving in. More Silvereds began streaming out from the sides of the Great Dome, carrying weapons of their own that fired loudly, tearing some of the Roranians explosively apart. They wore black panelled uniforms, with faceplates similar to the bulky Tug Masks.

"Why would the Administration do this?" Ilouden gasped, rushing over to them, his mouth agape.

"It's not them. It's far too disorganised, and too obvious," Kera replied, surprisingly calmly. "It's the Anti-

Vaesian Movement." She looked at them both, shaking their arms roughly to get their attention. "We need to go, now."

"But we can help—"

She silenced Ilouden. "We're more likely to be killed in the crossfire. The real Silvered soldiers haven't arrived yet."

Other Roranians, walking jerkily, evidently not yet well-accustomed to the flips, appeared from various entry points on the concourse with their small hand-held weaponry. They fired indiscriminately at the Vaesians and their towers. The air began to turn dark and hazy, accompanied by the smell of burning.

Thunderous bolts of pure white appeared from thin air, branching out and striking many of the Roranians forcefully, vaporising them into clouds of matter. A low hum, the same hum Diyan had heard many times now, began to permeate all around them, along with the smell of muvaeyt. The terrified Roranians shouted to one another and concentrated their bursts of fire on where the bolts were coming from. At some of the places their fire was concentrated, heavily armoured Silvereds suddenly appeared, lying dead on the ground, blue wisps escaping from their mouths.

Kera grabbed Diyan and shouted to Ilouden, "I said we need to go, now!" She pulled Diyan forcefully towards a part of the concourse edge that seemed devoid of activity. Ilouden ran just behind. The hum grew in intensity. Diyan instinctively tried to stop as what looked like hundreds of armoured Silvereds appeared around the perimeter of the concourse, just ahead, again from thin air, but Kera pulled him again. The humming grew louder as they drew closer – it was coming from the approaching Silvereds. Each had thick, blue, muvaeyt-wisps clouding around their heads. Up close, the armour they wore was like nothing Diyan had seen before; unlike that of the other Silvered soldiers from around the Great Dome, the armour worn by these Silvereds covered their entire bodies, and appeared to be made from what looked like a very dense matte of their own hair. It shone brightly, so brightly that Diyan felt he was looking into a kindling star. As with the noise of the hum, the closer Kera pulled him towards them, the brighter their armour became – so much so that he tried to turn away, unable to quell his rising panic.

"I'm Kera – we are with the Vaesian Union!" Kera shouted.

The Silvered soldiers said nothing, but moved to the side, allowing them to rush through the light blue fog. Some of the Silvereds stepped back, as though impacted by something, but only one fell, before almost immediately getting up again. The humming intensified. Diyan looked to the side – a group of the Roranians were firing their weapons at them. But these Silvered soldiers seemed unconcerned, unworried. They advanced forwards, quickly. As they passed, the heat from their armour lightly singed the fine hairs on Diyan's exposed skin. He looked back once they had passed through the mass of Silvered soldiers – they were engaging the Roranians. The true battle was beginning.

Loud explosions in other parts of the city caused the three friends to twist and turn with every noise and flash. It was not just the Great Dome or this concourse that was under attack.

"Why have they done this now?" Ilouden shouted, gesturing to the Roranians from the Anti-Vaesian Movement.

Kera ignored him. "This way."

She led them through various narrow passageways and stairways, discretely woven around the city. Everything appeared almost normal as they ran; only the sounds of the raging battle reverberating all around them felt out of place. They passed by several groups of terrified-looking Silvereds, as well as some of Sunsprit's Roranian citizens, without stopping to speak. Kera shouted at them to continue.

"Where are we going?" Diyan huffed to Ilouden, who ran beside him. Kera was just ahead, regularly glancing back, hurrying them along.

"I don't know. I've never been here before, I…" Ilouden struggled for breath. "I wasn't ready for this."

"Kera?" Diyan shouted. "Kera, where—"

"To see Osr."

"But…Osr was in the…next to the Great Dome, with

the others. They're probably—"

"Holos, most of them," Ilouden said, puffing. "Probably all…except us. They would never have met all together like that."

"Something useful they copied from us," Kera said. They turned around another corner, and she suddenly slowed down.

"Why're we stopping?"

Humming. The blue muvaeyt haze. All around. It grew louder and more intense. From out of nowhere, just like the Silvered soldiers on the concourse, an enormous Silvered appeared before them, towering over Diyan.

"She's expecting you."

"Good," Kera replied.

The Silvered took a step to the side and disappeared again. The blue wisps quickly dissipated too.

They rushed through where the Silvered had been standing, along an empty, narrow passage. Another Silvered, equally as large and accompanied by the hum and the wisps, materialised before them, again blocking their path. Staring Kera briefly in the eyes, the Silvered stood to the side – Diyan was expecting another disappearance, but the Silvered did not fade away. Instead, the side of the tower disappeared, and an entrance was revealed that appeared to be the mouth of a long, dark passage. Two large Silvereds stood on either side of the entrance, wearing the thick, matted armour of the Silvered soldiers on the concourse. While their armour did not glow, their tensirs did, and small balls of light the size of a fist rolled about at their tips. Thick blue wisps streamed from their mouths.

Kera, Diyan and Ilouden stepped through the entrance. The gap behind them immediately resealed, becoming the side of a tower again. Looking at the two Silvereds, where their necks extended up from their armour, Diyan could see their bodies emitting a faint silver light, casting greyish hues on the swirling muvaeyt wisps. The seemingly ever-present hum surrounded them.

"They're readying themselves," Kera said, walking quickly forwards. "Takes time." She led the other two into the darkness, and soon, the glow from the Silvereds at the entrance was almost indistinct. A new flicker of light up ahead captured their focus.

"They are not as weak as the Administration thinks," Ilouden replied, although his comment seemed more for his own benefit than a genuine observation.

"Where are we?"

"Nearly there," Kera said. "Osr's going to help us. She has to."

The speck of light enlarged. Diyan quickly realised it was another pair of Silvereds, also emitting a faint glow from their bodies, with the same blue wisps as the others.

"Those soldiers from the concourse were much brighter," Diyan whispered, as they drew close. "The hum coming from them, it was so loud…"

"But they weren't as ready as they could have been,"

Kera replied. "It takes practice, but the longer they have to prepare, the more dangerous they are. Muvaeyt helps them focus."

They reached the two Silvereds at the end of the dark passage. The Silvereds stood motionless, barely registering their presence. They were in what appeared to be a small, cylindrical room, with brown walls. The ceiling was not visible, and it was impossible to tell how high it rose. Immediately, Diyan looked towards the centre, and on seeing a small circular base, walked towards it.

"It's going to take us to Osr, isn't it?"

Before he could reply, an explosion of sound and light made them turn back. The other end of the long passage was exposed, the wall gone again. The Silvereds were shining brightly and their movement was rapid, it was difficult to see what was happening. A moment later, Silvered bodies lay motionless on the ground – all lights emanating from them extinguished. A two-legged figure with thick, black-plated armour walked forwards. Unmistakably Roranian, and with strangely familiar movements.

"How is that possible?" Ilouden asked, shocked. "Nothing can do that to them."

The armour shimmered and the Roranian moved fluidly, with unnatural speed, before coming to an unexpected halt. A section of the armour around the warrior's head shimmered into transparency. Diyan gasped. Paran's face stared back at them. Despite being at the far end of the passage, Paran's fury was obvious, unadulterated. His easy smile was nowhere to be seen; his face contorted with rage.

"Paran!" Diyan shouted.

Paran raised his arm, pointing at them. "I saw you," he shouted, without moving. His voice boomed, amplified by the suit, echoing around the passage. "I saw you, before their *Great Dome*." He almost spat out the last two words. "I'm so glad you were able to become reacquainted while Yena and I were being tortured."

The two Silvereds beside Kera, Diyan and Ilouden moved forwards, advancing towards Paran, their bodies glowing bright silver – almost white. Balls of energy rolled at their tensirs.

"No," Kera shouted, moving after them, towards Paran. "You're mistaken." She pulled at the arm of one of the Silvereds. "Don't – Paran's with us!"

"You betrayed us! Both of you!" Paran shouted.

Diyan moved to keep up with Kera and the two Silvereds. "Paran, we didn't betray you. Whatever the Administration has told you is a lie. We were coming back to get you and Yena! I found Kera, and—"

"Liar! You found her and you did nothing! I came to save *you*, and this is what I find?"

"Paran." Kera raised her palms in a conciliatory gesture as the two Silvereds finally stopped, although they did not let her pass. "Please understand, what we need to do is too important. You can help us, we can get Yena. But first we need to get—"

The transparent section of Paran's armour shimmered again, returning to pure black. "The Administration gave me one rule. I take Kera in, or Yena dies. Loten is destroyed. Rememox is destroyed. Wiln is destroyed! You made me do this. Kera, come with me. Diyan, I won't let you stop me."

"We can stop them together."

"It's too late for that."

The Silvereds visibly tensed, brightening even more. Kera and Diyan stopped, frozen. Suddenly, Paran began to walk quickly towards them. The Silvereds began moving forwards again, just as fast.

"Diyan…I…" Kera stopped, taking a hesitant step backwards and pulling Diyan with her. "Diyan, I think we need to go."

"But—"

"Whatever the Administration have told him, we're not going to be able to convince him now. What we have to do is too important." For the first time, she sounded worried. "Come on, we need to go!"

Diyan tore his gaze from the advancing Paran, turning back with Kera, towards the small cylindrical room.

"You're not the same as us, Kera!" Paran shouted. "We all know it. And you've betrayed us, Diyan. You've betrayed us! You always wanted her for yourself."

A bright light exploded as a ball of energy from one of the Silvereds expanded enormously and hurtled towards

Paran. Diyan turned and shouted instinctively, but the ball of energy merely bounced off Paran's armour and ricocheted destructively against a wall of the passage, causing a thick chunk to fragment explosively, spraying the air with a cloud of debris. The other Silvered released another blast of energy, which the armour did not manage to deflect, but Paran was merely knocked off balance. Judging by his jerky movements, it looked as though a flip in his area had also just occurred. The Silvereds took the opportunity, lunging towards him. Immediately, he ripped one of them off, throwing the Silvered forcefully against the wall.

"Diyan – they're not going to be able to stop him," Kera shouted. They both picked up their pace, running back to Ilouden at the end of the passage, and the three of them stepped onto the circle at the centre.

"How long does it take?" Diyan asked, his eyes fixed on Paran's fight with the Silvereds. Unfortunately for them, the Silvereds were losing. They seemed helpless against Paran's onslaught and were being thrown about mercilessly.

"It's not designed for all of us," Kera shouted. Fortunately, a moment later, they began to rise in the air, slowly. They watched helplessly as the Silvereds battled valiantly to stop Paran advancing towards them. He was moving impossibly fast, fighting them without weaponry, as though he were enjoying it. By the time they were high enough that he had disappeared from view, Paran had almost reached the cylindrical room, and one of the Silvereds was dead.

"Level seventeen combat technology, from our Great Ship. Maybe even eighteen," Kera muttered. "I'd assumed they were all destroyed by the Haze Rings. I wonder what other secrets the Administration has kept."

"That's Paran?" Ilouden said, levelly. "He seems different to how you described."

Diyan ignored him, looking over the edge, breathing fast. Everything was pitch black again and quiet. It was not possible to discern how high they had risen.

"How did Paran get here?"

"The Administration," Kera said. "They must have helped the Anti-Vaesian Movement gain entry to Sunsprit – all deniable, of course. They're testing the Vaesians while protecting themselves from reprisals."

"And they publicly denounce the Anti-Vaesian Movement anyway, so can't be held accountable," Ilouden said angrily.

"Exactly. They probably helped them build up their presence here in Sunsprit ever since they sent you, as their failsafe option. And they've also sent a highly motivated Paran."

"That's one way of describing him," Ilouden muttered.

The dim outline of a passageway became visible to one side, and the platform moved slowly across to connect to the wall. They rushed off. The corridor was short, quickly opening out into a dimly lit room – about half as long as the corridor they had left Paran in. The room was saturated with a thick hum. On the other side of the platform, more than a dozen glowing Silvereds waited, motionless, bright spheres of light shining beneath their tensirs and wisps of blue wafting about their heads. There were also other, non-glowing Silvereds dotted around them, holding heavy weaponry.

"He's coming for you," Kera said loudly, walking towards them. Diyan and Ilouden followed cautiously behind her. The Silvereds parted to allow them through. "And you won't be able to stop him."

"We'll protect Osr," a growling voice replied.

They walked into a smaller room behind the Silvereds. Osr was alone at its centre, facing away from them as she paced. She was surrounded by holos, each depicting events that were happening in Sunsprit.

"Quite the predicament we find ourselves in," Osr said.

"It is," Kera replied, quietly.

"The question is, can I trust you, Kera?" Osr turned around. "Can we trust you?" She looked at Diyan. "I had hoped to make your reacquaintance under difference circumstances, but I'd like to say that I did enjoy our conversations on the way to Sunsprit. Until all this happened, I had thought we might be able to persuade you to stay in Sunsprit. But now, our options have changed."

"I…" Diyan was unsure what to say as he wiped a bead of sweat from his forehead. Ilouden was just as bewildered and was likewise sweating. It was as though they were standing next to the hot bodies of the shining Silvereds again. The thought made Diyan's body rigid and he sniffed about the empty air suspiciously.

"We don't have time," Kera said coolly. "And you only have one good choice. The Roranian coming through behind us is better equipped than we are used to, you will not be able to stop him."

"And you led him here."

"I had no choice."

The Silvered guffawed and looked at the holos, shaking her head. "You've always been so perceptive, Kera. Whether it's my kind or yours, you always know what everyone's thinking. You always have a plan."

"Kera's on our side," Ilouden stated, hastily. "She fights against the Administration."

Again, a guffaw. "Of the latter point, I have no doubt. But Kera fights *everyone*. I fear it's just that, up to now, her path has aligned with ours." Again, Osr turned her attention back to the holos and pushed her tensirs against some of them. "But that is not to say that you are not correct, in this instance. There really isn't another choice. If you are right about the dummy node and what it contains, it's too valuable to fall into the Administration's clutches, and yet, we need to use their influx network to decode it. A group of Vaesians is unlikely to be able to enter Fadin now, especially Silvereds. You are our only hope. You three. I have no better options." Osr made a gesture with one set of tensirs and four Silvereds appeared from nowhere, surprisingly unaccompanied by blue wisps. Each shone brightly, and the Roranians were forced to avert their eyes. When they looked back, one appeared to be passing something to Osr, before all four disappeared again. Osr held the object towards Kera.

"The dummy node," Ilouden said, reverently.

Kera took it. Deep, booming cries and sounds of battle rang out from directly outside the room. Paran was there. Flashes of heat passed Diyan. The four invisible guards had joined the fray.

"You could leave, too. You could come with us," Kera said, staring into Osr's eyes.

"My place is here."

"Why are you—"

"I can take care of myself. Now you must go. Hespinr waits by my glazer and will escort you to the edge of our city so that you are not misidentified as enemies of Sunsprit."

"You knew I would come here."

Osr guffawed. "Everything contributes to my tetibat, even now. Information builds us. Anyway, I assume the Administration's current actions in Sunsprit mean Diyan's deal with them no longer holds. Therefore, you will need to sneak into the city and find a way to access the network. The necessary equipment to enter Fadin is stowed in the glazer." She glanced through the entrance. The shouts and grunts coming from the Silvereds fighting Paran were becoming more pained, and flashes of bright white punctuated reality. The structure around them shook with the violence. "It doesn't appear we have long. You must go."

A Silvered materialised beside a section of the wall that could not be seen from the entrance. The Silvered's eyes flickered closed, briefly, and the side of the wall disappeared, revealing another route out. Osr turned around, away from them, and raised an arm.

"Leave now, I have work to do. Don't get caught in Fadin, else all may be lost."

Further screams from the Vaesians jolted the three of them into action, prompting them to rush through. They ran along the sequence of corridors, finally exiting as a Silvered appeared and opened another section of wall for them. Hespinr waited next to a glazer.

Chapter 30
Violent Journey

Nearby screams, muffled by the glazer's sides, filtered through to Diyan, Kera, and Ilouden. Outside, Hespinr strode in front of the glazer, directing Silvereds away from their path. If she had been a Roranian, her speed could only have been achieved by running, but she did not appear to be pushing her body at all. Her speed was only dictated by how quickly she could clear the mass of Silvereds who congregated and rushed about in their way, as well as the occasional Roranian local. Her head whipped about from side to side as she shouted commands. A few other glazers crossed their path, travelling along other routes. Colourful lights from violent explosions flickered all around, visible through the spaces between the towers and above. Sometimes the glazer rocked from the force, its old dampening systems overcome. Darkness was setting in.

Ilouden sat in the front, manipulating the glazer's controls, while Diyan and Kera were squeezed awkwardly into the back, their shoulders pressed together as they watched the mayhem.

"Is Hespinr safe out there?" Diyan asked.

"She can more than take care of herself," Ilouden replied.

"She's very fast."

"Properly trained, the Vaesians are…formidable."

"And she's a Silvered," Kera said, managing to shrug despite their confinement. "They're even stronger than normal Vaesians."

"Where's Paran?"

Kera sighed. "Hopefully Osr has managed to slow him down, although I don't think she'll be able to stop him. We need to get ourselves as far away from him as possible."

"It's such a mess," Diyan muttered bitterly, clenching his jaw. "Everything's such a mess now."

The glazer shuddered violently as the luminous ground around them visibly rippled, and the two large towers beside the glazer began to sway dangerously. Silvereds rushed away. Hespinr picked up her pace and Ilouden increased the glazer's speed to match. A moment later, they turned a corner where, thankfully, none of the towers were swaying, yet.

Diyan pointed to a fast-moving group of Silvereds who had just disappeared down a narrow passageway. "I've seen what the Silvereds can do. They can appear and disappear. They can make walls materialise from nothing – and they're not holos, I felt them. Their bodies glow—"

"Being Silvered can sometimes afford certain Vaesians special…abilities," Kera said. "It's what's allowed the Vaesian Union to remain strong, despite the Administration believing differently."

Ilouden turned sharply around. "Kera…"

She waved a hand, almost lazily. "He knows most of it already, he's seen it, and Osr's allowed you to tell him a lot more already. And if the Administration capture and interrogate him, they'll probably have us as well, so they'll find out anyway." She looked at Diyan, and despite the carnage outside, he looked back. "A minority of the Silvereds have propensities towards certain abilities. And an even smaller minority are able to harness those propensities and develop them." She took a deep breath. "Matter and energy manipulation, under the right conditions, with the right aptitudes, and with the right guidance, well…you've seen what they can do."

Movement outside took their attention. Hespinr rushed quickly – so much so that her body became a blur. When her form resolved again, she was standing in front of a group of nearby Silvereds, who had their weapons pointed at the glazer. One of the Silvereds had their central leg raised slightly off the ground.

"Don't worry. They heal quickly, even faster than we

do," Kera said.

A moment later, Hespinr was back in front of the glazer as though nothing had happened, and the Silvereds in the group were no longer interested. Hespinr's head swivelled around, atop her long, thick neck, in continual motion.

"What can Hespinr do?"

Kera shook her head. "As far as I know, she's just very able. Being Silvered results from an overactivation and proliferation of their cell-scales, to various degrees. Some cases are far more pronounced than others, some less noticeable."

"And the matter manipulation? The—"

A series of loud booms interrupted their conversation, as tall clouds of dark smoke rolled high into the air, reaching the lofty heights of the dome and fanning across. The darkness increased.

Kera resumed talking, calmly. "It's impossible to predict whether a Vaesian will have a special propensity or not, or even when it might surface. It appears random, as far as they know. That's what happens when technologies we barely understand are tinkered with."

"I thought it was Roranian technology that we used to help them?" Diyan said, drawing his eyes back to Kera.

She chuckled. "Roranian? Almost everything we have came from Tapache, don't forget that. And anyway, when I was with the Nesch, I saw similar technologies to the cell-scales. It is possible other debris came down with the fragments of our Great Ship, when it was destroyed, that didn't originate from Tapache." She smiled. "And if it did come from the Nesch, who knows where the Nesch came across it."

"Then why would we give it to the Vaesians?"

"Whoever was in control of Fadin before the Administration probably wanted to test the cell-scales on them before they used them on us. Our longevity and the other qualities Tapache imbued us with are precious. Presumably, they wanted to see whether the cell-scales had a detrimental effect. But it was pointless. The cell-scales don't work on us."

A lone Silvered appeared beside Hespinr. The two conversed briefly before the Silvered ran off, the blur of movement only just visible. Hespinr changed direction, leading them off sharply through a narrower part of Sunsprit. A moment later, there was a loud explosion from where they had originally been headed.

"Being Silvered has advantages," Diyan said, slowly.

Kera nodded. "They have far shorter lives, but—"

"They live beautifully," Ilouden interrupted. He swerved his head around, surveying Sunsprit. "For the most part."

Kera nodded. "That's right. They're less constrained. The non-Silvereds, and most Roranians, they're indecisive. They prefer to wait, to withhold action. To protect their long lives."

"It sounds like you're saying the Silvereds are free,"

Diyan suggested.

Kera smiled and shrugged. "They live more brightly and they die sooner. Some consider it a plague, others a gift."

Further rumbling in the distance pitted their conversation, rocking the glazer – although its dampening systems seemed to be coping for the moment, just.

"What about Osr?" Diyan asked.

Kera did not reply immediately. "You've noticed her little tricks already, haven't you?"

He nodded. "She can hide herself. Her hair becomes white. Is that something she's doing, or—"

"Probably not as easy as it looks. She's old, and smart. Amongst the first to actually choose to become Silvered."

"And when those Silvereds kept bumping into me, or when I fell over the edge of Upper-Sunsprit and was caught...all those times when I could feel them searching my body...they were doing something, weren't they? It's something to do with their abilities."

"They were checking you, perhaps a little over-zealously at times. Some can detect certain devices the Administration uses. Tracers, recorders. Things like that. They might not have been active, but they'd have been passively gathering information, ready to transmit it back to the Administration at the first opportunity. We needed to ensure they were all disabled. You can never be too careful."

A group of Roranians holding weapons ran towards

the glazer. They stopped and aimed them at Hespinr. Ilouden shouted, bringing the vehicle to an immediate halt, but before there was time for anything else, Hespinr had disappeared in a blur of motion and the Roranians lay motionless on the ground. Hespinr reappeared in front of the glazer and beckoned Ilouden to continue taking them forwards.

"Muvaeyt helps them, doesn't it?" Diyan said, turning away from the Roranian bodies.

"Helps them concentrate, that's all. They don't all need it."

"And the Vaesian Union has kept this a secret? That the Silvereds are capable of all this?"

"The vast majority of Vaesians think of Silvering as a plague, it's not a hard secret to keep. The Administration, in their hubris, have never delved into it," Kera replied.

"Most Vaesians really do view Sunsprit as a lost cause, but it's the seat of their power," Ilouden added. "Without it, the Vaesian Union would crumble into separate, untethered cities. Sunsprit makes a show of wanting Roranian technologies – holos and the rest – but it doesn't want them anywhere near as badly as the Administration believes. It can manufacture most of what it needs itself."

"Exactly," Kera said, glancing outside the glazer. "The Anti-Vaesian Movement won't be successful. Sunsprit was caught unawares, but it'll survive. The difficulty is that they don't want to reveal too many of their capabilities in case any of the Anti-Vaesian attackers survive. It wouldn't be good for the Administration to learn what the Silvereds can really do."

They turned and entered a large concourse. The dome sharply met the ground a little way off, and judging by the quantity and magnitude of the flips, Diyan knew they had to be near the edge of Ringscape, if not almost right upon it. There was no fighting, no other Roranians or Vaesians in sight, just the three of them in Osr's glazer, led by Hespinr. The concourse was lined with thin, low-level towers, facing the dome wall, and two stubby walls that joined the last of the towers to the dome itself, sealing off the bounds of the concourse. There were no obvious exit points from the city.

Hespinr raised both arms towards a nearby section of wall, gesturing with her tensirs in a waving motion. Almost simultaneously, the wall dematerialised, leaving a dark hole in its place. A group of six heavily armed, brightly shining Silvereds waited on either side of the newly exposed exit. Through the thick atmosphere, it was obvious that the breached boundary looked out over the edge of Ringscape. An array of tubes and thin structures lined the sides, some of them dropping over the edge towards Under-Sunsprit.

Hespinr motioned for them to go through the gap, and Ilouden directed the glazer towards it.

"Wait! You can't be serious?" Diyan exclaimed, his voice rising with alarm. "The concourse floor doesn't extend over the gap." He looked at Kera, who merely grinned back. Outside the glazer, Hespinr stood to the side and raised an arm. Ilouden raised his arm in return, while Diyan looked back and forth between them in confusion. "Isn't Hespinr coming with us?"

"Hespinr's staying here," Kera informed him, shuffling down into her seat and pushing lightly against Diyan as she pulled up her facepiece. "Let's settle down."

As the glazer's speed began to increase, Diyan had no choice but to acquiesce, the acceleration forcing his body backwards into his seat. He could do nothing but stare in disbelief as the glazer sped out, over the edge.

Chapter 31
Revealed Understanding

Diyan turned around, watching the faint lights of Sunsprit diminish in the darkness. The signs of the attack were no longer distinguishable. The glazer was still travelling along the side of Ringscape – the strange region between the underside and upperside, where flips occurred constantly. The edge of Ringscape, which lined its upperside, was only a short distance to Diyan's left, whilst a dark, endless expanse lay to his right. His stomach was in a quasi-permanent state of lurching and settling, which was not wholly down to the flips. Without the Vaesian city and its structures around them, the perplexing nature of the flips and the sheer scale of Ringscape was terrifying.

Suddenly, Ilouden swerved the glazer to the left. It clunkily flipped across, perpendicular to the upperside, and they quickly left the edge behind, travelling further into the upperside. The flips diminished rapidly, and soon they were non-existent. Diyan pulled his facepiece down.

"The glazers don't require the magnetic paths after all, do they?" he commented. "We've not used a single path since leaving Sunsprit, and we even stuck to the side without them, despite the flips."

"The Administration thinks they do," Kera explained, making a tsking sound.

"The Administration seems to think a lot of things about the Vaesians," Diyan muttered.

"And the little things add up," Ilouden replied.

Diyan nodded. "But we're not headed towards Fadin yet, are we?" He gestured around them. "Sunsprit's that way, and Fadin's past it. We've been going in the wrong direction."

"Makes less sense to escape *towards* Fadin, doesn't it? And no one would have expected us to escape *along* the edge," Ilouden replied. "Safer this way, for many reasons. We're going to make a big arc back now and travel the long route to Fadin." He turned around and flashed them both a grin. "Happy for the flips to be gone?"

"Will Hespinr be okay?" Diyan asked.

"Hespinr can take care of herself," Kera said.

"And Paran?"

Kera did not reply, setting the tone for quite some time afterwards, leaving Diyan to silently gaze out at the monotonous landscape. Ilouden piped up every now and then, pointing out the directions of other settlements and the occasional vehicle in the distance, muttering all the while about suspected Administration internment centres. He was taking them along a route where they would be unlikely to encounter any others.

Slowly, the gentle vibrations of the glazer rocked Diyan to sleep. His dreams were permeated by the screams and explosions rocking Sunsprit, and Paran's angry face. Someone was shouting his name. And Kera's.

*

"Diyan." It was Ilouden. "You drifted off a while ago." The Roranian turned back to face the front. "Both of you." It was daytime.

"I didn't *drift off*," Kera said testily. "I was resting on purpose."

Diyan rubbed his shoulder, trying to remove the sensation that something had been pressing against it. He noticed Kera moving awkwardly towards the other side of their small, shared seat.

"If we continue on this trajectory, we'll reach the outskirts of Fadin soon."

Kera nodded, twisting back as she began fiddling with one of the glazer's internal compartments. She leaned back towards Diyan, in order to prise it open, then stuck her arm inside.

"Here." She passed Diyan his original footwear. "Give me yours, I'll put them in here." Kera pointed tangentially to the direction they were travelling in. "Ilouden, we need to go there."

Ilouden nodded and the skimmer began to swerve to the side.

"But that's away from Fadin," Diyan said.

"Just a precaution."

"The Administration probably won't have publicised the attack on Sunsprit," Ilouden explained, upon Kera's silence. "They'll have downplayed it as some small Anti-Vaesian protest or other. But still, we can't just barge through. Better to enter unnoticed."

"Where are we going?"

"You'll see," Ilouden said. His wide grin was visible from the side of his face. "I've guessed it."

Kera stared intently at the scenery, moving her head purposefully, clearly looking for something. She tapped Ilouden's chair. "Here." The glazer stopped.

Ilouden and Diyan exited the glazer, watching with their facepieces around their necks while Kera remained inside, rummaging through various internal compartments. The glazer's front fold and both back folds were raised, allowing the atmosphere's cool air to flow through. Somehow, Kera had managed to manoeuvre the back-seat forwards and was delving into an exposed compartment below.

"Ilouden, there's something I'd like to ask," Diyan whispered.

"What is it?"

"Are there any Vaesian males, or are they very different

from us?"

Ilouden laughed. "In a way, yes, to both. They're not actually female right now, it's simply how we distinguish their states. They change state every cycle."

"How long's a cycle?"

"About ten standard years."

"And what happens after that?"

"They're still them, and they look the same, but their bodies produce chemical substances that allow new life to be fertilised and grown within them."

Diyan nodded slowly. "To allow them to reproduce?"

"For the most part. Usually, at least three cycles are required."

"Why's that?"

Ilouden chuckled. "They're not Roranian, Diyan. Don't think about their reproduction in our terms. It's quite different."

"How should I think about it?"

Before Ilouden could reply, Kera emerged from the glazer, looking irritated.

"What is it?" Ilouden asked.

"Osr only left us one wing-pack," she said, heaving a bulky, black pack with her trailing arm.

"A single wing-pack?" Diyan asked, nonplussed, looking between them.

Ilouden grinned. "Well, it's not like you haven't used one in tandem before. Remember your...fall, over the edge..."

Kera swung the wing-pack around across her back and tightened its straps across her front. She stretched her body and shuffled lightly to check the pack's restraints, then strode over to Ilouden. "Well, here's where we part. Good luck on your return." They embraced briefly.

"Sunsprit will be fine," Ilouden assured her, moving over to Diyan and patting him warmly on the shoulder. "And don't you go getting yourself killed. You're not so bad, I should like us to meet again."

"Why aren't you coming with us?" Diyan asked.

"Someone has to take the glazer back." Ilouden walked towards the glazer. "Besides, I've never visited Fadin before, I'd stick out immediately. It's up to you two to have all the fun. Take the dummy node, figure out what you can, then return to the Vaesian Union. Return to Sunsprit. We can't let the Administration win." He walked around the glazer and pulled the two back folds down, then sat in the front. "Don't make all of this have been for nothing." The front automatically folded down.

Kera and Diyan watched the glazer until it disappeared from view.

"Come on," Kera said, turning briskly and pulling her facepiece over her mouth. "This way."

Diyan did the same and walked after her. Kera barely spoke as they walked, seemingly fixated on their surroundings. Every time Diyan attempted to draw Kera into conversation, he received a shrug or one-word answer. She was concentrating. So far, they had not seen

301

anyone else, although their surroundings were noticeably changing.

"There," Diyan said, pointing to a large pole sticking vertically up from the ground. He looked at Kera's wing-pack. "We're going up that, aren't we?"

Kera shook her head. "Not that one, no."

Diyan frowned as they continued walking. Soon, he spotted another.

"That one?"

She shook her head again.

"Why?"

"Better to go solitude gliding as part of a group."

"*Solitude gliding?*"

"That's what it's called."

He looked up sceptically. "Are you sure we should be doing this in tandem?"

Her head was turned so it was difficult to see clearly, but he thought he noticed a brief smirk flicker across her face.

"Used to be for observation and reconnaissance. As Fadin grew, it became unnecessary, other than as a leisure activity," she explained.

They resumed walking. The third pole they spotted was surrounded by small, moving figures. As they moved closer, they saw there were seven of them – all Roranians. Each wore a wing-pack. Almost immediately, Kera's demeanour changed. She began to look tired, as though the wing-pack was heavier than before.

"Can I help?" Diyan asked.

"No," she snapped, keeping a weary but amiable smile across her face. "Just play along."

He nodded.

The group of Roranians noticed them on their approach, and by the time they reached them, some of the group had already disappeared up the pole and were gliding in the skies above. Only three were left at the base, alongside three nearby skimmers. Kera raised an arm in greeting.

"Everything okay?" one of the three asked once they were within talking distance, walking a few steps towards them. He was slim, with short brown hair and a friendly smile, and had pulled his facepiece down. Kera and Diyan did the same.

Kera nodded. "Our skimmer malfunctioned," she said, in mock exasperation. "With all our things inside. The silly old thing went straight back to Fadin before we were finished. Who knows where they've ended up!"

The man nodded and shook his head knowingly. "Happened to me once before. Very irritating. The network's got its problems, eh?" Behind him, one of the other remaining two was thrust high up the pole, into the sky. "It's because the signal's not so good out here. Why didn't you request another skimmer from your pole?"

Kera shook her head. "Took too long, so..." She grabbed Diyan's arm sweetly. "We thought we'd take a stroll." She looked back at the man. "Almost had to wrestle the wing-pack off him, he insisted on carrying it most of the way."

"Ah," he grinned, looking at Kera's single wing-pack. "Tandem. A little dangerous. Romantic, though." He glanced up then took a step back and pointed at the pole. There was a small interface visible at head height around its circumference. "You can request a skimmer here if your stroll's finished. I should be going now!"

"Actually, we might follow you up," Kera said eagerly. "One more flight." She gazed into Diyan's eyes dramatically. "What do you think?" She kissed him quickly, on the lips. "Another flight?"

Confused, Diyan nodded. "Yes, I, err...one more flight would be good."

"We'll go after you," Kera said to the man. "We may need a little time down here first." She pulled Diyan closer to her.

The man's grin widened. "Up to you." He strolled back to the pole as his last remaining friend was pushed up and into the air, then began strapping himself in. "Just make sure to watch out for the Silvereds!"

"What?" Kera's eyes blazed with momentary fierceness.

"You haven't heard? Sunsprit's had an outbreak. A more aggressive cell-scale strain. We've been told to report any we see trying to sneak into Fadin."

"Oh," Kera replied, slowly. "And the Anti-Vaesian protests there?"

The man shrugged. "I haven't heard of them but..." He tipped his head to the side. "It makes you think...maybe they've got a point." Before he had time to say anything else, he was flung up the pole. Kera released her grip of Diyan, her jovial countenance evaporated.

"The Administration's blamed it on a new cell-scale outbreak and not the Anti-Vaesians," Diyan ruminated.

"Seems they want more control over Sunsprit than I thought they'd dare. An outbreak means quarantine. Quarantine means control."

"Is that bad?"

She grimaced. "Worse, probably. But Osr will have considered this outcome already. Sunsprit isn't unprepared." She walked towards the skimmers. "We're taking one of theirs."

"We're not going up?" Diyan asked, eyeing the Roranians soaring above them, attempting to hide his relief.

"No. That's not the plan."

"Then why did you tell me it was?"

"So that our story would be believable."

"Believable? I looked terrified!"

Kera smirked. The nearest skimmer opened automatically for her. She reached inside and began pulling out anything that belonged to the group above.

Diyan looked up nervously. None of the soaring Roranians seemed to have noticed. "Why didn't we just call our own skimmer?"

"Safety," Kera replied. "These are pre-registered to them. The less we interact with the influx network the better. Glazers don't do secondary checks mid-journey, and with any luck, that protocol hasn't been changed yet. We'll barely be scraping the influx network's surface. Come on, get in."

Diyan followed her into the skimmer, which closed behind him. "Where to?" he asked.

"Probably wherever one of them lives," Kera said, with a shrug. "We just need to reach an influx node."

Chapter 32
Hidden Action

Diyan glanced around nervously. The room was messy, with clothing and objects strewn about the place. It was only a little larger than the accommodation he had been given upon first entering Fadin, although clearly stamped with someone's identity. Possibly the man they had spoken to at the base of the pole. Some faint music played in the background. The lights were a warm orange, half-dimmed from daylight levels. He looked back as the entrance closed behind them with an audible thump.

"How did you get us in here?" he asked. "You just placed your hand on the door. Is that how you took the dummy node in the first place? The augmentations from the Nesch?"

"Questions, questions." Kera walked straight to the influx node. "Soon, we'll have some answers."

"Are you sure this is a good idea?" Diyan asked,

looking around.

"There's no internal surveillance," Kera replied, settling onto a white stool in front of the node. A holo interface appeared and she began manipulating its controls while reaching into her pocket.

"That's not what I mean. What if the Tugs did something to it?" He motioned to the dummy node now in her hand.

"That's exactly what we hope happened," she replied. "The Tugs stored their information on this device, and we need to know what that information is." She reached forwards and placed the dummy node at the centre of the influx node.

Diyan sighed and settled on the stool beside hers, watching as the dummy node became enveloped in a bright, yellow glow from the base up. A holo sphere wrapped around Kera's head and her speech became muffled. Diyan tapped the influx node, raising up another interface.

"Diyan…" Kera's voice sounded far away. "Are you seeing this?"

"In a moment, I'm just joining," he said, moving through the controls, trying to remember the sequences he had been shown. There was a strange smell coming from the dummy node, as though it was lightly smoking. "Kera, something's wrong with the dummy node." She did not reply. He tapped the controls and joined her. A holo wrapped around him, but it was pitch black, empty.

"Kera, it's not working for me. I think the device is compromised; it's not allowing additional entrance."

"It's not what we thought, at all," he heard her murmur in response. "What if I'm not right?"

"What isn't?"

"The Haze Rings, Barrenscape, Ringscape...nothing. It's all a giant machine, and it's filled with *them*. They're here, *with* us."

"Who's here?"

She did not reply. Diyan exited the holo. Kera's hands were trembling. She was still enveloped in the simulation.

"Kera—"

"It's not what we thought at all," she repeated, her voice still muffled. Her entire body began to convulse. "It's not a wave of death for the machines...it takes them and...it's storing them..."

"Kera!" he rushed to her side. Immediately, the holo dissipated and she slumped forwards.

"We...need to destroy the Source. I was right about that...I think. I can predict the exits. I can stop it, but we can't stop it from in here...they know we're here now. They're coming!"

The entrance to the room disappeared behind a flash of light, replaced by smoke. A shadowy figure walked through, coming to a stop just a few short strides from where Diyan and Kera were sat. The smoke swirled momentarily, uncovering his face. He wore a white facepiece, which he pulled down. It was the same man who had appeared to Diyan as a holo before he had been tasked with finding Kera. A large, dark, armoured figure came into view behind him. A section of the armour at the head shimmered to transparency as the figure stood behind, a little to the side. Paran. His eyes were narrowed, and his jaw was clenched. He was smiling tightly, but the expression did not reach his eyes. Other, more typically armoured Administration soldiers filed in around them.

Kera raised her head to look at them. "No…" She looked at Diyan with empty, dejected eyes. "What have you done?"

"I'm sorry," Diyan said, with a tear rolling down his cheek. "I had to."

The man from the Administration took a step closer. "Kera," he said, with the same smug, jovial condescension as before. "We finally meet."

Diyan was grabbed from behind and taken from the room.

GLOSSARY

Administration – Roranian regime in control of Fadin.

Aenoun – Vaesian city on Ringscape.

Aesia – Roranian city on Ringscape that was combined with Harmend, taking the latter's name.

Air terminals – Filtration facilities that purify Ringscape's air, which is slightly less than optimal for Roranian respiration. In the absence of air terminals, regwear facepieces can be used to filter Ringscape's (and Barrenscape's) air. Roranians may experience mild headaches from prolonged exposure to unfiltered air.

Aivinr – Member of the council that directs the Vaesian Union.

Alpuri – Mysterious isolationist species that has been settled on Ringscape for an unknown period of time. Little is known of them.

Annexe – Expansive private areas within the Roranian Great Ship, allocated to each individual. They can be altered and redesigned according to the whims of the individual they belong to.

Anti-Vaesian Movement ('Anti-Vaesians') – Subversive group of Roranians who believe the Vaesians are hiding secrets about Ringscape and the Source itself. Due to this belief, the group exhibits a deep hatred towards the Vaesians, especially Silvered Vaesians. They have a presence in Fadin, and some of the other large Roranian cities, as well as in many of the smaller settlements. The Administration publicly denounces them.

Aura – Coloured glow surrounding the c-automs that can be used to help identify them. It also acts as a visible indicator of where the c-automs physical activities are concentrated.

Barrenscape – One of the three known parts of the Source (the other two being Ringscape and the Haze Rings). It appears like a vast tube that has been drawn into a circle, connected at both ends, and then squashed in on itself from two opposite sides. Another way of visualising it is as a malleable ring, held between two fingers, where both fingers have pushed the sides inwards, towards each other. Unlike Ringscape, Barrenscape has no edge, since it is cylindrical. It has a total surface area many orders of magnitude greater than that of a typical life-supporting planet orbiting a star. Aside from the debris that sometimes rains down upon it through the Haze Rings, it is thought to be too dangerous to occupy and is therefore uninhabited, aside from the Breaker.

Behind the Veil – Group of Vaesians who believe there is something in Ringscape that they cannot see. Members are referred to as 'Veilers', who usually remove a piece of bodily hair to signify their status as members.

Berthing – Process by which c-automs can undergo the machine-equivalent of biological stasis, and have their intellects stored safely. Berthing can be used to escape harm. During normal activities on a Wanderer vessel, the commanding craft-lects sometimes 'sleep' during long periods of solitude and allow specially selected c-automs to also sleep by being berthed, rather than being destroyed.

Biological sentient ('biological') – Non-exotic living entity that has naturally evolved, or would have been able to, and that also possesses an intellect.

Bloom propulsion unit ('bloom') – Wanderer propulsion method powered by vacuum energy.

Bomera – Female Roranian who lives within Sunsprit and is willingly governed by the Vaesian Union. She is primarily engaged with studies involving the Tugs.

Breaker – Name given to an entity that is believed to be confined to Barrenscape, and which destroys almost everything it comes into contact with. It is the principal reason that no permanent settlements have been established on Barrenscape. It is thought to be able to manipulate gravity. No accurate scans or images exist of it, and very little else can be deduced aside from its rough location. While very powerful, it was unable to penetrate the casket-ship, or unwilling.

Casket – Protective, spherical cocoons used to grow young Roranians aboard the Great Ship, replacing the need for biological birth. Constructed from triamond-derivative materials, the caskets are very hardy, able to withstand many types of attack, as well as empty space. The caskets are able to sustain Roranian occupants for extremely long periods of time, even once fully grown, either in stasis or awake, and also have a variety of other features. The casket walls are generally coloured dark red, though can be set to be transparent, translucent, or opaque with ease.

Casket-ship – Makeshift vessel created by Wiln, Loten, and Rememox, from three separate caskets joined together.

C-autom – Machine-lect sentients, typically used as crewmembers aboard a Wanderer Ship by the commanding craft-lect. Each c-autom aboard the

Roranian Great Ship has been tasked by Tapache with looking after a specific Roranian charge, or to serve as a backup to look after a Roranian charge should the prior c-autom be destroyed. The situation aboard the Roranian Great Ship is atypical, with most c-automs in existence serving aboard Wanderer ships with the commanding craft-lect actually present.

Cell-scale machines ('cell-scales') – Extremely small machines that live upon and within Vaesians, making their bodies stronger and better able to cope with Ringscape's gravity. Although the technology was given to the Vaesians by the Roranians, it is not entirely understood, and there are instances where the technology fails – the cell-scale machines over-proliferate, drawing too much energy from their hosts. This leads to a condition called 'Silvering' where, aside from Vaesians becoming silver in colour, their lifespans are significantly reduced. Those with Silvering are known as 'Silvereds', and there is no known cure. Transmission rates are low, and while most Vaesians believe the condition to be a plague, they are not generally fearful of catching it through brief contact. Cell-scale technology does not work on Roranians.

Combat regwear ('combat suit') – Reinforced regwear worn for the purpose of combat. There are many different levels of combat regwear, with any Roranian aboard the Great Ship able to access up to and including level thirteen.

Communication channel – Messages that are broadcast, via technological media, to specific groups or individuals. Communication channel requests must be accepted by the end-recipient in order for the channel to be established, unless the initiator has a higher level of security access over the transmission medium.

Competitions – The collective name for many of the activities that Roranians can choose to undertake on the Great Ship, generally for leisure.

Corun – A c-autom from the Roranian Great Ship.

Craft-lect – Type of Wanderer machine-lect that is typically tasked with detecting and destroying incidences of Sensespace infection within the galaxy.

Craft-lect fleet – Wanderer ships under the control of craft-lects.

Craft-lect-like activities – Detection and elimination of incidences of Sensespace infection within the galaxy.

Cutter – Makeshift machine used by Roranian salvagers that has triamond-tipped needles, capable of penetrating triamond-derived materials.

Databanks – Wanderer memory technology.

Diyan – Roranian male from the Great Ship, accompanied by the c-autom Wiln.

Docking ring – Segmented structure used to dock Vaesian ships. They now sit as relics around and within Vaesian cities.

Drone – Automated instruments that are typically not sentient.

Dual city – Cities with permanent settled presences on both sides of Ringscape, such as Fadin and Sunsprit.

Dummy node – Information storage device related to the influx network. It was created by the Administration and then stolen by Kera.

Echoes of Gravity – Mysterious presence in Sunsprit that Vaesians sometimes use to help percolate their thoughts.

Edge (or Side) of Ringscape – The wedge of surface that separates Ringscape's upperside and underside. A region of anomalous gravitational behaviour.

Electro-boost platform – Surface whose vertical movement can be manipulated in order to take those standing on the surface to different heights.

Electro-clamps – Clamps that can be used to secure metallic objects to other surfaces. They are useful in ships that have poor inertial dampeners and/or inadequate gravitation emulation technologies.

Entry events – Low probability instances during which

the Haze Rings allow penetration into the Source from external space. Typically, only mangled debris makes it through, if anything. Entry events that allow life to penetrate the Source are exceedingly rare.

Fadin – Largest and most influential Roranian city on Ringscape, under the rule of the Administration. It is a dual city, comprised of Upper-Fadin and Under-Fadin.

Flip – Gravitational fluctuations that occur with greater frequency and intensity the closer one is to an edge of Ringscape. On the edge itself, the flips are continuous. They are strongest at the midpoint between the upperside and the underside. The gravitational fluctuations can be used to generate power using gradient transducers.

Gelirn – Member of the council that directs the Vaesian Union.

Glazer – Vaesian transport vehicles, similar to skimmers.

Gradient transducer – Devices that can be used to generate power from the gravitation fluctuations ('flips') near and along the edges of Ringscape.

Gravitometer – Simple Vaesian devices used for gravity observations and measurements within the Tug Field.

Graviton – Elementary particle of the gravitational force.

Gravity strings – Gravitational force constructs that have been found deep within Sunsprit, along an edge of Ringscape. They emanate from spiked structures that rise vertically up from the ground, together referred to as the Tugs. Assumed to be sentient.

Great Dome – Grand building in Upper-Sunsprit that supposedly serves as a meeting place for the quarrelling Silvered faction leaders.

Great Ship – Usually used to refer to the Roranian Great Ship, an enormous vessel given to the Roranians by Tapache in order to carry out the quest set for them. Although Tapache is a Wanderer and designed the vessel itself, it predominantly used Roranian-derived technologies where possible. The Roranians aboard the ship are looked after and taught by c-autom helpers.

Gronwenthian cloth – Type of clothing created by the Gronwenthians, whose manufacturing instructions are available to Roranians within their Great Ship's databanks.

Harmend – Roranian city on Ringscape. It was once a smaller city but was combined with Aesia to form one large city.

Haze Rings – One of the three known parts of the Source (the other two being Ringscape and Barrenscape). The Haze Rings are rotating structures around Ringscape and Barrenscape that create an almost impenetrable barrier, even capable of destroying bloom propulsion units. They keep everything within the Source *inside*, and everything outside the Source *mostly outside*. Sometimes, external penetration into the Source is allowed, and these events are called entry events. The Haze Rings go through periods where entry events are more common. During entry events, aberrations in the detected wavelengths emitted by the Haze Rings have indicated that they are comprised of many single hyperfine loops, rotating extremely fast. The Haze Rings also create the periodic light (often referred to as 'daylight') that immerses Barrenscape and Ringscape, as well as the pernicious haze winds that can make daytime travel between Barrenscape and Ringscape impossible. It is thought that the Haze Rings are responsible for the Source's 'thick atmosphere', whereby signals, including visible light, scatter much more quickly than the typical laws of physics allow. It is for this same reason that long-range information transfer is extremely inefficient and energy intensive.

Haze winds – Dangerous winds that are generated by the Haze Rings during their light-emission 'daytime' phase. The haze winds limit travel between Ringscape and Barrenscape.

Hespinr – Silvered Vaesian residing in Sunsprit.

Holo – Umbrella term for different types of holographic technologies used by many species and civilisations, including the Roranians. Often used as a prefix to specify a certain type of holographic technology. Can sometimes be interacted with and are responsive to physical motions.

Ilouden – Male Roranian who lives within Sunsprit and is willingly governed by the Vaesian Union.

Influx – Responsive unit of the Administration's information network.

Influx network – The Administration's information network, available to Roranians living in Fadin.

Influx node – Physical structure through which the influx network is accessed.

Irido – Member of Kera's salvaging crew.

Kera – Roranian female from the Great Ship, accompanied by the c-autom Otherness.

Learning centre – Building in Fadin used for the community teaching of Roranian children.

Lect – Living entity that possesses an intellect and is therefore sentient. Usually an affix to a machine intelligence.

Lellara – Female Roranian who lives within Sunsprit and is willingly governed by the Vaesian Union. She is primarily engaged with studies involving the Tugs.

Loten – C-autom from the Great Ship and companion of Paran.

Machine-lect – Machine-based intelligence.

Magnetic paths of Sunsprit ('magnetic paths') – Paths that lead to and join up at Sunsprit, forming a great surface that runs under much of the city.

Muvaeyt – Substance chewed by Silvered Vaesians, releasing a blue mist. It has no effect on non-Silvered Vaesians or Roranians.

Neural conjoiner – Technology used by the Administration to exact information from other Roranians, although the mind can be irreversibly damaged as a result.

Orb-body – Physical form created by Tapache for the c-automs, which are also able to exist in non-corporeal form. Each orb-body emits its own unique glow.

Osr – Silvered Vaesian residing within Sunsprit, member of the council that directs the Vaesian Union.

Otherness – C-autom from the Great Ship and companion of Kera.

Paran – Roranian male from the Great Ship, accompanied by the c-autom Loten.

Prietman – Cloaked creatures seen in both Fadin and Sunsprit. They are rare, and not thought to be of high intelligence.

Probability wave of death ('probability wave') – Theorised but undetected wave, thought to be emitted by the Source, that can result in the death of machine-lects. The closer a machine-lect is to the Source, the higher the chance of death. No machine-lects can exist within the Source due to this phenomenon.

Recruitment centre – Administration buildings where eligible Roranians in Fadin can apply for certain types of work.

Regwear – Roranian clothing from the Great Ship that has smart capabilities like air filtration and thermoregulation.

Rememox – C-autom from the Great Ship and companion of Yena.

Ringscape – One of the three known parts of the Source (the other two being the Haze Rings and Barrenscape). It is where the majority of sentient life that has entered through the Haze Rings is thought to reside. It is ring-shaped and flat-surfaced, with both sides (upperside and underside) habitable.

Roranians – Humanoid species whose remnants were

found by the Wanderer, Tapache. From the materials and information found in the remnants, Tapache was able to resurrect the species by creating a new 'batch' of Roranians, whom it placed aboard a Great Ship it designed for them. In return for completing Tapache's quest, they are informed that Tapache will aid them in discovering what became of their civilisation, and whether anything remains.

Selo – C-autom from the Great Ship and initial companion of Yena.

Sensespace – Enemy of the Wanderers. It is an infective and hostile presence that appears to be drawn to sentience. Most Wanderer craft-lects are tasked with traversing the galaxy to seek and destroy it.

Sentient – Living entity possessing an intellect.

Side (or 'Edge') of Ringscape – The wedge of surface that separates Ringscape's upperside and underside. These are regions of anomalous gravitational behaviour.

Silvered Vaesian ('Silvered') – Vaesians whose cell-scales have overactivated and proliferated to the extent that their bodies have taken on a silver colour. Their lifespans are severely impacted as a result. The condition is difficult to pass on, although many other Vaesians still give them a wide berth. Sunsprit is the only city with a predominantly Silvered population.

Skimmer – Roranian transport vehicles. Aboard the Great Ship, they are capable of aerial travel, however, this ability has not been unlocked on Ringscape.

Sky-factory – Manufacturing structures that have been placed high above Ringscape's surface, to which they are attached by great tethers. There are six in total – three attached to Upper-Fadin, and three attached to Under-Fadin. The heat and noise they emit make them unsuitable for Ringscape's surface. They are guarded by the Administration's drones.

Sky-factory capsules – Vehicles that run along the tethers connecting the sky-factories to Ringscape.

Sky-factory tethers – Strong linear attachments that connect the sky-factories to Ringscape.

Soft-graviton emulators – Roranian technology that produces an artificial gravity field.

Soji – Member of Kera's salvaging crew.

Solitude gliding – Roranian leisure activity whereby those wearing wing-packs are flung high up into the air, whereupon the wing-packs unfurl, and gliding can commence.

Source – The origin of the probability wave of death for machine-lects. Its builders are unknown.

Standard time – Roranian time measurement system.

Sunsprit ('City of the Silvereds') – The only Vaesian city predominantly occupied by Silvered Vaesians. It is also the only other known dual city on Ringscape, besides Fadin. The two parts of Sunsprit are far more tightly physically joined than Fadin's two parts.

Tapache – Powerful Wanderer craft-lect (a type of machine-lect intelligence).

Tensirs – Small finger-like fronds that extend from the end of Vaesian arms. They are highly adhesive and more numerous than fingers.

Tetibat – Vaesian principle, concerning acting to increase one's stability in life, in all measures, literal and metaphorical.

Thermal ejection rifle – Roranian weapon.

Thick atmosphere – Quirk of the atmosphere inside the Source, whereby signals, including visible light, scatter much more quickly than the typical laws of physics allow. It is for this same reason that long-range information transfer is extremely inefficient and energy intensive. It is thought that the Haze Rings are responsible.

Triamond – Wanderer material used by Tapache as part of the Roranian casket casing.

Tug Field – The expanse deep within Sunsprit where the Tugs are found.

Tug Mask – Vaesian head gear that allows visual observation of the Tugs' gravity strings. Conscious observation is required to activate the mask's fuel.

Tugs – Assumed sentient beings that exist, hidden, deep within Sunsprit, along an edge of Ringscape. They are comprised of spiked structures that rise vertically up from the ground, and gravity strings that emanate from the tips of the spiked structures.

Underside of Ringscape ('underside') – One of the sides of Ringscape.

Council of the Vaesian Union ('Council') – The leading group of Vaesians directing the Vaesian Union.

Upperside of Ringscape ('upperside') – One of the sides of Ringscape.

Uthrit – Vaesian city on Ringscape.

Vaesian Union ('Union') – The aggregate Vaesian collective governing the Vaesian settlements and their people.

Vaesians – Sentient species that inhabit Ringscape alongside the Roranians. The Vaesians consider the Roranians to be new to Ringscape since their own history of occupation is far more extensive. Upon entering the Source, the Roranians displaced the Vaesians as the main authority.

Veilers – Secretive members of the 'Behind the Veil' Vaesian group, joined in the belief there is something in Ringscape that is not currently seen.

Viewing platform – Platform within the Roranian Great Ship overlooking the caskets.

Void technology – Name sometimes given to the theorised technology that could be the cause of the probability wave of death, emitted by the Source.

Wanderer fleet – All of the fleets of different Wanderer ships within the galaxy, often used to refer to the craft-lect fleet, which is the largest.

Wanderers – Civilisation predominantly comprised of machine-lect intelligences, and the principal force in the galaxy attempting to destroy the Sensespace.

Water Musk – Scent from Diyan's annexe on the Roranian Great Ship.

Wiln – C-autom from the Great Ship and companion of Diyan.

Wing-pack – Pack worn about the back that can be unfurled to reveal a large set of wings, used for gliding.

Yena – Roranian female from the Great Ship, accompanied by the c-autom Rememox, following the loss of Selo.

Message from the Author

I hope you enjoyed reading Echoes of Gravity. Please consider leaving a review or subscribing to the mailing list on my website.

www.jamesmurdo.com

CPSIA information can be obtained
at www.ICGtesting.com
Printed in the USA
LVHW021509200621
690709LV00001B/112